*For all you hardcore Dracula lovers, who want
nothing more than to see him happy.*

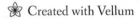 Created with Vellum

PROLOGUE

ALL RIGHT, boys and girls, listen up, cuz I'm only going to say this once.

When someone says your plan is downright stupid, perk up those ears and start taking notes. Otherwise, you might end up like me, cornered in a filthy alleyway, staring down the business end of a pair of fangs.

Let me back up a moment. Don't worry, this won't take long. Fang-face here will just have to wait the few seconds it'll take me to fill you in. After all, I want you not only to mourn my death, but learn from it as well. Maybe this lesson will save your ass one day.

Where should I start? Not the beginning—that's

boring. No one wants to know my life story. So, let's fast-forward twenty-four years to tonight. The night I die.

First, an important note: It's been a week since the vampire community came out of their bloody coffins, so to speak. Which means everything is still so fresh. Humanity has no idea how to cope. Well, most of humanity. The small percentage of remaining Goths are walking around rubbing everyone's faces in the knowledge, like they've always been part of the cool kids' club.

As if.

And the second: I'm a professional vlogger. Or *was*, anyway. Maybe that doesn't mean much to anyone, but I swear it's relevant to *all* of this. See, I thought it'd be a fantastic idea to use my vlog as a media source for all things "vampiric." To learn all I could about these elusive blood drinkers and post it on my vlog for the entire world to see. Use their popularity to bolster my fame. I mean, what do we truly know about vampires? We've all read the books and watched the movies, but those were fantasy. And this is reality. As a social media influencer, it's my responsibility to shed a little light on the truth, right?

Unfortunately, during my search, I attracted the

attention of a very unfriendly vampire—the kind who stars in horror films. I honestly hadn't expected to run into such an animal. Naïve, I know. Clearly, vampires aren't the friendly beasts the media portrays. My ex-boyfriend warned me this would happen, but I never believed someone would actually turn me into a Happy Meal.

Nothing but a comedy of errors led me to this dreadful moment.

Maybe you should look away now, because I highly doubt my death will be a pretty one.

"This is so stupid. Remind me again why I always go along with your plans?"

I huffed and rolled my eyes. I loved Lucy. She was the best friend a girl could ask for. But damn, sometimes she was a real stick in the mud, always cautioning me to smarten up and think things through. Well, where was the fun in that? Last thing I wanted was to tiptoe through life. Live fast and free, I always said. Gotta grab life by the horns. Yadda, yadda, yadda.

"We'll be fine, I promise. Let's go! It'll be fun." I gripped Lucy's hand and dragged her to the front of the ridiculously long line.

Still, she dug in her heels. "You do know they don't allow cellphones in the club, right?"

She was referring to Fallen—New Orleans's hottest new vamp club. Of course, since vampires had only recently come out of their coffin-closets, who knew which club would make it to the very top of the five-star list. For now, this was the *one*.

In the week since I'd learned about this club, I'd researched the hell out of it, and came across some very interesting, albeit mildly disturbing, information. If my sources were trustworthy, this club had been around for a while, disguised as a Goth club. But true horror lay in the underbelly of this beast. A "blood farm," as the dark web called it.

Apparently, all the big-named bloodsuckers frequented this establishment. And why? Because the owner/manager supposedly supplied the club not only with the newest synthetic blood products but also, as rumor had it, the *real* stuff too. The *good* stuff. As in, bottles of fresh human blood drained directly from the tap. Further digging revealed that someone had also sent an anonymous tip to the police, but the club had managed to clean up before the authorities had arrived. Imagine my surprise when I stumbled across that juicy nugget of gossip. The perfect story just *waiting* to be revealed.

"Earth to Anna," Lucy said, tapping the back of my head. "Did you hear me?"

I gave a casual nod. "I did. And I do know about their no cellphone rule. It'll be fine."

"Fine?" Lucy laughed. "Girl, I haven't seen you go five seconds without your phone since you bought your very first one. You expect me to believe you're okay with this? Ms. Modern Vlogger? Ms. Can't Go Two Seconds Without Retweeting Someone?"

I snorted a laugh. "Oh, shut up."

Sadly, she wasn't wrong. Far from it, in fact. But I'd planned for this. The club definitely didn't allow any form of cellular devices, but since I absolutely *needed* my phone tonight, I'd taken some precautions. My very dreams hinged on the success of my plan.

It'd been a week since vampires had made their startling debut, announcing their so-called "peaceful" presence to the world. A moment that would surely go down in the history books. In that time, there'd been mass confusion, a little hysteria, definitely some full-blown panic, and a whole lotta online chatter. While most people were still confused, wondering if this was some kind of prank, others—like myself—remained skeptical. Literary vampires had been around since long before the

7

modern era, though the current stories seemed to focus on dramatic teenage romance. Some "lucky" girl who caught the eye of a big, bad—but actually good—vampire.

Pfft. I highly doubted such a thing existed.

There was no way a species that fed off human blood could be qualified as "peaceful." In one night, these creatures had restructured the entire food chain, knocking humans down a peg. Sure, they'd tied in the release of their synthetic blood line with their show-stopping announcement, but I wasn't fooled.

And that was the whole purpose behind Lucy's and my presence here tonight.

I wasn't a professional journalist—I lacked the credentials—but I still possessed a hungry appetite for uncovering the truth. And luckily, we lived in a digital age where any mook with decent equipment could build a story and slap it up on their website.

Enter, *moi.*

Despite my best efforts, the world had yet to discover me. But after tonight.... Imaginary stars shone in my eyes. After tonight, I would be famous. Celebritized. Viral. If the rumors were true, I would be the one to crack this story wide open. Just imagine, an exposé on vampiric blood slavery on *my* vlog. Everyone would know I'd scooped it. Not the police. Not the real journalists. Me. An eager twenty-four-year-old armed with a cellphone.

I shivered with excitement—nothing would stop me tonight.

Clutching Lucy's hand, I dragged her into the line, butting in front of three women wearing more makeup than a burlesque performer and racy outfits that blatantly exposed their throats. In the last week, I'd seen so many articles about women like this— desperate for a nibble, flagrantly flashing their jugulars with the hope of catching a vampire's attention. It didn't surprise me. Too many vampire romances out there, glorifying sexy love bites and eternal life. I couldn't imagine ever letting anyone— man or beast—sink their teeth into my throat. Didn't these people realize how many germs the mouth contains? *Yeesh* and *shudder*. No thanks.

"Hey!" the woman closest to me shouted. She grabbed my arm, her dangerously sharp nails catching my skin. Make no mistake, these cougars were on the *prowl* tonight. "Back of the line, bitch!"

I ignored her shrill voice and instead stared up at the bouncer. I instantly knew he was a vampire, and my breath caught in my throat. Wow. I'd never seen one up close before. He was, in a word, impressive.

I'd expected muscles—bouncers were always ripped. But this guy went beyond muscular to downright bulging with veins.

His keen gaze caught mine, and he watched with a raised brow as I grabbed a crisp hundo and slipped it into his pocket. After a slight hesitation, he gave an almost indecipherable nod and pointed to our purses. "Gotta check those. No electronics allowed inside."

Damn, his voice was *deep*. The sort of deep that awoke something in the lady bits area. But now wasn't the right moment to let his voice distract me. He needed to check our purses, and I most definitely had a cellphone in there. If found, they would ban us from the club. I couldn't let that happen. We had to get inside. So, earlier today, I'd sewn a small pocket into the liner, hidden from sight—or rather, human sight. Then, just in case, I'd dumped silver shavings I'd purchased online into my purse and covered it up with a Styrofoam container chock-full of garlic bread.

I had absolutely no idea if this would work. I was working under the assumption that the myths were true. Supposedly, silver weakened a vamp's senses, and they were apparently all allergic to garlic. Personally, I loved garlic. But I could see how someone with an enhanced sense of smell might not appreciate it.

I only hoped these two things combined convinced him not to look too closely.

The bouncer leaned in to inspect our bags. I popped mine open and shoved it toward his face. With a choking gasp, he staggered backward, clutching his nose. Even in the dark of night, I saw his lip curl upward as he wafted the air near his face.

"Oh!" I feigned horror. "I'm so sorry! My friend and I grabbed some pizza along the way. A girl's gotta eat before drinking, you know. It came with free garlic bread. I wasn't thinking when I put them in my purse. Just let me throw it out, then you can take another look."

The offended vamp garbled something I didn't understand, then pointed at the doors and waved us inside. If I wasn't mistaken, the poor guy looked to be tearing up. I was tempted to lean closer and study his face, fangs and all. But seeing as how my dream had just been delivered to me on a silver platter, I choked back my curiosity and hurried inside.

Darkness and deafening noise instantly consumed us. The emphatic beat of what sounded like horrible techno music echoed off the walls and thumped beneath our feet.

I grasped Lucy's hand and dragged her farther inside. A dimly lit staircase greeted us, leading us down to a sunken dance floor. Once we braved the first step, the entire place suddenly lit up with colorful strobe lights, as though the club had simply been waiting for us.

I grinned and squeezed Lucy's hand. This was what I lived for. The excitement of a new story, the energy of chasing a lead, and the thrill of experiencing a new adventure. My mama always called me an adrenaline junkie with a penchant for gossip, which made me laugh, considering it described me to a T.

At the bottom of the stairs, mystical fog swirled around our feet. I snickered—trust vampires to be stuck in the past. Techno music and fog machines. Could they be any more '90s?

"It's loud!" Lucy shouted over the incessant noise.

I was used to clubbing and the expected deafness that tended to last for days afterward. Lucy often tagged along, seeing as I never gave her a choice, but she always remarked on the noise. I suspected she preferred dark and dank bars. Quiet, lonely, withdrawn—all the words I often used to describe her. How the hell we'd ended up friends, I had no idea.

I turned my attention toward the surrounding crowd and clapped my hands with delight. Now, *this* was a club. Everywhere I looked, I saw someone writhing and grinding against another person, their hips gyrating shamelessly. It reminded me of the movie *Dirty Dancing* when Baby first stumbled across the *real* dancers. The brazen touches, the heated embraces... hell, someone was actually necking off to the side of the room. And at closer inspection, fingering. Yup, that's right. Some random guy stood pressed up against a woman, her skirt hiked up to her hips, his fingers boldly going where I assumed every man had gone before.

"Well, that looks fun," I shouted, nudging Lucy's shoulder and gesturing toward the scandalous couple.

If I had to guess, the no cellphone rule likely encouraged such dirty behavior. Easy to be naughty if there weren't any repercussions to fear.

"Oh. My. God!" Lucy cried out. If the woman owned pearls, no doubt she would have been clutching them right now.

I grinned and shook my head.

Mr. Shameless ground against the woman, then

slid his knee between her legs and pushed her panties down. With her ass and other goodies bared to the entire club, he continued to ravish her without a care in the world. And she seemed quite content in the moment.

Vampires, man. Guess they really did see things differently than us mundane humans.

It was difficult to tear my gaze away from the couple. They were like a freaking car crash. You kept looking back to see if things got worse, and every time I snuck a peek, they most definitely were. I had a feeling if we didn't stop watching now, we'd catch the full act in a matter of minutes.

Every fiber of my vlogger-being wanted to whip out my phone and film this. It'd definitely get me some hits. Everyone loved a good sex scandal. But that wasn't what we were here for, and I couldn't risk exposing my cell for something so mediocre. No, we were here to investigate illegal bloodletting. I couldn't allow something like this to distract me, not when there was a real story to unearth.

We had to dance if we wanted to blend in with the crowd. Any nearby vamps had to believe we were here for the same reason as Mr. and Mrs. Shameless over there. If they got even the slightest whiff of my true intentions, they'd shut me down faster than a restaurant infested with rats.

I led Lucy out onto the floor. With a teasing grin, I buried my hands in my hair and started dancing, swaying seductively to the beat. Lucy mimicked me, though her movements were stilted. Her attention seemed elsewhere, like she was imagining a million other places she could be right now.

Some sidekick she was turning out to be.

"Hey!" I tugged her hand and placed it on my hip. Touching didn't bother me. We'd seen each other in our birthday suits more times than I could count. "Loosen up!"

She grimaced, her gaze still roaming the club.

I shook my head and chuckled under my breath. Typical Lucy. Here we were, in New Orleans, for crying out loud, getting our groove on in the hottest vampire establishment, and she still couldn't relax and have a little fun. Most of our friends back home called her Mother Hen. Always pecking at us, nagging us to take our vitamins and wear sunscreen, because vitamin deficiencies and melanoma were two very serious problems. I loved her to death, but sometimes I wanted to shake the sensibility right out of her.

With an impish grin, I cupped her hips and drew

her close, hoping to evoke some sort of reaction. Instead, she leaned forward and pressed her lips to my ear. To any common observer, I knew it looked sexual. Like she was taking a little taste of Anna. The guy beside us laughed and gave us two massive thumbs up.

Men.

"Vampire," Lucy said, distracting me from Douche McDoucheson. "Up above. Your six o'clock."

Excitement stirred my blood. I quickly spun and pressed my back flat against her chest, my hands now gripping her thighs and my booty shimmying against her abdomen. McDoucheson cheered and lifted his beer in our direction. I ignored him, like most men, and let my gaze stray across the upper floor. Sure enough, a single vampire prowled above.

Pardon the expression, but *holy shit*. This vampire looked *nothing* like our bouncer outside. Our bouncer had looked friendly. Muscled, yes, but in a way that suggested he worked out. Nothing dangerous had stuck out to me.

But this guy? He had a giant invisible sign above his head with a flashing arrow that read *Vampire*. Everything about this one screamed *predatory*. The vamp was tall, broad, muscular, everything my lady bits generally wanted in a man, but I didn't like the way his hungry gaze raked over the crowd. In search of his next meal, maybe? One would assume Fallen's patrons knew what they were getting into by frequenting this type of club, but I had to wonder if they'd come for the thrill or to be a snack.

Legally, a vampire had to get permission before feeding on a human. It was the quickest I'd ever seen a law pass. So quick that I, and many others, had our doubts. Maybe the government had known a little something-something in advance. Maybe they'd taken the time to pass this law before announcing to the world that vampires existed.

My wannabe-journalist brain didn't believe a law could be passed in under a week. Government never agreed on anything. Seemed unlikely they'd agree on a law insisting on consent when cases involving rape were still being thrown out of court.

"Anna," Lucy hissed in my ear.

I whirled around to face her.

With a pinched expression, she pushed her hands through her hair and quietly gestured over her shoulder. My gaze followed, and sure enough, another vampire was serving drinks behind the bar. His movements were downright fluid, and damn if I wasn't jealous. My ballet instructor had tried for years to impart that particular lesson on me. It'd never stuck. I was as graceful as a drunken gazelle wearing six-inch heels and a purple tutu.

I scanned the crowd in search of more. Now that I'd seen the two of them, I knew what to look for. Impossibly pale faces, smooth complexions, thick luxurious hair, devastatingly seductive smiles. As though their exclusive club only accepted the incredibly beautiful. Well, that left me out. Lucy could make the cut—the woman's skin was pale and flawless and her eyes as vivid as emeralds. Me? I was a mess. Tousled dirty-blonde hair tossed up into a sloppy bun and boring hazel eyes that never caught a man's attention. Not with Lucy standing right next to me. I didn't care though, or so I'd convinced myself a long time ago. Lucy was gorgeous, and she knew it, but thankfully, she wasn't the sort to rub it in other people's faces. And I appreciated that about her. She possessed a modesty and kindness that many lacked.

Focusing back on the task, I danced around Lucy in a tight circle and scoped out the rest of the club. Four doors that I could count. Emergency exit, two bathrooms, and then an obscured door toward the back of the dance floor guarded by a single vampire. A storage room, maybe? But why guard a storage room? Unless that's where they kept all the blood. I could definitely see a need for a guard then, to ensure no one made off with their supply.

I studied the rest of the club. My attention landed on the bartender, and I watched as he served order after order. I'd never seen someone mix drinks so quickly before. And his martinis looked downright delicious. But now wasn't the time to get distracted by yummy gin and vermouth.

Interestingly, though, he never seemed to serve blood. Every customer at his counter had been human so far.

So then where did the vamps get their drinks?

Or were *we* the drinks?

No. My intel had specifically mentioned illegal bloodletting. That had to mean a back room somewhere. My gaze drifted back to the guarded room. Maybe it wasn't for storage after all. Really, there was only one way to find out.

"In about two minutes, I want you to create a distraction," I shouted to Lucy.

Her sweaty brow creased. "What?"

"A distraction. You know, a ruckus. Big enough to attract *everyone's* attention." I slyly gestured to the lone guard near the back of the dance floor. I needed him to abandon his post so I could sneak in.

She closed her eyes and muttered something to herself, something I couldn't catch with the music droning in my ear. But I imagined it was something similar to "why am I friends with you?"

"Two minutes," I reminded her, holding up two fingers.

"What do you suggest?"

I shrugged. Then, with a naughty smile, I danced my way toward the women's bathroom, all the while silently talking myself up. Oh yeah, tonight was gonna be *the* night. I was about to crack this story wide open. I was gonna show the world that vampires were far from the docile little pets they wanted us to believe they were. That their friendly neighborhood PR couldn't save them. One video was all it would take. If something unsavory was happening in that room, I was gonna be all over it like white on rice. They had fangs, for cripes' sake. Fangs meant to sink into our fragile little throats and drain us dry. I mean, humanity could barely tolerate mosquitoes sucking at our veins. How the hell were we planning on cohabitating with vampires?

I paused in front of the women's room door and peered back into the crowd. By my Mississippi counts, Lucy had thirty more to go. Hoping not to attract any unwanted attention, I bent down and fiddled with my shoes. Men didn't understand heels. They simply enjoyed the look of them in the bedroom. I could play with them for minutes, and no one would be the wiser.

At twenty Mississippis, I heard it. A scream. A shout. The crowd roaring with excitement. Then, suddenly, the music cut off with a grating screech. I watched as everyone turned toward the center of the dance floor, where my bestie stood eye-to-eye against Douche McDoucheson. Even from back here, I could hear her screaming a series of unflattering names that would have deeply offended his mama.

When she reached "self-righteous motherfucker," the vamp guarding the sketchy door broke protocol and wove through the crowd to sort out this new problem. I, however, skedaddled my pert ass toward the newly abandoned door and gripped the doorknob. It turned without resistance, startling me. Who left a guarded door unlocked?

Whatever. Not my problem.

I snuck into the room, then skidded to a stop, my jaw slack.

This was *not* a storage room. Nor a kitchen. Nor a frickin' back office.

No—this was a damn whorehouse. I honestly couldn't think of a better term.

Naked women everywhere. Writhing. Moaning. And on top of the naked women were naked men. Naked *vampire* men.

A blood orgy?

I needed a second to adjust. Except, I didn't have a second. *This* was my bloody story. The club wasn't providing bottles full of fresh human blood. No. They were providing their vampire clientele with *victims*.

Holy guacamole.

No wonder I hadn't spotted a single vamp buying a drink out on the dance floor. Why buy when you could get fresh from the tap back here, holed up in a room that looked like the decorator had taken notes from Hannibal Lector, their greedy mouths latched onto the women?

And the sounds.

My God, the sounds.

I'd seen porn, and this didn't compare. The sucking, the lapping, the moaning, the groaning, the thrusting... I couldn't decide if I needed to throw up or slip someone a twenty. How the hell had they kept this so quiet? And no wonder they'd stationed a guard. Gracious! Imagine if an unknowing customer stumbled across this.

Someone like me!

I rifled through my purse and freed my phone from its fancy hidden pocket, then activated the camera. I had *just* hit record, and hadn't even looked at the screen yet, when one of the closest vamps positioned himself between a pair of long legs. An unconscious woman lay beneath him, her head turned to the side, brandishing a fresh bite wound.

Oh hell no!

I refused to stand here and let *that* happen. Dead or alive, rape was rape. But before I could so much as move, he thrust into her.

Indignation rose hard and fast within me. I aimed my camera at him and opened my mouth, about to scream something—*anything*—when an ice-cold hand clapped over my mouth.

How quickly my rage turned to fear. Before I could so much as react, another arm snaked across my waist and dragged me back against a hard chest. His arms were like vices, too strong for me to struggle against.

He wrenched me backward, and my Jimmy Choos caught against the tiles, falling off my feet. The second my bare feet hit the floor, instinct flooded me. I would *not* become one of these women! I would not become some pin cushion for them to sink their fangs into while they sank something *else* in down below.

I dropped my phone, then screamed and kicked, slapped and bit, twisted and struggled. But no one so much as batted an eyelash in my direction. Hell, no one even bothered to look up, so consumed with their conquests to notice a woman in distress. Doubtful they even cared. And my attacker? All he did was laugh, the vile prick.

He dragged me down a dark hallway, and I heard him kick open another door. Fresh, cold air assaulted me, cooling my fear a few degrees. Maybe it was just the bouncer from out front, kicking me out for breaking the rules. Or maybe the guard had returned to find me inside and was ridding the club of a little problem—namely *me*. Honestly, I didn't care which, so long as they didn't hurt me.

My abductor spun me around and shoved me backward. I staggered from the force and toppled into a metal fence.

Gasping for breath, I clutched the fence and finally glanced up.

A vampire stood in front of me. And it was neither the bouncer nor the guard. And from the looks of the dumpster next to me, he hadn't dragged me out into the street. No, he'd dragged me out the back, into a freaking alleyway.

This wasn't good. Vampires weren't legally allowed to feed on the unwilling, but hey, when did laws ever stop someone from doing what they wanted? And watching this predator pace in front of me didn't fill me with any reassurances.

The vamp lifted his head, his eyes closed, and inhaled. "I love that smell."

His voice. Oh God. He sounded like Death.

"Do you know what fear smells like?" he continued, enjoying his little monologue.

I didn't bother answering. Instead, I searched for something I could use as a weapon. But apparently Fallen liked to keep their alleyway squeaky clean. The *one* time I wouldn't have minded being thrown into a garbage pile.

Without waiting for my answer, my attacker darted forward. Ivory fangs flashed in the pale streetlight, his face terrifyingly monstrous. He slapped the fence by my head, then lifted his other hand and gripped my throat.

Fear snaked down my spine as a million thoughts raced through my mind.

Can't breathe!

Can't scream!

Lucy!

Help!

"You smell like peaches," the vamp rasped, his rank breath brushing against my throat.

Mouth gaping like a fish out of water, I beat him with closed fists, kicked him with bare feet, clawed at his face and arms, *anything* to get this monster *off* me.

Instead, he leaned forward and nuzzled my cheek. He gave another painful squeeze, then released the hold on my throat. I reared back, coughing, choking, gasping. But before I could so much as catch my breath, he struck. Like a viper, his fangs plunged deep into my neck.

I screamed, the hoarse sound likely to be the last thing I ever heard.

Because I was going to die here.

Strange how fast the darkness came. And when it completely consumed me, my last thought was *I should have listened to Lucy.*

Reckless—that was the word Lucy always used to describe me. And every time, I grinned and nodded. I couldn't help it. I liked that word. It suited me perfectly.

For instance, in fifth grade, one of my classmates had dared me to hang upside down from the monkey bars for the entire recess. If I fell, I had to cough up my lunch money. If I won, I got hers. Maybe that didn't seem like a crazy bet, but for a bunch of ten-year-olds, it'd seemed insane. When I won, because of course I did, I used my classmate's money to buy lunch for the homeless man down the street. Lucy and I hadn't been friends at this point. In fact, we'd classified each other as archnemeses. She'd hated me, and I'd hated her. Elementary drama and whatnot. But she'd heard the story from everyone in the school. I was the *wildcat* who'd hung upside down for fifteen minutes without losing my breakfast.

In eleventh grade, I'd punched my soon-to-be ex-boyfriend in the face when he'd spread the rumor that I was a minx in the sheets. Wasn't long before the *truth* had spread around the school. Dude had been too scared to touch me, let alone steal home base.

In twelfth grade, I'd egged *and* toilet-papered our hometown's mayor's house. Now, before anyone starts judging me, I feel like it's important to note that the mayor was—and still is—my father. And like the upstanding citizen he is, he'd just cheated on my mom and kicked us out, so I'd been feeling a little vengeful. And how had my so-called wonderful father responded? He'd called the cops and had me picked up for littering and vandalism. Thankfully, no charges were ever laid, but as a punishment, I'd had to clean up the mess, thereby forcing me to spend time with my father's new she-bat of a mistress who'd moved in soon after my father had kicked us out. I'd returned the favor by giving the bitch's overpriced Agent Provocateur lingerie a spin in the washer and dryer—and *not* on delicate mode.

Her horrified screams had kept me grinning for a year.

My point to all this was that sometimes I don't think things through. I occasionally react rashly. Like, *maybe* it hadn't been such a great idea to storm a vampire club in the middle of the night. And *maybe* it hadn't been such a great idea to film an illegal blood orgy instead of getting the hell out of Dodge and calling the police. My quest for fame had gotten me into trouble more than once, but this time, things had gone a little too far.

Unfortunately, I was now paying the piper. Because, believe me, there was no romance in dying. True death wasn't anything like in the movies. No weepy music as I sucked in my last breath, no final peaceful sigh as my eyes closed, no one gracefully sobbing as they begged me to wake up. Instead, there was a hell of a lot of screaming, some horrible slurping sound echoing in my ear, and the indecency of being discarded in the alleyway like I was nothing more than a piece of garbage.

And the worst part? The absolute catastrophe on top of my horrendously shitty night? I somehow could see all this happening. I'd heard of out-of-body and near-death experiences, but I never believed they were real. It didn't seem possible that your soul or essence or whatever could take a little vacation from your body.

Well, now I knew it was possible.

I stood there and watched as that asshole drained me of almost every last drop of blood, slavering over me like a starved dog drooling over a Big Mac. And when he was done, he wiped his hands on his pants like I was filthy or something and casually strolled back into the club, not a hair out of place. I glared at him the entire time, committing every detail of his face, down to that stupid hairy mole on his chin, to my memory. I wanted to memorize the murderous bastard, because I had every intention of haunting his stupid ass for the rest of my incorporeal existence.

I'd seen *Ghost*. I knew what was happening here. Knew I'd be trapped here until I solved my murder. That was how these things worked, right? Ghosts were the definition of unfinished business, and oh baby, was my business now unfinished. I just needed to find someone nearby who could speak to the dead. This was a club full of vampires, for shit's sake. If they existed, and I, a ghost, existed, then surely there *had* to be a psychic somewhere who could talk to me.

Right?

Except, weirdly enough, things were growing a little... hazy. Was that normal? It felt like a fog had settled over me, like it was trying to erase me from this world.

I rubbed my eyes and turned back to my body, crumpled and broken against the cold cement. Strangely enough, I could feel my connection to it weakening. I wasn't *fully* dead yet, but I could feel the inevitable moment closing in on me. Like a phone counting down the minutes until it died. I estimated I had about four percent left on my life's battery.

Coldness crept into my center. I clutched my chest and staggered toward my body. This was bad. Like, *really* bad. Why punt my soul from my body just to watch this happen? That had to rate pretty high on the torture scale. *Here, kid. Just stand here and watch yourself die, knowing you can't do a single thing about it. Sound good?* No! It absolutely did not!

The closer I got to my body, the more everything faded. The edges were dark-gray now, and it continued to creep inward, robbing my world of all the color. I couldn't see much beyond my body, and even that had begun to blur.

Two percent remained, which I assumed equated to a few minutes.

I kneeled next to my body and reached for my hand, only for my fingers to pass right through. I wanted to scream and curse, but when my lips parted, no sound emerged. Stupid deathly rules.

I was so focused on my situation that I barely noticed when the back door suddenly slammed open. But I definitely noticed when a shadow fell over me. I gasped and shot to my feet to find a stranger hovering over my body.

For the first time, a sliver of hope pushed back the darkness. I knew it was too late for anyone to actually help me, considering I was ninety-nine percent dead now. But at least now, I wouldn't die alone. And for some reason, that comforted me.

I squinted through the foggy haze to find a man crouching next to me. Everything about him was dark, from his hair to his shoes. So dark that I wondered if he was Death himself. I'd always pictured the Grim Reaper cloaked in black with a face so skeletal it scared people to death. Maybe this was him? I couldn't see the man's face, hidden from sight as it was, but everything else fit.

In one fluid movement, he scooped me into his arms and rose. I looked so small, so broken, pressed against his chest.

Less than one percent remained now. I was hanging on by a thread. Barely.

If this guy meant to help, it was too late. No one

could survive such extreme blood loss—even I knew that.

At half a percent, the man moved. I couldn't see what he was doing, but if I strained really hard, I could catch a hint of his face. He stood utterly still, but I'd never forget his eyes. So dark, so piercing, like black coal burning in the darkness. And for one brief moment, I let myself believe he was staring through the veil *at me.*

He shifted his weight, then pressed something against my mouth, something I couldn't make out. But the instant we connected, I *felt* it. A strange electrical current zipping through my body. It almost felt like a horse had kicked me in the chest. I gasped and wrapped my arms around myself.

Another zap. Stronger this time. And with it came a little clarity. Like there was a light at the end of the tunnel, barreling right toward me.

When the third jolt came, I was ready. Excited, even. With every little kick, I felt stronger, alive, and pissed as hell. I had no idea what was happening, and I didn't care. All that mattered was my countdown had begun to reverse and my battery meter climbed upward. Like he'd plugged me into the wall. Half a percent became three; three became ten; ten became thirty; thirty became fifty.

At seventy-five percent, my soul slammed back into my body and my eyes flew open. I sucked in a sputtering gasp and choked. Something warm and bitter filled my mouth. It tasted like pennies and ambrosia mixed into one strange cocktail. I coughed as the liquid trickled down my chin. But none of that mattered when I caught sight of the man holding me. The man with eyes as dark as night.

He stared down at me, his mouth curved upward. I caught sight of his *sharp* pearly whites, but for some reason, they didn't scare me.

"Ah, there you are," he said in a voice as smooth as silk.

Mm, I'd always loved a man with an accent, and his was to die for. I tried to think of a witty response, something biting and hilarious to break the tension. It wasn't every night a girl woke up in the arms of a beautiful man who'd saved her life, after all. But my savior chose that moment to unleash his hypnotic gaze on me once more. Damn, it was mesmerizing. I couldn't tear my eyes away. They seemed to swirl like dark, warm chocolate syrup. So delicious. So manly. So beautiful.

"Thank you," he said with a wide smile.

Shit. Had I said that out loud?

"Shh." He repositioned me in his arms. "You're safe now, Anna. Sleep."

He didn't need to tell me twice.

🦇

A SHARP JAB in my ass startled me awake.

I sucked in a startled breath and froze. Oh fuck. Was that... a dick? Was there a *dick* poking me in the *ass*? That was impossible, right? Except, it felt distinctly similar. The hardened tip, the long ridge—holy shit, that *was* a dick! There were so many things wrong with this scenario, the most important of which was that I had no idea whose dick it was! I couldn't recall *anything* from last night after Lucy and I infiltrated Fallen.

Wait, wait, *wait*. Fallen was a vamp club.

Oh. Oh no.

Did I get drunk and fuck a fanger? No. No! Surely, Lucy would never let me go home with a vamp.

Unless... what if we'd been enthralled? Enraptured? Hypnotized? Whatever they frickin' called it. I'd heard vamps could do that. Tamper with our minds, make us believe things, make us think we were attracted to them—their own personal form of Ecstasy and Rohypnol.

Oh, this had all the potential for an epic disaster of catastrophic proportions.

Okay. The most important thing at this moment was not to freak out and certainly not to move until I figured everything out. I couldn't afford to wake the beast attached to the wanker still knock-knock-knocking at my backdoor.

Think, Anna. Think!

If a vamp had hypnotized me, I wouldn't be aware of it. And I certainly wouldn't be in the right frame of mind to question what had happened. So, by that twisted logic, it seemed safe to assume I hadn't been mind-raped.

Was there a second option? A possible drunken fling with some junkie human obsessed with vamps? I didn't *feel* hungover. And I knew without a doubt I hadn't taken even the slightest sip of alcohol last night. I never did when working, because I liked a clear mind.

Regardless, I needed to get the eff out of here and find Lucy. Vamoose my poor violated ass out the front door and never look back. Thankfully, the hard member digging into my backside hadn't so much as twitched, meaning my bed partner was

DATING DRACULA

still snoozing away. It also meant I needed to be careful. Quiet. Sneaky. But first, I had to crawl out of this bed without waking anyone, which might be a little difficult, considering it was absolutely pitch-black in here. I was surrounded by so much darkness that I couldn't see an inch in front of my face. Whoever lived here owned some killer sun-blocking curtains, which would make escaping super difficult.

I only hoped to hell I never gave him my phone number.

I reached out a hand, searching for the edge of the bed, but cursed when my fingers slammed into a wall.

Uh... okay. That was unexpected. And more than a little nerve-wracking.

I flattened my palm against the wall and followed it upward. But when my palm found a corner and took a sharp forty-five degree turn inward, I sucked in a panicked breath.

What the *hell*?

Fuck this. I didn't care anymore if I woke someone, so I flipped onto my other side and felt around. That thing jabbing me in the ass? My damn shoes. The stupid heels I'd worn to the club last night. But that didn't make sense. I remembered them falling off my feet at some point. So how were they here?

On the upside, at least I wasn't in bed with some stranger.

I reached out, hoping to find the other edge of the bed, but instead, found more wall. A wall that climbed upward and took another forty-five degree turn inward.

I started shivering and gasping for breath.

There was only one thing that explained the walls surrounding me. But it couldn't be happening. I wasn't trapped inside a....

Cripes, I couldn't even finish that thought.

What the hell happened last night? Had a serial killer kidnapped me? Locked me in a box and left?

I inhaled through my nose and froze at the unmistakable scent of pine and satin.

Now fully panicking, I patted the material beneath me and the plush pillow under my head.

Holy effing hell.

Either someone had placed bedding inside this box, or I was locked in a *coffin*.

Yup, I screamed. And when my breath ran out, I screamed some more. This was everyone's worst nightmare come true. Had someone buried me alive? Or was this some sort of horrible joke? Like a hazing?

And if so, who the hell would play such a cruel prank?

It didn't take long for me to realize that screaming was likely using up all my air. Eyes wide, even in the darkness, I clapped a trembling hand over my mouth. This was bad. So very, very bad. And I had no idea what to do. No one ever taught a class on how to escape a coffin. Tied to a chair, I could handle. Self-defense, sure! I could kick a guy in the balls better than any woman. But this was *beyond* anything I'd ever imagined possible.

Someone had *buried* me. In a coffin.

Okay. Calm down. Think your way out of this.

I waved a hand near my face just to feel the air move, to convince myself I hadn't used it all up screaming. Scenario: what if I'd died last night? Was that why I couldn't remember anything? No, that didn't make sense. Dead people didn't come back to life.

Or rather, not *all* dead people.

Vampires sure as shit came back to life.

Except, I didn't feel like a vampire. I felt like *me*.

And where the hell was Lucy? My blood ran cold just thinking about her also being buried somewhere out there, screaming my name, worrying about me as I was her.

No. I had to get out of here. If not for me, then for her. I couldn't let my best friend die out there all alone.

Coffins were made of wood, evidenced by the smell. That meant they were breakable. It might hurt like hell, but I could handle that. I tightened my hand into a fist and pulled it back next to my head. There wasn't enough room for a solid punch, and there wasn't enough room to pull my knees up for a decent kick either. Who the hell designed these things? And why were they so small? A girl needed some leg room to kick her way free, right?

Breathe, I told myself. *You can do this. You've taken self-defense classes. You know how to throw a punch. It's gonna hurt, but hey, a broken hand is better than suffocating to death.*

Nodding to myself, I struck, then gasped when my fist punched right through the top of the coffin. *Whoa.* Wood splinters rained down on me, but I didn't stop to contemplate what that meant. My hand was *outside* the coffin, and that was all that mattered. I pulled it back, then peered through the jagged hole. I'd expected dirt, mud, cement, but instead, I found only air.

So I hadn't been buried then. Relief loosened my muscles. Things were looking up. I could handle this now. Just knowing I wasn't entombed six feet under soothed my frayed nerves.

Palms flat against the lid, I gave it a hard shove. It slid off without resistance. Huh. Maybe I should have tried that first before going all Chuck Norris on the coffin's ass. Meh. I felt surprisingly little guilt. Whoever had pulled this shitty little prank could pay for repairs, because I sure as hell didn't find this amusing.

I gripped the edges of the coffin and launched myself over the edge, landing silently on my toes. I cocked my head and stared at my feet, surprised by my sudden cat-like nimbleness. That sort of move usually landed me on my ass, listening to people laugh as they uploaded the embarrassing video online.

I shook my head and turned away from the coffin. I needed to focus on location. Where was I? At first glance, I appeared to be standing in the middle of what looked like an attic—albeit a reinforced one. I groaned and shuddered. Nothing like waking up in a creepily enclosed room, complete with a coffin to freak a girl out.

So then whose attic was this, and why was I here?

"Anna!"

I whirled toward the familiar voice, a grin spreading across my face at the sight of Lucy barreling toward me. Thank heavens she was fine! At least now I knew she wasn't trapped in a coffin somewhere too. But why was she here? She never would have arranged this little stunt, considering she didn't possess a single funny bone in her body. These sorts of pranks weren't her style. Lucy lacked *all* imagination for such things.

She screeched to a stop in front of me, her cheeks streaked with tears.

Whoa, what the hell? Had someone hurt her? If so, I felt a sudden need to punch that specific person for hurting my Lucy.

"Are you all right?" I demanded, then froze when something sharp scraped across my tongue. I instinctively reached for my mouth but paused when Lucy started rambling.

"Me? Are you insane?" She wiped her snotty nose against her arm. "I should be asking you that question! Asks *me* if *I'm* all right...."

Huh? A deep frown pinched my eyebrows. I felt fine, considering my recent circumstances. Yet, she still seemed quite upset by something.

She took a deep breath, then ran her hands over her hair and exhaled. "Okay. Are you okay?"

"I'm fine. Why wouldn't I be? Oh, because I just woke up in a fucking *coffin*?"

She paled. Like visibly paled. I'd never seen someone do that before. All the blood just suddenly drained from her face. It was mesmerizing. I stared at her cheeks, fascinated by the tiny veins and arteries beneath her skin.

Lucy took a giant step back and glanced behind her. "He... he said it was necessary."

"Who said?"

"Now, don't get mad."

"Girl, I'm already spitting. Out with it already."

Lucy swallowed. My gaze dropped to that little hollow in her throat, and I watched the seductive movement. I'd never noticed how beautiful her neck was before. So lean and graceful. And warm. Wow. She looked *very* warm. We'd never been more than friends, but I suddenly felt a strange desire for her.

I wanted to bury my face in her throat. It looked so inviting. So delicious. So—

"Lucy, step back," a male voice commanded, one that sparked a hazy memory, almost like a dream.

Dazed, I tore my gaze from her newly flushed neck and flicked a quick glance at the shadow hovering near the doorway. I barely paid him any mind, my focus all for Lucy. She was all that mattered right now. Eyes half-lidded, I stumbled forward and mindlessly reached for her. Distantly, I heard myself mumble something incomprehensible, with absolutely no idea what I was trying to say. I just knew I needed her. I needed something *from* her.

She turned away from me and glanced over her shoulder. "What?"

"Step back. Now," the shadow ordered.

Lucy bolted out of reach, and instantly, full-blown anger erupted within me. It took control of my body, rising hard and fast like a volcano. I'd never felt this monstrous presence before. It seemed to invade every inch of me until all that remained was a senseless creature with one thing on its mind.

To feed.

My lips peeled back, and with a savage snarl, I lunged forward, my clawed fingers swiping at my best friend's throat.

The shadow man swept into my path, but I ignored him completely. I saw his arm rushing toward me. I meant to duck beneath it, but instead, he turned his hand and grazed his wrist against my mouth. He must have nicked himself against something sharp. I knew it the second his skin split. It was like my senses kicked into overdrive. I *smelled* the blood before I saw the wound—I'd never noticed how mouth-wateringly delicious blood smelled before. Never craved something the way I craved *this* right now. It was like Lucy didn't exist anymore. The only thing that mattered was his blood.

I snatched his arm and yanked it to my mouth.

With a soft sigh, my lips closed around his wrist, and I sucked. The instant his blood coated my tongue, I sank into mindless bliss. I barely registered the feel of his fingers stroking my hair or the sound of Lucy sobbing in the corner. The only thing I knew was this incessant hunger and endless thirst.

Guess I really had died.

3

WITH EVERY GULP OF BLOOD, I felt my sanity returning. But with it came this annoying yammering sound, and it took a few more swallows for me to realize it was coming from Lucy. My eyes were closed, but I could smell her. She stood—more like hovered—nearby, fretting over every damn little thing.

"Should she still be drinking?"

OMG, yes.

"Hasn't she had enough yet?"

Not nearly.

"Why is this taking so long?"

Because I'm thirsty!

"Shouldn't you be doing something?"

He is! Calm your tits!

This man's—whose name I *still* didn't know—blood was so sweet, so fulfilling. Every mouthful made me want more. A part of me never wanted to let go, but there was a smaller part of me, the lingering human part, that screamed wordlessly in my head.

I was drinking *blood*, for crying out loud. From a stranger, no less.

What had my life become?

My senses slammed back into place, and I reared back from the bleeding arm with a choking gasp. My stomach instantly roiled, so I clapped a hand over my mouth and spun away without so much as a thank you. Just like that, the blood turned sour in my gut. I couldn't believe this. I just drank someone's blood. Their blood. Their blood! No matter how many times I repeated it, my brain refused to comprehend.

Yesterday, I was a normal girl. Lucy and I had left our hometown and driven to New Orleans with a single goal in mind: getting into Fallen and busting open the truth. We'd rolled the windows down as we drove, singing into the wind as we sped toward the city. We'd left all our problems back home—including my freshly minted ex-boyfriend of one week—with the grandiose expectation that I'd be famous upon return.

Oh, I was going to be famous all right. Or maybe infamous was the better word.

The first resident of Perish, Louisiana, to be turned into a vampire.

A *vampire*.

My mama had always told me my busybody nose would get me into trouble one day. I absolutely hated the idea of returning home to prove her prediction true.

"Anna?" Lucy whispered.

"Stay back." My voice shook with strained effort. I could still smell her. Hell, I still craved her. If she so much as took another step, I might lose control again. And I refused to let that happen. She was my best friend—no way in hell I'd be responsible for her death.

Of course, she didn't listen. Lucy never did. She did what she wanted, when she wanted.

Her footsteps practically echoed in my ears, but it was nothing compared to the sound of her thunderous heartbeat. Saliva pooled in my mouth, and it took every ounce of restraint I possessed not to seize her by the throat and drain her dry.

"Anna?"

"I said stay back!" I shouted, whirling around to face her.

The pungent stench of fear splashed me in the face. Eyes wide, I cupped my cheeks and staggered backward. That damn monster had risen inside me again. Was that the vampire within? Would it always be this hungry?

"I—I'm sorry." I shook my head over and over, hoping it would help clear my thoughts. I reminded myself again and again that I didn't *actually* want to eat Lucy. I didn't want to eat *anyone*. Unfortunately, though, it seemed like I no longer had a say in that matter.

This was too much.

I needed to focus on something else—*anything* else.

So, instead, I turned toward the man who'd just fed me his blood. The second our gazes clashed, my jaw dropped. I recognized him! He was the shadow from the alleyway. The man who'd saved me. Even now, his eyes burned, enthralled, in a way I'd never seen before.

"You," I whispered.

He matched my stare with a faint smile. "Me."

"You two know each other?" Lucy asked. "From before all this, I mean?"

I shook my head. I seemed to be doing that a lot tonight. "No, I don't *know* him. But he saved my life."

"Um, I think he failed," Lucy snapped, her frustration painting her cheeks with a lovely splash of color. "Epically."

"No, he saved me," I whispered as memories assaulted me. This was the man from the alley. The one who'd jump-started my heart and saved me at the very last second by apparently turning me into a vampire. The evidence was undeniable at this point.

"Can someone *please* tell me what the hell is going on here?" Lucy demanded, her voice shrill. "And start at the damn beginning please, because I have no fucking clue what happened."

I winced at the sound of Lucy cussing. I'd only heard her swear maybe once or twice in our life. She'd always been the nice one. Not me. I cussed as much as possible.

"Start at the point where you insisted I cause a distraction," she said.

Right. The distraction. The club. The vampires. The orgy. It was strange—I remembered it all, but it felt like the memories were from another life. All hazy and dim, like my brain was already struggling to forget the traumatic event. Self-preservation, perhaps?

"Well?" Lucy insisted when I didn't immediately respond.

"Give me a sec. It's hard being dead."

"Undead," my savior corrected.

"Same diff." I rubbed my eyes and groaned. "Okay. So, I had you cause a distraction to draw away a vamp guarding the back door. When I snuck in, I found a blood orgy. I got a little video, but before I could leave, someone grabbed me."

"A vampire?" Lucy asked.

I pinned her with a droll look that clearly said *duh.* "He dragged me outside and... killed me."

"Almost killed you," the stranger said.

I caught his gaze again and felt my nerves settle. There was something odd about him. Something calming but equally mysterious. I didn't even know his name, but I owed him so much. Without him, I'd be flat on my back in a morgue right now with a lovely tag dangling from my toe.

Even more interesting, I felt a strange fluttering in my chest when I looked at him. It wasn't my heart, because sadly, that little gem was long dead. I hadn't noticed it at first, but now that I knew I'd crossed into the undead, I realized my body was *quiet.* As a living, breathing human, I'd never paid attention to my heart unless it did something funky like skip a beat. But now, my entire body felt hollow. Nothing beat beneath my breast, no blood flowed through my veins. I was walking and talking like it was any other day, but my body seemed to be firmly dead.

I cleared my throat and refocused my attention. "You knew my name."

My savior quirked a thick, dark brow.

"After you changed me. You said my name and told me to sleep. How did you know who I was?"

His expression shuttered. I watched, mesmerized, as his mouth flattened into a grim line and his eyes narrowed, as though he didn't want to answer my question. "Does it matter?"

"Definitely. Especially to me."

"And me," Lucy chimed in.

My savior sighed, his broad shoulders rising and falling with the dramatic movement, considering we didn't *need* to breathe other than to smell things. I pulled my gaze from his face and inspected the rest of him. He'd draped himself in black clothing, right down to his shoes. The dark shade contrasted against his pale skin but blended with his ear-length, wavy, midnight hair and obsidian eyes. Monochromatic or not, I had to admit, he made it look good, like an avenging dark angel.

"You wouldn't believe me if I told you."

Laughter burst past my lips. "That evasion might have worked yesterday, but not so much today."

The stranger stepped toward me and extended his hand, as though inviting me to touch him. And for some unknown reason, I wanted to. No doubt about it. I reached out and brushed my fingers across his palm. The instant we connected, warmth bloomed within my chest. For a brief moment, I wondered if my heart had restarted. But then the moment passed, and I realized it was nothing more than a wave of attraction for a man I didn't know.

Interesting.

His fingers closed around mine, and he pulled me toward him, murmuring quietly, "I heard your name in my head."

I peered up at him with a small frown. Had he just admitted to being able to read minds? Because that was impossible—said the newborn she-vamp. Was there even a word for us? Besides monster?

"You what?" Lucy asked, saving me the embarrassment of asking him to repeat himself.

He brushed his fingers along my knuckles, then

released my hand and stepped back. "I heard her name. It was whispered to me."

"Like you can read minds?"

"No, I don't have that ability." I wanted to dig deeper into this whole hearing my name in his head thing. Because that didn't seem natural. But he pressed onward. "When I realized Anna was in trouble, I stepped in."

"And turned her into a vampire!" Lucy accused.

"Her options were that or death. Perhaps you would have preferred a deceased best friend? Someone to bury six feet under?"

Lucy's mouth snapped shut.

I choked back a laugh, knowing she wouldn't appreciate it. I understood her concerns, but really, she couldn't complain about his methods. I'd been there. If he hadn't turned me, I would have died. That other vamp had done quite the thorough job. He hadn't drunk every last drop, but he hadn't left me enough to survive the ordeal either.

And speaking of which... "Do you know the other vampire? The one who killed me?"

"Almost killed you," my savior intonated. "And no, unfortunately not."

"Super handy," I mumbled. "So, what are the rules here? Do I file a complaint somewhere? Or even better, get to hunt the bastard down and kill him for killing me?"

"If that's your desire."

I blinked. "Which one?"

His mouth curled into a small grin, leading me to believe he'd been referring to the latter.

"Okay. Good. I want to kill him back." I could already imagine it. The second I got my hands on that asshole, I was going to break every bone in his body and shove something super long up his dickhole. No one killed me and got away with it.

"What? Are you insane?" Lucy screeched. She rushed forward, grabbed my hands, then gasped and stared down at them. "Holy crap, you're ice-cold."

"No, I'm not. You're just boiling hot." I drew my hands back and wiped them down my shirt. "Geez. Do you have a fever or something?"

"Human temperatures run around ninety-eight degrees," my savior commented. "Vampires run much cooler than that. It's noticeably different."

"Fun," I muttered.

"Just more information to store away for later." Lucy hugged her arms around her waist and shook her head. "Look, I know you want to kick your murderer's butt and all that, but don't you think that's maybe a little dangerous? And reckless? He *killed* you last time, remember?"

"Almost killed me," I said at the same time as my savior. We shared a private grin, then I turned back to Lucy. "I think I'll be a little more equipped this time."

Lucy's face hardened. "What about your family?"

I froze. "What about them?"

"Don't you think they might deserve to hear what happened? To see you? To grieve you? If you go off guns a-blazing, and *he* kills *you*, you'll be really dead this time. Like *dead*-dead."

"So, you'd rather I just let this go?"

"Yes!" She threw her arms up into the air. "Anna, you got off lucky this time! Okay, something bad happened, and yes, your life has been irreparably changed, but you're *alive*, sort of. Walking and talking. Maybe you drink blood now, but that's better than a tombstone! If you go after him, I'll be the one returning home with the news that you're truly dead."

"Oh, don't be so dramatic. I'm only half-dead."

"Undead," my savior clarified.

"Yeah—that." I waved a hand. "So, why does it matter when I tell them? Don't you think someone should track this guy down? What if I'm not the only one he's killed?"

"So what? Aren't there vampire police who can handle this?"

"I have no idea. I just woke up, remember?"

"We have a protocol for these situations," my savior commented. "Someone who will open an investigation on your behalf."

"There!" Lucy cried out. "See! Someone else can handle this."

"Maybe I don't want someone else to handle this," I growled, remembering how vulnerable I'd felt in that alleyway, how broken. That vamp had stolen everything from me. He'd sunk his teeth in my throat and drained me—and he'd *enjoyed* it. I didn't want some vampified cop dealing with this. I wanted to be the one who ripped out my murderer's throat. How many victims got that chance in life?

Lucy scoffed and shook her head. "This is so stupid. You're risking your life, *again*. You dragged me to that club. Then left me without any idea as to what you were doing. When you didn't come back, I had no idea how to find you! Do you know what that felt like? They kicked me out when I started making a scene. I luckily found this guy holding you in the alley"—she stopped and released a slow exhale—

"and you're doing it again. Your half-cocked ideas got you killed once, and now they're going to get you permanently dead."

"Lucy—"

"I'm not staying," she blurted out.

Betrayal stabbed me in the chest. "What?"

She met my gaze with tears brimming in her eyes. "You think I want to stay here and watch you hunt down some vamp in the name of justice? Sorry, vengeance. What if he wins the fight? What then?"

"Lucy." I walked toward her but froze when she waved her hands in the air and spun around, giving me her back.

The scent of her anger was rich, like a sweet perfume filling the air. But beneath it, I caught the scent of something more primal, bitter. Grief, I realized. Strange that I could smell emotions now.

I caught the sound of her soft sobs. They were almost deafening now with my sensitive hearing.

I wasn't sure how to process all this. Lucy and I had been best friends since high school, after we'd finally buried our frenemy hatchets. We were Lucy and Anna, sisters from different misters. Our parents had often remarked how we were always attached at the hip. She'd never said no to me before, and certainly had never abandoned me in a moment of need. Then again, my shenanigans had never gotten me killed before, and I'd never tried to hurt her before.

Seemed my death had put a small damper on our relationship.

"I'm sorry," she whispered with her back still to me. "I just.... You died, Anna. You're *dead*."

"Undead," my savior clarified for like the third time.

"It's still dead!" Lucy snapped.

Even I glared at him. Now wasn't the time for his little comments.

"I—I don't know how to handle all this. Do I grieve for you? Or celebrate the fact that you're still walking around? You're a vampire, Anna. For frick's sake, do you know what that means? You drink blood, you sleep in a coffin... you aren't *you* anymore. How am I supposed to handle this?"

My dead heart shattered. "You're supposed to accept me as I am," I said, struggling to keep my voice steady. "We're sisters. Always. Forever."

"Except always and forever means two very different things to us now," she said.

I forced myself to swallow. From the sounds of it, Lucy was breaking up with me. Which almost made me laugh. She was my longest relationship ever. And she wanted to walk away from it? All because of an accident I had no control over?

I ran a hand down my face and turned toward my savior. Someone whose name I *really* needed to learn. I couldn't keep referring to him as my savior or I was going to develop some major hero worship issues.

"Anna, I'm sorry," Lucy repeated. "But I think I need some time to process all this."

I nodded, all the while keeping my gaze trained on my savior. He was the only thing keeping me calm right now. The thought that I might lose my best friend over all this was too much. I couldn't show her how much this hurt, because if I did, I might never recover. Lucy had stormed into a vamp club at my side, but apparently, she drew the line at death.

And honestly? I didn't blame her. This time, tears really did spring to my eyes, but I blinked them back before they spilled. If I started crying, I had a feeling I'd never stop.

"I'm going to head back to the hotel," she said. "I've been staying there the past few nights." Wait, what? Past few *nights*? But before I could question that little tidbit, she continued speaking. "Do you want me to call your parents for you? Explain what happened?"

"No," I rasped. That wasn't her responsibility. If anyone was going to tell them about my transformation, it would be me.

"I'll text you," she mumbled, but her voice was already fading. She was leaving.

Text me. Ugh. Why not just tell me you hope we can still be friends?

I hated this. What happened to best friends forever? I'd like to think that if this had happened to her, I'd still be standing by her side. Lucy was my world. Nothing could have convinced me to leave her.

"I'm sorry" was her final comment before I heard the door shut.

I took a few minutes to absorb everything. Thankfully, my savior let me brood in silence. I appreciated that. I wasn't in the mood to hear platitudes right now.

Once I was sure I had schooled my expression, I turned toward him and nodded. It was embarrassing to have someone witness a break-up, but there wasn't anything I could do about that now.

I needed a distraction. I didn't want to think about Lucy right now. I'd reserve that for later, when

I was alone and could process everything myself. Instead, I stared up at him, once again stricken speechless when our gazes met. Why did I find him so enthralling? So fascinating? It felt like I could stare at him for hours.

Clearing my throat, I rubbed the bridge of my nose and asked, "Well, do you have a name?"

His brows shot upward, and an amused smile claimed his lips, exposing the tips of his fangs. Intrigued, I reached for my own, poking them with my fingertip. They must have been what scraped my tongue earlier. Seemed they were a permanent fixture too. I'd have to remember that when talking and laughing. Vampires might be public knowledge now, but as seen by Lucy, humans weren't one hundred percent ready to accept them yet.

"Forgive me," he said, his voice deliciously rumbly. "I'm so accustomed to being recognized wherever I go that I often forget to introduce myself."

So, he was like vampire royalty or something?

Fangs still peeking out from behind his lips, he gave an old-fashioned bow, one he executed flawlessly, then peered at me through long, dark lashes. I shit you not, the boy almost breathed life back into me. He was just that gorgeous.

"My name is Vlad." He took my hand and lifted

it to his lips before brushing a gentle kiss across my knuckles. "But most know me as Dracula."

I wish I could say I absorbed that information with grace and poise. But that would have been a lie. Instead, I burst out laughing, and said, "No shit!"

Did he just say Dracula?

Like... *the* Dracula? *I vant to suck your blood,* Dracula?

My shoulders shook with gentle laughter, but the more I thought about it, the more hysterical this seemed. Dracula! The big guy himself. I was hardly a fan of bloodsuckers, but even I had to admit, I was starstruck. This guy was positively the most famous man in the world. Hell, maybe even more famous than the British monarchy. Everyone knew Queen Elizabeth, sure, but Dracula had stuffed dolls, movies, TV shows, books.... He even had Halloween costumes based after him!

I snorted with laughter—a very unappealing

habit, I admit—then laughed harder when I caught sight of his wide-eyed expression. My first night diving into the world of vampires, and I meet the Count himself. What were the chances?

As for dear ole Drac, he seemed a little put out by my reaction. If I'd thought his expression dark before, it was nothing compared to now. Rage flashed across his noble countenance, and his nose crinkled like a pissed-off lion. At the sight of his whetted fangs, my laughter morphed into a choking cough, and I covered my mouth with the back of my hand.

"I'm sorry, I'm sorry," I sputtered. I waved my hand in front of my face, then reached toward him. Unsurprisingly, he stepped out of reach. "It's just... wow. I mean, Dracula."

"I prefer Vlad," he growled. And damn, the man could growl. Ever heard a human attempt that before? It always made me laugh. We—or *they*—weren't designed to truly growl anymore. But the sound rumbling deep in Dracula's throat made all my little hairs stand on end. Seemed wise to remember not to piss him off.

Before I could attempt another apology, Dracula —sorry, *Vlad*—grabbed my hand and pulled me out of the room. He didn't grip me hard, but he pulled with enough force to keep me skittering after him.

Clearly, he wasn't impressed with me right now, and I couldn't blame him. I wouldn't appreciate someone laughing at my expense either. I needed to try apologizing again. You know, when my sides weren't hurting from laughing so hard.

He led me down a flight of winding stairs, then guided me through a series of rooms. He refused to let me peruse, so I studied each room fleetingly, catching sight of things like four-poster beds, ornate bathtubs—yes, there was more than one—marble flooring, and oh yeah, regal statues of him everywhere. Pretty much everything one would expect to find in Dracula's estate.

As we hurried down another flight of stairs, I caught whiffs of humans, and my mouth began to water. Despite the fact that I'd just fed on him, my stomach twisted with hunger. Thankfully, Dracula tightened his grip on my hand and tugged me along, away from the delicious humans. Before I could thank him, he took a hard right-hand turn into a sitting room.

And holy crap on a cracker, what a sitting room it was. It had to be bigger than my entire apartment. I stepped forward, noting that he held onto my hand as long as possible before finally releasing it.

"Fuck me," I whispered.

Like, holy shit, maybe even twice as big as my apartment. The ceiling was at least two-stories high, and in the middle hung a glimmering chandelier. Whistling softly, I spun in a slow circle and studied the rest of the room. Beautiful paintings and elegant sconces graced the warm-toned walls, and across from me was a wall-to-wall fireplace gently flickering with small flames. I stepped closer, only to hear the charred wood popping away. Which meant someone had to attend this freaking fire *all night long*.

Must be good to be rich.

I returned to Dracula, then grimaced when I caught sight of a truly horrendous pair of couches behind him. Fainting couches, I believe they were called. I'd seen them in movies before—usually historicals—all velvet material and wooden framing. Ugh, I *hated* velvet. Even though it suited the slightly Victorian décor, it screamed *uncomfortable*. Clearly, this room wasn't meant for relaxing. I felt drab in comparison, my naked feet leaving a slight dirt trail thanks to the frightening events that had led me here.

Guess no one had bothered to clean me up before slapping me in a coffin.

A quick glance down revealed my unkempt condition. My outfit was in tatters, my feet bare and filthy, and blood crusted my hair. I must have looked quite the fright. Thankfully, Dracula—ugh, *Vlad.* Man, I really needed to get into that habit—didn't seem overly concerned about my current state compared to his pristine room.

Which had me wondering... "Live here long?"

He followed my gaze and took in the surroundings as though trying to see the room from my perspective. "A few years now. I bought this place from a dear friend who wished to leave New Orleans. He'd grown tired of all the tourists."

"And would this dear friend be, oh, I don't know, the King of England or something?"

Vlad's gaze strayed from the chandelier to the plush fur carpet beneath our feet. "Another vampire, actually. He'd lived here for a few centuries and decided it was time to move. Grew tired of the famous life, I suppose."

"He was famous before vampires came out to the public?"

Vlad nodded. "He's a central character in a popular book series. People wanted to see his house, even if they didn't believe he was a real vampire. He left a few things behind after he moved, and I found I liked them enough to leave them."

My brows darted upward. Just who were we

talking about here? Another famous vampire? I only
knew of a couple, and Vlad was the main one.

Vlad waved a dismissive hand, clearly not the
sort to name-drop, much to my annoyance. I was
itching with curiosity, but I forced myself not to pry.
Seeing as how there weren't *that* many famous
vampires, I figured I could take an educated guess as
to who he meant. And if I was right, that would
explain the wolf fur draped across the back of an
antique dining chair sitting across the room and the
picture of a fancy violin hanging on the wall,
assuming those didn't belong to Vlad.

"Well then." Vlad crossed the room and took a
seat on one of those dreadful couches. "I imagine you
must have some questions."

He removed his jacket and flung it over the back
of the fainting couch, then gestured for me to sit next
to him. I grimaced at the sight of all that velvet. In all
my life, I'd never liked the feel of it. It made me itchy
just thinking about touching it. I didn't find it soft
like everyone else. It was like touching Styrofoam.
Whenever I *did* touch it, I felt this strange catch in
the back of my throat, almost like it was suffocating
me. Velvet and I certainly were not friends, and I felt
no desire to bridge that gap.

Instead, I skirted around the couch and perched

my big ole butt on what I assumed, and damn well *hoped*, was a stool.

Vlad gave an amused smirk but ignored my preferred seating and instead indicated that I should speak.

Right. Questions. I had so many I didn't know where to begin. My whole life had imploded. Where would I even start? Maybe with the simplest things? Then go from there? See where the conversation led us?

"So..." I tapped my fingers against my knee. "I guess I'm a vampire, huh?"

The corner of Vlad's mouth tipped upward. "Indeed."

"And just to be clear, you're the one who turned me?"

He inclined his head.

"And that makes you my... master?" I cringed when I said that word. I was a woman of the twenty-first century, I didn't dig the whole *master* vibe.

To Vlad's credit, he seemed equally horrified by the notion. "Not even remotely."

Thank goodness for that. Yuck.

"What does it make you then? Is there a title for someone who turns another into a vampire?"

"A sire," he said, settling into the couch. He

rested an ankle against his thigh and laid a hand on his knee.

Sire. That sounded fancy. While the last thing I wanted to do was fangirl in front of Vlad, I had to admit, I found this part fascinating. Not the dying bit, of course, but the being turned by him. Imagine what this could do for me and for my vlog. Bloody freaking Dracula. Vlad the Impaler, for cripes' sake. If I could interview *him*, the man himself, imagine how my popularity would skyrocket. People all over the world would tune into my vlog because of my personal connection to the most famous vampire in history. Hell, the most infamous tyrant, if you considered his human life.

"I'm not him," Vlad suddenly said, interrupting my inner monologue.

I blinked. "Not who?"

"Vlad Tepes."

"I thought you said you couldn't read minds," I accused.

"I can't. But your expression is quite transparent. Not to mention, I have quite a bit of experience in this area. When I tell people my name, they tend to jump to this first conclusion."

"Okay, but you did say you're Vlad."

"My birth name is Vlad Vasek," he said, his other

arm now stretching along the back of the couch. He looked the picture of comfort and ease. Every bit of me was dying to video him during this line of questioning, but considering I'd just woken in a coffin, I had no idea where my phone was.

"I'm far from the man you're thinking of," Vlad continued. "Tepes was a cruel, vindictive monster. Unfortunately, Vlad was a common name at my time of birth. It might interest you to know I'm older than Tepes, by about a decade or so. It's difficult to keep track of the years when you're as old as I am, but I remember someone telling me a decade once."

I stared dumbfoundedly. "But you called yourself Dracula."

"Indeed. There are those among your kind who associate Dracula with Tepes. And why not? The man was as bloodthirsty as they come. They would be wrong, however. Dear Mr. Stoker wasn't writing about Vlad Tepes. That's an assumption made by scholars, fanatics, even family members."

"Stoker was writing about *you*?"

Vlad nodded. "He was an insightful man and saw through my guise in minutes. He lived at a time when humans believed in the supernatural. Most feared ghosts and goblins, and they certainly feared the undead. In fact, where I'm from, graves were often reopened after five or so years and the corpses checked for vampirism. Things like simply not following proper burial procedure could result in the rising of a vampire. Humans lived in fear of a great many things back then. The concept of staking a vampire came about from the belief that staking a body to the ground would pin the monster to their grave, leaving them unable to rise.

"Stoker sought me out to learn about such creatures. To this day, I'm not sure when he figured out I was a vampire, but he soon offered me a sip of his blood. I was younger then, foolish even, and I took him up on that offer. To him, I was the confirmation of all his pursuits.

"However, while visiting my country, he came to learn of another man. One truly long-dead but equally intriguing. Vlad Tepes fascinated him. I cautioned him against writing his book, warning him that others of my kind might not appreciate the release of our secrets. But Stoker's imagination would not be silenced, and I found him too engaging to kill. Thus, Dracula's legend was born."

Huh. That put a small damper on my buzz, but not entirely. "So, you're not Tepes."

"No."

While slightly disappointed, I was also relieved. I

couldn't imagine being tied to such a tyrant for the rest of my existence. "And Tepes is not Dracula."

Vlad shook his head. "People made their assumptions, but we vampires know the truth. Especially considering quite a few of us were born before Tepes and knew the man himself. Cruel, yes. Vampire, no."

I bit my lip and considered my next question. Finally, after a moment's hesitation, I decided to go for it. What was the worst thing he could say? "Would you be willing to let me interview you?"

The sight of his widening eyes brought a shy smile to my lips. Had my question surprised him?

"Interview me about what?"

"Just you. The truth behind Dracula. Let the world meet the real you and not the fictional character in the books and movies."

"And how, might I ask, would you interview me?"

This time, I was the one to wave the dismissive hand. "I have a vlog."

His blank stare wasn't encouraging.

"Um. Like a movie, except I'm filming you and asking questions for the public to view."

Understanding dawned on Vlad's face. "I'm afraid that won't be possible for two reasons."

I tried not to show my disappointment. This was exactly the sort of thing my vlog needed. A human— well, vampire—interest piece with someone famous. I knew a journalist would push for a yes, but somehow, I also knew Vlad wasn't the sort to concede.

"The first is that every vampire in the country has been given a hush order," Vlad continued. "The queen felt it was time to announce our existence to the world, but under no circumstances are any random vampires to give interviews without her express consent."

I'd learned of the vampire queen a week ago when she'd signed a peace treaty with our president, but it still sorta blew my mind. "But you aren't a random vampire."

"I am to her," he said. "While I might possess notoriety, I am not part of the queen's inner circle and have no power beyond my own."

"I wouldn't think something like that would stop you."

He offered another fangy grin. "Tell me, Anna. What do you know about vampires?"

I shrugged. In my last week, I'd done some research, as journalists were wont to do, but the information always seemed to contradict itself. Some sites claimed they—*we*—could only subsist off human blood, while others claimed animals would do in a pinch. No one ever seemed to know the right answer.

No human, that was.

"I know vampires drink blood, as seen by our little interlude upstairs."

He nodded.

"One would assume sunlight is a problem, considering the coffin."

"Very insightful. Direct sunlight will reduce us to ash. Some vampires can tolerate dusk and dawn depending on their age. I've also heard of vampires who could remain awake during the day when under duress. But for the most part, the sun renders us completely useless, and our coffins provide us protection while in that state. Typically, vampires are traditional creatures. Coffins used to be the only thing that could provide us with enough cover both from the sun and humans. Some took a more direct approach and dug little nests in the earth while others hide in the walls. But those of us who preferred something more..."

"Comfortable?"

He nodded. "That'll suffice. Those of us who preferred something more comfortable relied on coffins. We hide them in our attics or secret rooms barred from within."

I nodded. Of those choices, the coffin definitely seemed preferable. "So if sunlight is a problem, I would assume that fire is too."

A twinkle sparkled in his eye. If I wasn't mistaken, he seemed almost proud of me. His newly born minion. And didn't that warm the cockles of my dead heart.

"And since decapitation seems to work for just about everything, I assume it can also kill us."

"Very good."

"What about stakes?"

A shadow darkened his face. "Regretfully, quite effective at killing us."

"All right. Did I miss anything?"

"A great deal, actually. I assume you've heard of our queen and her council?"

"Beyond the press release from a week ago, no."

Vlad nodded. "Very well. Regarding your previous statement, that you wouldn't think someone of my caliber would be bothered by the queen's decree, I need you to understand something. We aren't governed like humans. The queen is our law. And her laws are absolute. You cannot successfully imprison a vampire—even permanently trapping us in coffins is difficult. Therefore, when one breaks the law, death is often the immediate punishment. We're immortal. We can always make new vampires. But our queen refuses to allow wayward vampires to run amok in this world. So when I tell you she's issued a hush order, know that disobeying merits strict punishment."

I forced myself to swallow. "Okay, so she's a tyrannical queen."

"No." Vlad sighed and repositioned himself on the couch. "Genevieve isn't cruel or unforgiving, but she must remain stout and stand by her laws. Otherwise, the vampire world would descend into anarchy, and the humans will pay the ultimate price. It's our responsibility as loyal subjects to obey her laws, and it's her responsibility as our queen to maintain control of our people."

A spark of anger flickered within. Listening to him, Vlad made it sound so idealistic, so perfect. But I'd already seen the darker side of vampirism, and I wasn't yet a week old. "If your queen is so strong and vampires fear her, then how the hell did I stumble across a blood orgy? I know for a fact that the human government worked with your queen to pass a law stating no vampires may take blood from unwilling victims, and yet look what I found."

A shadow whisked over Vlad's face. He lowered his arms from the couch and braced his elbows against his knees. "I was hoping not to have this discussion with you yet. Not until you'd had more time to adjust. But perhaps it's best I tell you now. Those women weren't unwilling."

I sucked in a sharp breath. "What?"

"The scene you stumbled across was sanctioned. It's not ideal, I'll admit, nor is it good PR, considering we've only been made general knowledge within the last week, but each attendee there signed a consent form. Those types of parties have been around for centuries."

My mouth gaped as I struggled to find the words. This was insane. Surely those people wouldn't have signed away their rights like that. The things I'd seen in that back room. Most of the—what? Customers? Patrons?—hadn't been aware enough to know what was happening. It honestly seemed no different than taking advantage of a drunk person.

"How...?" I shook my head in an attempt to clear my thoughts. "How do you know they all signed consent forms? Have you seen the documentation?"

"I know it's in your nature to distrust—"

"Of course I'm distrustful!" I shouted. "You're sitting here telling me about this mysterious tyrannical queen that holds complete power over every vampire subject beneath her, who *allows* these blood orgies to take place because the humans consented. Well, hello? Do you not see me sitting in front of you? I absolutely did *not* consent to this. That vampire, whoever the hell he is, literally dragged me out of the club, threw me up against the fence, and drained me dry before discarding me next to a fucking dumpster like I was trash. And you expect me to trust you? To believe you when you just say those people consented? I saw those humans with my own eyes. I saw the delirium, the lack of inhibition, the complete and utter lack of awareness of anything going on in that room."

Tears welled in my eyes, and I bit my lip to silence my shouting. Vlad didn't deserve my anger. He was just the messenger. But this whole situation was becoming incredibly distressing and not at all how I expected my weekend in New Orleans to turn out.

"Anna." Vlad cupped my hands. The instant we connected, I felt a sense of calm wash over me. Something about him soothed me, as though he could reach inside and ease my nerves. "As a general rule, humans crave a vampire's bite. It can be erotic, sensual, and heighten the pleasure one feels while engaged in intercourse."

My cheeks burned. Hearing Vlad utter things like "erotic" and "sensual" gave me some naughty visuals. Ones I didn't find particularly welcoming right now.

"Fallen has been hosting those blood parties for a very long time, so I assure you, those who joined in were vetted. Most, I imagine, already belonged to other vampires."

"Wait, what the hell does that mean, belong?"

"There's so much you don't know yet. So much I have to teach you."

"Well, we're in it now, so you may as well continue."

He squeezed my hand and nodded. "Vampires tend to employ humans, keep them on 'staff' as part of their harem. Many of us dislike hunting. It's exhausting to constantly be on the prowl. So, it became common practice to keep a few humans in our homes to feed from. These people are always made aware of their circumstances and sign an NDA agreement on threat of death should they break them. Usually these people are in need of help. Homeless, drug addicts, et cetera. We meet their needs while they feed ours."

"So you extort them," I accused.

Vlad held my gaze without a flicker of remorse. "Yes, we extort them. But it's a symbiotic relationship that's worked for millennia. These people prefer their lives with us as opposed to living like a junkie on the streets. I've heard of these little blood parties, and more often than not, they're attended by those particular humans. Those employed by a vampire. Believe me when I tell you, no innocents were harmed."

No, no innocents were harmed. None whatsoever.

Except me.

My breath caught in my throat, and tears pricked at my eyes. Suddenly, this wasn't fun anymore. I no longer cared who Vlad was or about his past. Now, I wish he'd just left me to die. Surely that would be an easier pill to swallow than these truth bombs he kept lobbing at me. At least then, I wouldn't be a walking, talking monster from beyond the grave who'd apparently died for *nothing*.

I pulled my hands from his and scrubbed my cheeks before my tears fell.

Later, I'd cry. In the safety of my own hotel or whatever. Not here. Not in front of Vlad. He might have turned me, but that didn't mean he got to see me at my most vulnerable.

I pressed the heels of my hands against my eyes and released a slow breath. "And your second reason?"

"Pardon?"

"At the beginning of this conversation, you said you couldn't give me an interview for two reasons."

"Ah, right. The second reason." He injected a little humor in his voice. "Well, have you ever seen any vampire movies? Or read any novels about us?"

"Of course."

"Good. If you were to name off let's say five things most commonly understood about vampires, what would they be?"

Great. A trivia game. Just what I wanted right now. "I don't know." I waved a hand in the air. "Aversion to sunlight, sleep in coffins, death by stake, allergic to garlic..."

He raised a brow. "And the last?"

I wracked my brain, then focused specifically on the latest book I'd read as part of my research. My eyes slowly widened, and I met Vlad's gaze. "No reflections."

He inclined his head.

But why would that matter for an interview?

Unless... I made a small disbelieving sound. "You expect me to believe that we don't have reflections? Even in videos?"

"They're all reflections."

I blinked. "So mirrors, cameras?"

"Water, windows. All of it. Our clothes are visible, but not *us*."

"Our clothes?" I repeated, flabbergasted. I suppose in a way it made sense. Our clothes weren't magical. We bought them in stores, for cripes' sake. I sat there, completely silent and entirely flummoxed. I had no idea what to make of all this. It was so much information in such a short amount of time. Almost like he'd given me a lecture in Vamp 101.

"It's a lot," Vlad said, as though he actually could read my mind. "Why don't you get some rest and digest everything you've just learned."

"Um." I hesitated at the sound of my voice, breathless and weak. "Yeah, maybe a good idea. You didn't happen to find my things at Fallen, did you? Phone, purse, all that stuff?"

Vlad nodded.

Relief flooded me. At least that would save me some money. "Then if you'll just tell me where they are, I'll head to my hotel."

"Ah. About that."

All my hopes suddenly deflated. His tone was very telling, even if he hadn't spoken the words. Seemed I wasn't the only one with a bit of transparency issues. "I'm not allowed to leave, am I?"

"Not yet."

I gave a slow nod. "I'm too tired to argue about that."

Emotion flickered in Vlad's eyes, but I couldn't read it. I didn't know him well enough yet. A part of me guessed it was pity, and that only enraged me further. I didn't need his pity.

"Your friend Lucy placed your things in one of the spare rooms one level up. It's your room to use as you see fit for as long as you need. I've asked my servants to steer clear of your space for now until you've had a few days to adjust. In the meantime, sunrise is in"—he peered at a massive grandfather clock across the room—"approximately seven hours or so. Might I suggest you take the time to unwind, perhaps clean yourself up, and check your emails. From what I understand, you'll have one in particular awaiting you from the queen."

"What?"

"Well, it'll say it's from the queen, but rest assured, it isn't actually from her. One of her inner circle members is responsible for registering new vampires and providing them with all the material needed to make this adjustment. As your sire, it was my responsibility to register you as a newborn vampire upon turning you. Your friend Lucy assisted by providing your contact information. The queen is very determined right now to make a good first impression with all new vampires. I'm afraid I have no idea what they've sent you, but I do know you've been sent something. Lucy confirmed the arrival of the email the night I changed you."

If I wasn't already overwhelmed, this might have done me in. To think I'd been registered and my personal information handed over to the queen's flunkies without so much as a request for permission just chapped me the wrong way. But bitching about it would accomplish nothing. The damage was already done.

"Thank you," I forced out. "If you don't mind, I'd like to just...."

Vlad rose from the couch in a fluid motion that rendered me speechless. "Of course."

I rose from my stool and approached the winding staircase. Before taking the first step, I glanced over my shoulder to find Vlad standing in the sitting room, his dark gaze trained on me.

"Find me before sunrise," he said. "I'll escort you to your coffin."

Because that sounded like a barrel of laughs.

I quickly climbed the stairs and found the room he'd mentioned. It was quite simple, actually. I'd recognized the scent of my purse, interestingly enough, and found it sitting on the bed when I entered. Not in the mood to peruse my surroundings, I crossed the room and snatched my phone from the bedspread. It seemed Lucy had even plugged it in for me. Maybe there was still some hope for our friendship.

I activated the cellphone screen. My finger hovered over the camera app, the last thing I'd been using before that asshole had killed me. Part of me didn't want to look, too afraid of what I'd see in my last moments. But after a while, curiosity got the better of me, and I entered my gallery. The video was the last item in the folder, and with a trembling hand, I quickly tapped it, then hit play.

Except, it was nothing like I remembered. I could see the woman closest to me moaning and panting, her eyes half-lidded like she was high. But Vlad was right. Not a single vampire was visible in the video, except for their clothes. The air sort of distorted around them, like watching a bad television feed. A few seconds later, the video jerked, and fear crept up my spine as I watched myself being dragged through the club, Jimmy Choos abandoned on the tile.

Terror grabbed hold of me, and I soon found myself on my knees gasping for unneeded air. Seemed the video of my murder had inspired a panic attack. At the sound of my screams rising from my phone, I scrambled for it and shut it off. Then I dragged myself to the bed and let it all out. One ragged cry after another.

Everything that had happened to me was all for nothing.

I'd *died* for *nothing*.

Those words kept echoing in my head until I finally threw myself onto the pillows and gave into the tears.

TEARS WERE the bane of every man's existence, regardless of age.

A few seconds after I broke down, I heard a gentle tap on the door. I hadn't welcomed Vlad into my room, but I felt the bed dip as he sat beside me. He offered a few words of encouragement, murmured a few helpless platitudes, but I still asked him to leave. It wasn't that I didn't appreciate him saving my life, but I firmly believed sobbing was a private affair. I'd never been one to share in the misery, so once the tears started, I just wanted to be left alone. And Vlad was so eager, he practically blurred from sight as he made his escape.

I didn't blame him.

No one wanted to be trapped with a hysterical person.

Truth be told, Lucy was the only person I wanted to see right now. In all our years together, this was the first time one of us had bailed on the other. I wanted nothing more than to reach out to her, to convince myself that she was still my best friend, that I hadn't done anything too damaging. But I knew I needed to give her space.

Death was difficult. While I hadn't *truly* died, I was now an official member of the undead country club. And Lucy wasn't. Were the roles reversed, I could only imagine how I would feel. And regardless of my current undead status, this had to be causing her some grief and loneliness.

Had she stuck around, though, she would have seen I was struggling with this as well. This change would not be easy for me. I had to come to grips with this new reality and learn who the hell I was now. Because, damn it, my life had taken a complete one-eighty.

Once my tears dried, I slowly sat up and wiped my cheeks. A flash of red caught my eye, and I stared down at my palms, flabbergasted. I looked like Lady Macbeth, my hands utterly stained in blood.

I cried out, darted to my feet, and bolted into the

nearest bathroom. Careful not to stain the sink, I ran the hot water until it steamed up the mirror. Only then did I plunge my hands into the basin and scrub, all while muttering, "Out, damned spot."

Even though they didn't take long to clean, I still felt the blood on my skin. It was all in my head, and I knew that, but it didn't change anything. Exasperated, I grabbed a nearby cloth, rinsed it, then scrubbed my cheeks until my skin felt raw. The thin material was covered in blood, even after I washed it out. I stared down at the tinged water and sighed. I needed to relearn everything about life and what it meant to become a vampire. I'd always loved surprises, but this was one thing I felt I needed to be prepared for. Maybe that would help me adjust to my situation a little better.

Finally clean, I dragged my soggy ass back into my bedroom and plopped down on the wooden bench resting against the bed's footboard. I fetched my phone from the floor and, once again, unlocked the screen.

The first thing I noticed this time was the date. April fifteenth. Good lord. Lucy and I had infiltrated the club three nights ago. She'd mentioned that earlier, that it'd taken a few nights for me to wake, but I hadn't been able to give it much thought yet. Or anything for that matter. Had I really slept in that coffin for that long? Was that how long it took someone to become a vampire? Ugh. I really needed to learn what else to expect.

I pulled down my notifications bar and grimaced at the sight of them all. Texts and missed calls from my parents, a few texts from my ex-boyfriend checking to make sure I was still alive—oh, the irony —some Facebook notifications, and sure enough, an email from "The Queen of Vampires."

The email was quite sparse. They welcomed me to their lifestyle—like I'd had a fricking choice— issued me a username and temporary password for their website, and included a few links to what looked like an online forum.

Curious, I clicked one of those links first. It took me to their website and prompted me to sign in using the name and password provided in the email. Once logged in, I pulled up their forum and began to investigate.

When I first started researching vampires after their big announcement, I'd noticed Google only consisted of personal websites and a bunch of Wikipedia pages based on vampire *myths* and *fiction*. At the time, I'd found it all entertaining. Now, I wanted the real info. The nitty gritty.

This site was far more professional than the blogs. Clean cut, easy to read, with a look about it that screamed *government*. Everything was categorized into a beautifully organized Q&A, followed closely by what looked like personal accounts.

I settled in for some quality learning time.

HELP. I've been changed into a vampire. What do I do?

Well, first off—let us offer both our congratulations and our condolences. We understand this choice is a personal one. If you've willingly been changed, we suggest turning to your sire for any assistance you may require in adjusting. By Queen Genevieve's law, your sire is required to mentor you for three months after your awakening. If, unfortunately, you were not turned willingly, please contact the council as soon as possible. You will require a great deal of support, and we have people who can help. Click here to be taken to our contact page with a list of applicable emails, phone numbers, and addresses.

. . .

I PAUSED at the sight of those emails and numbers before finally jotting a few down. Maybe there was *something* they could do to assist me with this change, other than handing me a website and sending me on my way.

I glanced at the next question.

WHAT CHANGES SHOULD I expect once I've been changed?

Vampires are extraordinary creatures. Over the first week, your body will undergo extreme changes. Anticipate an immediate awkward stage as your body learns to adjust to its new abilities. The initial change takes three nights, during which you'll remain unconscious. Upon waking, you'll begin to experience heightened senses, strength, and most importantly, hunger. While becoming a vampire is a majestic transformation, it, of course, does not come without challenges. And a newborn's hunger is unlike anything you'll ever experience. The queen recommends that you sequester yourself from all loved ones for the first week as a means of protecting them and yourself while you adjust. Fear not, though.

This hunger will eventually pass. And soon you'll become a normal, functioning vampire.

For more information, <u>click here</u>.

I IGNORED the link for now and instead contemplated what I'd just read. Maybe it was for the best that Lucy had left. I'd never forgive myself if I hurt her. Or anyone else, for that matter.

After promising myself that I'd text her once I was finished, I finally clicked the link and groaned when I saw the stupid headline.

YOUR VAMPIRIC BODY AND YOU!

This is one of the most common discussions, so we felt it best to dedicate an entire page to this topic. The vampiric body is nothing like a human's. Our breed is stronger, faster, and deadlier. And whereas humans weaken as they age, vampires grow stronger. Take heart in knowing that you'll never be as weak and useless as you're feeling right now.

I SKIMMED THE ENTIRE PAGE, noting interesting little tidbits like how newborn vampires could

immediately lift upwards of five hundred pounds. Further research concluded that since our bodies were able to take more damage and heal faster, we were less encumbered by things like strained muscles.

I couldn't help but think about Vlad. If newborns were already that strong, and vampires only grew stronger with age, what did that mean for someone who'd lived for more than half a millennium?

The rest of the article continued in the same vein, mentioning how vampires can count the craters on the moon and hear approximately ten miles away. I hadn't been given the chance to experience any of that yet, but I also hadn't left the house. Unluckily for me, our fangs were *not* retractable, and it was our responsibility to try and hide them while speaking— to avoid scaring the normies. Guess that meant I'd have to learn how to speak without chomping on my lips and tongue. And even worse, yes, we cried blood tears now. Repulsive. I made an immediate mental note to stop crying entirely. Some women were attractive when they cried, but I had a feeling female vampires weren't among them.

The next question gave me a hard pause.

CAN VAMPIRES PRODUCE CHILDREN?

No.

THAT WAS IT? No further discussion on the topic? I hunted around on the page but found nothing. So, I opened a new Google tab and searched this specific question. The answer wasn't encouraging. According to one of those horrid blog sites, even though vampires were classified as the undead, the fact remained that the body *did* die. As such, all natural bodily functions cease, such as a female's reproductive system. The dead couldn't give birth to the living.

My chin wobbled as I read the words, but I banished the traitorous tears that threatened to spill. I was twenty-four years old—I'd never really given thought to children. However, I absolutely hated that the decision had been stolen from me. There were upsides, though. No more monthly cycle, which, yay! And no more using the bathroom. Another plus. Still, the sting of that particular loss lingered.

I moved on before any dark thoughts took root.

Is it true that vampires are immortal?

Yes and no. All vampires are long-lived, but

you're only as immortal as you allow yourself to be. Therefore, we recommend living your everlasting life in such a way that doesn't result in someone cutting off your head.

Good undead life advice, there.

So, really, what they were trying to say was I'd spend the rest of my "long-lived" life lonely and barren, provided I didn't attract the attention of an axe-wielding lunatic.

This was fun, and yes, that was sarcasm.

Can vampires love?

Vampires are creatures of heightened and intense emotions. When we find our mate, it's chaotic, messy, and yes, eternal. Unfortunately, few ever find their true soulmate, but when they do, it's an unbreakable bond.

Oh boy, did this question stop me in my tracks. There were so many thoughts racing through my head. I'd often heard it said that vampires were soulless. That when they died, their souls passed on, but their bodies remained, reanimated by magic and a consciousness that lacked morals. If this was the case, wouldn't that mean us soulless monsters were incapable of love?

We were entering an existential philosophical debate here, and I had no one to argue with.

The most important question being: Did we or didn't we possess a soul? The debate hinged entirely on that answer. I wasn't a religious person—far from it, in fact. I was, in a word, an atheist. There was simply too much bad shit out there in the world for me to be able to believe in an all-powerful deity. And if our destinies were actually preordained, then the "Big G" up there truly hated us all.

But that didn't mean I didn't believe in souls. The thought that I might have lost mine twisted my insides. Without my essence, my being... what did that make me?

Ugh, all this research was giving me a headache.

I rubbed my temples, then froze when my phone buzzed, and a notification flashed across the top of my screen. I sucked in a sharp breath at the sight of Lucy's name and nearly dropped my phone in the mad dash to tap the bubble.

L: *Did you see that your hair and nails will stop growing? That every night they'll revert back to*

whatever you looked like when you were changed?
Good thing we got a manicure before coming here.

What? No, I hadn't read that part. And grateful for the distraction, I flicked a glance at my hands. Relief rounded my tense shoulders. Thankfully, I'd opted for a classic manicure with rounded tips and a clear polish before hitting the road. No need to ever work on these bad boys again. My feet, on the other hand, were a whole other battle. Rough heels and ugly nails. Guess I now got to spend eternity suffering through endless pedicures. Ugh. I hated when other people touched my feet.

Who was I kidding?

My feet were strictly a no-touchy zone for me. Ah well. Someone had invented socks for a reason, right?

I glanced back at my phone to see the three little dots on the screen. I hadn't yet responded to Lucy, but she was typing another message. I couldn't begin to describe how happy that made me. She'd left, but I clearly hadn't lost my best friend.

L: *Apparently all vampires are born with a special gift. Did you see that?*

A: *No, I haven't. Sounds rad, though. What kinda gift?*

L: *Dunno. Maybe that's how your dude knew*

where to find you.

A: *Did he ever introduce himself to you?*

L: *LOL. No. I never asked.*

Three nights and she never asked his name? Guess they hadn't spent much time together. And while I was thinking about that....

A: *What did you do while I was out of it?*

L: *Fretted, mostly. Sat in our hotel and stared at the walls. Read up on vampirism. You know, normal stuff.*

Nothing about that was normal.

A: *Did you tell anyone about what happened?*

L: *Yeah, right. I didn't even know what to say. Mostly, I just worried.*

Remorse swelled within me.

A: *I'm so sorry, Luce. I can't imagine what this must feel like for you.*

A few moments passed in which she didn't respond. Maybe she wasn't ready to talk about her emotions yet. Lucy was like that. I hated sharing emotions in general, but Lucy clammed up when something was too much for her. Like this.

The three dots popped up, and I waited anxiously, so grateful my best friend was still willing to talk to me.

L: *So, what's his name, then?*

A: *Vlad.*

L: LOL. *Of course it is.*

A: *What's that supposed to mean?*

L: *Aren't all vampires named Vlad, or Lestat, or Dracula, or something? Wannabe bloodsuckers, right?*

I bit back a laugh. She'd nailed two out of three already.

A: *He's the real Vlad. Also known as Dracula.*

The message quickly turned to *read*, but Lucy didn't immediately respond. My mouth twitched with amusement. I could only imagine how she was taking that little bit of information.

L: *You shittin' me?*

I snorted at her message.

A: *Nope. The legend is based on him. Insane, right?*

She left me on *read* again. I decided to change the topic.

A: *Have you left town yet?*

She didn't immediately respond. I sat perched on the edge of the bench, nibbling on my thumbnail. Finally, when the three dots popped up, I sighed.

L: *No.*

Relief bloomed through my chest. The site recommended a week's separation. I could handle that if it meant seeing her again.

A: *Are you going to stay?*

Another long pause. Clearly Lucy hadn't decided on anything yet and was making this up as she went. I knew my best friend better than anyone. I was no stranger to her thought process.

L: *Do you promise not to go after the vamp who attacked you?*

I considered her question and understood the implication. If I pursued my bloodlust for this vamp, she'd leave, and I'd likely lose my best friend. No matter what happened, nothing was worth that. So I gritted my teeth and answered.

A: *Yes.*

L: *Then yes, I'll stay.*

I fist-pumped the air. Everything was so strange right now. And there was so much to digest. But with Lucy at my side, I felt like I could do anything. She was my rock and always had been.

A: *Thank you. Love you, Luce.*

L: *Yeah, yeah, just don't think about ever taking another bite out of me, got it?*

A: *Yes, ma'am.*

L: *That's better.*

A: *The sites say we shouldn't see each other for a week. What are you going to do in the meantime?*

L: *I thought I'd go back to the vamp club, see*

what I can learn about your... well, that guy.

That guy, meaning the vamp who'd killed me. Adoration swelled within me. This girl was my life. And even though I'd been sorta murdered at that club, she was still willing to go back, if it meant helping me. I must have done something great in a past life to end up with a friend like her.

But no way in hell was I going to let her tackle that place without me. Or ever. It was too dangerous. And I loved Lucy way too much to let her risk her life like that, regardless of her reasons.

A: *No, absolutely not.*

L: *Girl, just cuz you're a badass vamp now, doesn't mean you get to tell me what to do.*

A: *Lucy, I'm serious. It's too dangerous. Promise me you won't. At least wait until Vlad and I can go with you. For backup.*

Yet another long pause. Finally, after a few minutes of me fretting over whether I was about to break quarantine to ensure her ass stayed put, she responded.

L: *Fine. I'll just go do some sightseeing during daylight hours then. You know, when all you little vamps are a-snooze in your coffins. Don't worry about me. Just focus on you. You're going to need to master* your control before we go home. You can't be munching on townies.

A: *Aww, why not? Bet Christopher tastes delicious.*

And wouldn't my ex-boyfriend just *love* me snacking on him.

L: *Har, har.*

Christopher had been my first *real* boyfriend. I couldn't use the word serious, because it definitely hadn't progressed to that, but our "relationship" had lasted longer than all the others I'd dated. Christopher and I had broken up a week ago, when he'd learned about my plan to come here in search of a vampire to interview. He'd warned me I was going to end up dead, and I'd broken up with him. Guess life really did have a way of punching you in the face. Still, if ever there was anyone who deserved a good necking, it was him.

L: *Go relax. Get comfy being in your own body again. I'll message you tomorrow night once the sun goes down.*

A: *Can do, girlfriend. Gab at ya later.*

Lucy sent a massive thumbs up, thereby ending the conversation. I took the time to scroll a few social media sites and reacquaint myself with the people from my hometown. Perish's population hovered

6

It seemed safe to assume, based on the cellphone laying smack dab in the middle of my face, that I'd fallen asleep while scrolling the feeds. Weirdly, I didn't recall drifting off. I remembered chuckling at something my former high school principal had posted in one of our town's local groups, then instant darkness. Not even a droopy eye to hint I'd been hovering on the edge of sleep. I could only assume it was because of the change. The Q&A I'd read had mentioned something about it taking a week for your body to completely adjust. Maybe it needed more sleep during the transition. Had to take a lot of work to reanimate a dead body.

I plucked the phone from my face and stretched

out my jaw. Then I lit up the screen and peered at the time through slitted, light-sensitive eyes. If the clock could be trusted—which, let's face it, I always trusted my phone—it was three in the morning. Or "witching hour," as my mother had taken to calling it. Two weeks ago, she'd never believed in the paranormal. But after the press release, she'd begun to take stock in everything. And witching hour had quickly become a time of night she now feared. Apparently, it had something to do with witches, demons, and ghosts being at their most powerful or some nonsense. All I felt was groggy. So guess there was no truth to that myth. She'd be so pleased to hear that.

And since the thought of telling my mom I'd been vampified filled me with abject terror, I chose to change my mental direction to something a tad less nerve-wracking—like personal hygiene. Because *blech*, I stunk. I guess three nights of marinating in my coffin hadn't done me any favors. Not to mention nearly dying. I had to imagine a body experienced some intense levels of stress when going through this sort of thing, meaning sweaty B.O. And since I was currently rooming with another vampire, taking a shower seemed a wise idea.

Yawning, I waddled my drowsy ass into the

closest bathroom. Though I was hardly an expert, I figured I had a few more hours until sunrise. Of course, even that raised more questions. It felt like every few minutes I thought of a dozen more.

What would happen? Would I "die?" Did I need to sleep in that damn coffin again? Would I immediately wake at sunset? Or did I need to set some sort of vampy alarm to wake me?

And if I did have to sleep in that coffin, why? There had to be other options. Surely these people weren't content with literally crawling into their death beds every night. I shuddered at the thought. Maybe other vampires were okay with that, but not me. I definitely needed to make some changes. Sunlight was a problem, but that was fine. I could work around that.

I didn't bother turning on the bathroom light, thanks to my newly improved vision. Everything was crisp and clear. Who needed light anyway, right? *Hello darkness, my old friend....*

The first thing I noticed was the mirror. There it sat above the sink, brazen as sunlight, as though taunting me to stare into it.

Nope. I wasn't ready for that.

It was one thing to *know* I didn't have a reflection. It was entirely different to experience it.

And somehow, I just knew that would be the thing to send me over the edge tonight. So, avoid the vanity.

The next thing I noticed was the massive amount of products stuffed onto the shelves next to me. Enough to stock an entire beauty salon. My gaze leapt from item to item, and I bit back a laugh. Had Vlad done this? Or had a servant done his bidding? Considering the four-poster beds and massive tubs that could fit a small house party, it seemed safe to assume he'd ordered someone to do it for him. I hadn't spotted any servants yet, but I sure could smell them. In fact, I could pick out their individual soap and shampoo brands. Thankfully, Vlad's blood still filled my tummy, so I wasn't feeling especially hungry right now.

I grinned when my gaze snagged an item of interest. My mouth felt grimy, seeing as how I hadn't brushed my teeth in three nights. It seemed my thoughtful host had anticipated my needs and provided me a toothbrush. Or at least what I assumed was a toothbrush. I grabbed it and held it up for inspection, laughing at the sight of it. Guess there was a special brand for vamps, one specifically designed for cleaning our fangs. It had this weird triple-sided head that formed a triangle. After a small experimentation—and yes, a Google search—I learned that I was supposed to insert my fang through the center. Once positioned, I pushed the button and listened to the electric hum as it cleaned and polished my dangerously sharp canines. Afterward, there was a button on the side that once pressed, opened the triangle up into a flat brush for the rest of my teeth.

Handy.

Now with squeaky clean teeth, I rinsed it off, then snapped a photo of it and fired it off to Lucy with the caption "Fangtastic." After a few moments, in which I considered the other products, Lucy sent back a laughing emoji. Hey, we had to laugh about it. Otherwise, we'd cry, and I'd already established a no-crying rule. I couldn't break it on my first night.

Unable to resist, I picked up a tube of lipstick and chuckled when I spotted the name Eternal Blood. The mascara brand was Everlast. And the eyeliner? Yup. Undead Black. My laughter echoed through the bathroom. An entire line of makeup designed for the everyday vamp-girl. Including Bite Me perfume. I couldn't even make this shit up. But someone had. And likely made millions off the product. Man, it sure hadn't taken the marketing companies long to dip their toes into the supernatural pool, considering how recently the queen had made the announcement. Made me question so many things. Like, had some companies known in advance? Had they been prepared, waiting to jump on the opportunity the second the treaty was announced? It also made me wonder if they'd manufactured anything for the men. Something like Immortal Cologne for the undead man in your life.

I'd always been fascinated by makeup but sadly had never mastered it. I always ended up looking like a circus clown who'd gotten into a bar fight. The few videos I'd watched had intimidated the hell out of me. Contouring, highlighting, shadowing, and oh lord, the blending. So much blending. I wasn't a painter. I barely even knew what those things meant! Kudos to those who'd figured it out, though.

And hey, guess it didn't really matter anymore, considering the whole no reflection thing. Seemed like an impossible task to master the art of something I'd never be able to see again, right? Besides, if I hadn't learned how to perfect my makeup in the last ten years or so, I really didn't think the next hundred were going to make a difference. With luck, maybe a bar-fighting clown would be the look then. I just needed to wait for my moment to shine.

After snapping a final picture of the undead makeup line for Lucy, I ran the water and hopped into the shower. I instantly ducked under the hot spray and let loose a groan worthy of the bestest orgasms. The water felt amazing as it pummeled the top of my head and trickled down my body. I didn't realize how badly I needed this. I'd always heard water was a symbol of renewal and rebirth, and right now, I was eager for those things. But the best part was it washed that murderous bastard off me. With my new senses, I could still catch whiffs of him, enough so that I knew I'd recognize him if we ever crossed paths again.

I lathered up and washed the blood from my hair, then moved on to the rest of me. I scrubbed, scrubbed, scrubbed until I shone, then leaned back against the shower wall and closed my eyes. There was something about the calming sound of water that soothed my nerves. I had a feeling I could stay in the shower all night and not run out of hot water, but that seemed rude. Vlad was letting me stay here. I didn't need to take advantage of the amenities.

Once dried off, I brushed my hair flat. I generally tied or braided it back to keep it off my face and shoulders, but the thought of exposing my neck bothered me. A vampire thing, maybe? Or residual trauma from the attack? I couldn't say.

I stared at the products on the counter, then

decided on a whim to apply a little of the Bite Me perfume to my wrists and throat. I wasn't *trying* to catch Vlad's attention or anything—not that I would have minded it if I *did*. No, I was just curious about the smell, or so I told myself.

But when I lifted my wrist to my nose and sniffed, I winced. The bottle claimed the perfume possessed floral notes mixed with a hint of an aphrodisiac. All I smelled was sterile alcohol. *Blech.* I turned the sink taps, wet a cloth, then scrubbed it off as best as I could. The overwhelming stench didn't give me hope for the rest of the products. Maybe Vlad thought this was what vampire women wanted. Or maybe his servants had bought it all, and he hadn't the foggiest idea about any of it. Either way, I wouldn't be wearing any of this stuff.

I returned to my bedroom to find a set of pajamas laid across the bed. Someone had found some spare clothes for me, it seemed, and slipped them into my room while I was showering. I pulled on the sweats and oversized hoodie and took comfort from the soft material. Nothing like wrapping yourself up in fleece and cotton to make the world feel right again.

Once dressed, I set out to hunt down the Count. Sunrise was approaching. I could feel it in my bones. And he'd asked me to find him beforehand. It didn't take long to find him. I knocked on a pair of giant oak doors and waited for his acknowledgement. When it came, I pushed one open and strode inside.

The moment I entered, I was struck by the staggering amount of wood in the room. Seemed our man here enjoyed himself some mahogany bookshelves alongside cherry wood floors and furniture. From roof to floor, wood, wood, and more wood.

"Geez, you suicidal?" I asked.

Vlad sat in a cushy-looking computer chair. He spun around at the sound of my voice, his brow lifted in question.

I gestured all around us. "One would think a vampire wouldn't want to be surrounded by this much wood."

"One would assume I'd be safe in my own home," he retorted.

"You know what they say about assuming."

He rolled his eyes, effectively communicating that he did indeed know that saying, and he remained unconcerned. "I only welcome those I trust into my home."

"And me?" I asked.

A whisper of a smile crossed his face. "If I didn't, I wouldn't have turned you, wouldn't you agree?"

"But how could you even begin to believe you can trust me? We don't know each other. You appeared out of nowhere to save my life. And speaking of... why were you even at the club?" My eyes widened. "Were you taking part in the orgy?"

Vlad's eyes grew comically wide. After a moment's bluster, he shook his head. "I assure you, I have no need for blood orgies." He cocked his head. "Are you always this inquisitive?"

"Oh, definitely," I said, laughing. By habit, my teeth scored my bottom lip. I winced when my fangs punctured the flesh, then moaned when a drop of blood coated my tongue.

Vlad's eyes flashed—with desire or anger, I couldn't tell—but he half-rose from his chair before he seemed to realize he'd even moved. With great effort, he appeared to restrain himself. He closed his eyes and drew in a deep breath, his fingers digging deep into the armrests.

Eyes still closed, he tilted his head toward me and began to speak, his words a tad clipped, as though he found this entire conversation tedious. "Let's begin with the club. I was there waiting."

"For a meal?"

"No" was all he said.

When he didn't offer any more information, my

mouth opened with the intention of digging deeper, but the grim slash of his lips told me this topic was off-limits.

He swallowed, and my gaze dipped to his throat, mesmerized by the motion. It was no surprise that Vlad checked off everything I liked in a guy. Tall, dark, handsome, strong, severe, smart—I stopped myself from listing more adjectives and instead forced my gaze back up to his. Heat flared within his dark eyes, like embers flickering against coal. Maybe I was just hungry? Or *maybe* I was hungry for something more primal.

Vlad blinked, snuffing out the flames. "I knew when I saw you...."

"Knew what?"

He shook his head. "I'm explaining this wrong."

"Technically, you aren't explaining anything."

Vlad sighed and narrowed his eyes on me. "If you'd let me finish."

I bit back a chuckle and pantomimed zipping my lips shut. What could I say? I loved to needle him. He was needle-worthy. Few guys were worth poking.

"I was nearby when I spotted you in the crowd. You were talking to your friend, and your voice cut through the deafening din, so soft, so sweet."

Not words people usually used to describe me, but I'd take them as a win for now.

"I admit I followed you for a bit. Watched as you and Lucy moved through the club. I lost track of you for but a few moments."

And I could see from his deep frown that this flustered him.

"I followed your scent, curious about you. When I discovered you'd entered the back room, I knew you were in trouble. Then I found you in that alleyway. Broken, bleeding, dying."

"So, you just turned me? Without even asking?"

"Who would I have asked?" Bitter laughter slipped past his lips. "Who was there but me? Had I left you, you would have died."

No doubt. I remembered the countdown looming in my head.

"Would you have preferred that?"

Truthfully, I wasn't sure. So, I refrained from answering that question. "*Why* change me then?" I demanded. "Seeing me in the crowd was reason enough to turn me?"

"Yes." He caught my gaze again, his features smooth with compassion. "And no."

This time, I frowned. "What does that even mean?"

"I wouldn't wish this existence on my worst enemy."

Um, okay. Then what did that make me?

"But you're the furthest thing from my worst enemy. And the thought of losing you before I even had a chance to know you... I couldn't bear that."

Remember that little headache from earlier? It came screaming back with a vengeance. Nothing this man said made any sense. And I was getting tired again. Too tired to keep digging. I would have bet my last dollar that my newfound exhaustion was all vamp-related. But that didn't make it any easier.

I rubbed my brow and released a small sigh.

Vlad was on his feet and swept across the room, all majestically. "Are you in pain?"

"Only the literal kind."

His fingertips touched my cheek, and I had to resist the urge to lean into him. Cripes, everything was just so confusing.

"What hurts?"

"My head," I mumbled.

Without a word, his fingers brushed my cheek and settled on my temples. He rubbed them in small circles with just the right amount of pressure. I moaned and closed my eyes, sinking into bliss. The man knew how to give good head—massages, that was.

"It's part of the transition," he told me. "It takes about a week for our bodies to fully adjust."

"I know. I read the website."

"What website?"

If it weren't for my headache, I might have laughed. Of course Vlad knew nothing about a website. He was as ancient as they came. And from what I'd read in books, ancient ones always abhorred modern technology.

"The queen's lackey sent a link in the email you told me about," I replied. "Stuff about the changes our bodies go through, recommendations to listen to our sires, since it's their responsibility to guide us for three months post-change. And since you're my sire, I guess that means I have to listen to you."

"Heaven forbid. Sunrise is less than fifteen minutes away. We should get you settled."

I groaned. "Do I have to go back into the coffin?"

Vlad cupped my cheeks, and I opened my eyes, meeting his gaze. I saw the truth in his face, and my hopes plummeted. I *hated* that stupid coffin. As if it wasn't bad enough to wake up in it post-death, I had to look forward to it for the rest of my life.

Hmm. Or did I?

I mean, was there an unwritten law stating vampires must retire to their coffins every night? Some vampy nonsense about pine boxes and cramped living conditions?

Gently nibbling on the inside of my lip, I considered those questions. Maybe there was another solution now. "Now that you guys are public knowledge, why not just black out your windows?"

"Black them out how? With black paint? That's not exactly attractive aesthetically."

I nodded. "What about mesh liner? Or blackout curtains?"

Vlad considered me while lowering his hands. "You haven't experienced sunlight yet. Believe me when I tell you it's no laughing matter. We can't risk our lives for simple comforts."

"Then what's the point of living?" I mumbled. "Look, there has to be something better than a coffin."

"It upsets you," he stated.

"Duh. No one wants to be trapped in a coffin."

His gaze turned distant. "I've done it for so long I barely give it a thought now."

"Well, wouldn't you like to sleep somewhere more comfortable? Like a giant California king bed?"

A chuckle rumbled in his chest. "I'm not sure

I've ever slept on one."

"Trust me, it's worth risking being burned alive."

That chuckle turned into full laughter. "I'll take your word for it."

"What about an attic suite without windows? Could have a bed, a dresser, whatever. Something more comfortable."

"Building code states that all bedrooms must have windows for emergency access."

"Okay." I considered our options. Maybe I could try sleeping in the earth? Buried under a mound of soil. But that sounded horrible. I'd never been claustrophobic before. Guess I was now.

Vlad's thoughts were clearly elsewhere. After a few moments, he nodded. "I'll make some inquiries and see what can be done. There might be some new options now that we needn't hide our existence anymore."

Hope blossomed like a flower in my chest. "Really?"

"Give me a few nights to discuss our options with contractors. I have some ideas, but I don't know if they're possible. There are building codes we must abide by, unfortunately."

"You would do that for me?"

He studied me silently. I could tell there was

something he wished to tell me, could practically see the words hovering on the tip of his tongue, but instead, he merely nodded and strode toward his office door. "Let's get you settled. There's not much time left before sunrise. We can discuss this at length once I have some answers."

Together, we went upstairs, and I started to sink into depression. I really didn't want to sleep up here tonight, but I wouldn't push it any further. He'd already heard my complaints and promised to do something about them. I couldn't ask for more.

We entered the attic, and I spotted a second coffin sitting next to mine—now complete with a brand new lid. Curiosity piqued, I stole a glance at him to find him very studiously staring at the coffins.

"Do you always sleep in this room?" I asked.

"Yes" was all he said as he approached my coffin and eased the lid back. My shoes sat inside, tucked up amongst the silk lining. I'd completely forgotten about them and was dismayed to find the heel had snapped off one. My poor Jimmy Choos. It'd taken me *months* to pay them off, but a girl *has* to have a pair of Choos. Now I needed to save up to buy another. I could pay to have them repaired, but they'd always be tainted in my head now.

I removed them from the liner and set them on

the floor. Didn't need them poking me in the bum again.

With one hand holding the lid, Vlad offered me his other to help me inside. I climbed in, then stretched out on my back, my breath already hitching.

"My people know not to disturb us during daylight hours unless it's an absolute emergency."

"Thank you," I whispered, relief loosening my shoulders. The thought of being caged in the darkness again would have given me palpitations if my heart could beat.

"I'll be right next to you all day," he said, his voice soothing those lingering anxieties. "I wake an hour before sunset. You won't be able to yet, but just know I'll be here when you wake."

"Okay. Good morning?" I prompted, unsure of the proper terminology, since technically the sun was rising.

"Sleep well, Anna," Vlad murmured as he sealed me in.

Before I could respond, he'd vanished. I heard the soft sounds of his own lid being moved, then nothing but silence. I had a moment to wonder if I could crawl into his coffin with him, when the sun suddenly rose and knocked me out.

7

I never was a morning person. Usually it was
ten a.m. before I hauled my ass out of bed in search
of waffles and coffee. And my damn coffee mug
needed to be empty before I was willing to so much
as converse with another human being. Lucy had
always teased me about this, told me I was pissier
than a mama grizzly bear. She'd even made me a
special mug for Christmas one year that read
"Cranky Bitch Medicine."

But, thanks to my new *condition*, I didn't need to
worry about any of that anymore. The instant sunset
hit, my eyes popped open without a hint of lingering
grogginess. One moment, I was dead, the next awake

again. Almost like someone had flicked on my power switch, and now I was raring to go.

I palmed the coffin lid to the side, hopped out with all the elegance and grace I'd lacked as a human, and glanced at Vlad's coffin. It sat open and empty, the silk pillows fluffed and pristine. Guess he really did wake an hour before sunset, earlier than the rest of us plebs.

A quick glance down revealed pristine pajamas. Normally when I woke, I looked like I'd been mauled in my sleep. Rat's nest for hair, half-rumpled pj's, sheets tangled between my legs, drool stains on my pillow—though I'd never admit to that one aloud. But not anymore it seemed. My pj's looked like I'd just ironed them. Not a wrinkle to be found. Guess we didn't move around much during daylight.

I didn't want to think about that. Just the thought that I might actually be dead during the day gave me a ragin' case of the heebie-jeebies. I needed to adjust, and I knew I would with time, but that night wasn't tonight. Probably not even tomorrow.

One upside, though. I didn't feel an immediate need for a shower as I had when human. My hair was smooth and unknotted, no gunk in my eyes, no yawning or lingering grouchiness, and—after blowing a quick puff of air into my hands—no morning breath either.

Now *that* was a miracle.

I had a huge hate-on for halitosis. My number two rule—which came after removing your shoes in my house—was no making out until teeth were brushed. The human mouth was disgusting. I didn't think it was too much to ask that my boyfriend handle that situation before handling mine.

"Good evening, madam," a monotonous voice said.

My head snapped up, and I spotted a rather old man standing next to the attic entry, dressed in—I kid you not—a penguin suit with a white towel draped over his forearm. I bit back a chuckle as I inspected him. He *had* to be Vlad's personal butler with that appearance.

"The Count awaits your presence downstairs," he said, gazing down his hawkish nose at me.

"He does, does he? Well, the Count can wait until I'm ready to be seen."

"That would be unwise," the old man said, his British accent emphasizing his words. "My instructions are to bring you to him immediately."

I shook my head. "I'd like to change my outfit first, if that's all right with your lordliness."

"Your attire can be addressed after your meeting. Master Dracula wishes to bid you a good evening and ensure you're fed a quality meal before seeing to the rest of your night."

A quality meal? Like what? Raw steak and potatoes drenched in blood with a Bloody Mary on the side? I snickered against the back of my hand and nodded. But when I took a step toward Mr. Butler, he gave a distinguished gasp and stepped backward.

"Please, madam. I will leave first. You haven't fed, and I don't wish to upset your delicate appetite."

Delicate appetite? What the hell did that even mean? Besides, I wasn't even hungry. "It's fine, Beauregard."

"My name is Harold, madam."

"Honestly, I prefer Beauregard."

"Yes, I imagine you would."

Was that sarcasm? Seeing as how I was fluent in that language, I was definitely picking up what he was putting down. If I had to guess, I'd wager Mr. Beauregard didn't like me.

With a dismissive wave, I took a few more steps toward him.

Beauregard's eyes went comically wide, but it wasn't until he started to protest that a mouth-wateringly delicious scent smacked me in the face like a wet towel. Holy guacamole, it was wonderful. Perfectly sweet with a hint of spice. Saliva pooled in my mouth, and my eyes fluttered shut. It wasn't until I outstretched a hand that I realized the delectable aroma came from Beauregard.

"Should I leave?" he asked in a soft voice.

It took every ounce of strength I possessed, but I managed to hold my breath and nod. Maybe if I didn't breathe, I wouldn't be tempted, because him leaving was the last thing I wanted. No, I wanted to sink my fangs into him and suck him dry until nothing remained but a withered, empty shell.

Distantly, I listened to the sound of his retreat. Only when he was two levels below me and well out of range did I exhale. His scent rode the air and could lead me to him if I wished, like a giant bright arrow lighting up the way. I had to fight the urge to chase him down. Surely, Vlad wouldn't appreciate me chomping on his butler's neck.

No. Beauregard was a human. I didn't eat humans.

Yet.

Hopefully never.

I just wished they didn't have to smell so good. It

was like every food fantasy I'd ever had rolled into one delectable package. Beauregard had reminded me of chocolate ice-cream sundaes topped with Bailey's. My former favorite Sunday afternoon snack.

I needed to focus on something else—*anything* else. So, I took the stairs two at a time and hurried to Vlad's office, where I was sure I'd find him. I knocked, then slipped inside without waiting for a response. It had to be safer in here, under Vlad's watchful eye.

Vlad glanced up from his desk and gave me a slight nod. He held a phone to his ear but from the sounds of it was on hold. For some reason, that made me laugh. A house full of employed humans hired for exactly this purpose, but he was the one on hold.

"I'll just...." I pointed at his surrounding library.

Books, books, and more books, all in alphabetical order. Not a single trinket donned the shelves, as though he felt they were unwelcome amongst his library.

I casually perused his selection. His tastes differed from mine. Unsurprising, really. The man was from an entirely different era than me. He'd already died before authors like Voltaire, Austen, and Shakespeare wrote their works.

I preferred more contemporary fiction, with a taste for fantasy when the mood struck. I'd never been one to enjoy the classics. But to each their own.

"Very well," I heard Vlad say as I rounded one row of bookshelves and started down another. "Yes, that'll suffice. We'll see you then. Thank you."

At the sound of his call disconnecting, I circled back around the stacks. The nosy journalist in me wanted to pepper him with questions. What was he planning? When he said "we," did he mean me and him? Or did he mean the royal we? But the manners my mother had instilled within me as a young child flared up, and I bit my tongue.

"Apologies." Vlad tipped his head. "How are you feeling tonight?"

"I'm okay, I think. Not as tired as last night. Less frazzled."

Vlad nodded. "Good. Are you hungry?"

My mind instantly went to donuts and coffee. Ugh, I would kill for a glazed anything right now. Even just a nibble. Something to soothe the sugar-addicted beast within me. "Can we eat human food?"

"Ah. No. Our systems can't handle it."

A polite way of saying *now that you're dead, only the lifeblood of the living will keep you alive*. Cute. I tried not to let the disappointment bring me down, but damn it, I *lived* for crullers. What a cruel existence—to live forever without ever again relishing a donut or pastry. It had to be illegal.

"So, just blood?"

He gave a single nod.

"Great. An eternal liquid diet."

His mouth twitched with the hint of a smile. "I assure you, it's not so bad. The different flavors make it quite appetizing. And our hunger is not so easily sated. Believe me when I tell you, you won't ever grow tired of blood."

Ugh. I think that was the most unappetizing thing he could have said.

"Does it have to be human?"

Sympathy softened his face. "I know of some who subsist off animals. But believe me when I tell you, that type of diet will weaken you. I admit I don't know the science behind it, but human blood is the best nourishment for us."

"What about other vampires?" My stomach warmed with the thought of last night, suckling at Vlad's wrist. The honeyed taste of his blood lingered in my memory.

Some sort of emotion flashed deep in Vlad's eyes,

but it was gone before I could figure it out. For a moment, I wondered if it was rage—if my question had angered him. But then I wondered if it was lust. Was the idea of me drinking his blood again as erotic for him as it was for me?

And if so, what did that mean?

Vlad cleared his throat. "There are *some* vampires out there who feed off one another."

"And...?"

He sighed and rubbed the bridge of his nose. "It's usually reserved for lovers. They share blood in the heat of the moment."

Heat of the...? Ahh.

"Sharing blood can be thrilling for both parties. To give yourself wholly to someone you care about deeply. However, many choose not to partake in such a way. The older the vampire, the more powerful their blood—and unfortunately, the more addicting. Drinking from an ancient, for example, is harmful to younger vampires."

"I don't understand." None of this was explained in the forums I read last night, so I was a bit lost here.

Vlad sat in his desk chair with a pinched expression. "Vampires require blood to survive. We subsist off humans because their blood contains no magic or power beyond simply providing life. But vampiric blood contains an essence humans lack. Younger vampires who drink from older vampires tend to experience exponential growth of their own power. But often, their minds and bodies aren't prepared for such a thing."

"So, what happens to the younger vampire then?"

"They succumb to madness, unable to handle the power. We vampires develop our powers naturally over the course of centuries. Over the years, I've grown into two abilities. But when a younger vampire drinks from an older one, the process is accelerated. And their young bodies can't handle the transition."

"Then what about last night?"

"It was an emergency," Vlad said. "A few small feedings won't harm you. But we do need to tread carefully. I am over five hundred years old. And you are...." He gave a small shrug.

"Two nights old," I answered, if we didn't count the three nights I'd spent marinating in my coffin.

"The age-gap is dangerous."

"So no more feeding off you. Got it."

Vlad's jaw tightened, and for a brief second, I wondered if he actually wanted me to feed from him.

He'd mentioned sharing blood was addicting. Perhaps he wasn't as immune as he thought.

Which got me wondering... "What about those who are in a relationship and share blood while—" This time, I cleared my throat. I was a grown-ass adult, but for some reason, I couldn't say the word "fucking" in front of Vlad. And "making love" seemed far worse.

"Yes, well, there's always an exception, and those in a relationship make that choice for themselves. Sadly, we've seen situations arise where the younger partner needs to be contained, or even killed, due to sharing too much blood. Those are sad days."

My breath rushed past my lips. "You kill them?"

"We have no choice, Anna. We cannot allow rabid vampires to run rampant through the streets. And those who've lost their minds to bloodlust can't be reasoned with. Imprisoning them would be a life worse than death, since their minds never heal. Death is a blessing in that case."

Okay. *Definitely* no more drinking from Vlad. No matter how badly I wanted to wrap my mouth around him. It was strange how that disappointed me. I hadn't known Vlad long. Yes, he'd saved my life, but really, I didn't know anything else about him, other than his approximate age. And yet, I felt this loss keenly. A weight pressed on my chest, almost like I wanted to cry. I remembered how sweet his blood had tasted, how it'd brought me back from the brink twice now. Once the night of my death, then last night. Was this the addiction he'd mentioned? Why vampires began to crave one another?

It had to be in my head. He'd said a few small feedings wouldn't harm me. Probably boiled down to me just wanting something I couldn't have. Typical Anna Perish behavior—and yes, before anyone asks, my family name is the same as my hometown name. Thank my great-great-and-so-on-grandfather who'd founded the town.

Anywho, growing up, my parents had constantly used reverse psychology on me, because anything they said I couldn't have, I wanted. Seemed Vlad's blood was no exception.

I shoved those thoughts to the back of my mind. Focusing on them would only deepen the craving. "Okay, then what's on the menu tonight?"

"I had Harold fetch you some bagged blood. It's human. However, not fresh from the source. You may not like it, but you can't leave the house for the rest of the week, so I'm afraid this will have to suffice."

I grimaced. Bagged blood did not sound

appetizing whatsoever. "What about another vampire my age?"

This time, rage flashed across Vlad's face. "Absolutely not."

I blinked. "Why not? If the age discrepancy is the only issue, and I'm not allowed around humans for the rest of the week, wouldn't it make sense—"

"No, Anna," he snapped, his words edged with a growl.

I startled at the severity of his tone.

After a few tense moments, he drew in a deep breath and rose from his chair. "I apologize. I didn't mean to...." He sighed and raked a hand through his hair. "My emotions are a bit charged right now. Let me call for Harold. And we'll get you fed."

His emotions were charged? Why? Yet again, I bit my tongue to keep from asking him the question. My inner journalist was getting frustrated with me. She wanted *all* the answers, and I kept holding back. Afraid of his responses, perhaps?

Vlad strode toward the door, then pressed an intercom button and summoned Harold.

The minutes passed in silence, with Vlad's back to me, as though he couldn't stand to face me right now. Clearly, something had upset him. And even though I was dying for answers, I knew better than to push.

Finally, Harold appeared, as calm and composed as he was in the attic. He held a bag of blood in one hand and an empty wine glass in the other. I grimaced at the sight. Maybe a black cup would have been better for my first time, to hide the dark-red color.

Vlad took the supplies from him, then beckoned me closer. He still seemed so distracted, even as he opened the bag and poured it into the glass. Something was clearly bothering him.

Harold eyed me as I approached, but I ignored him. The scent of blood had reached my nose, and right now, it was the only thing I could focus on. Much like in the attic, it didn't smell disgusting at all.

Vlad offered me the glass. I held the stem between my fingers and gave it a swirl, like I'd seen wine aficionados do. The blood was too thick to swish, but it gave a small slosh, freshening the scent. I felt the monster within rise at the sight. Hunger grew within me until it was all I could think about. I wanted blood, *needed* it. And I didn't care how I got it. Even if it meant slurping it out of a glass.

I lifted it to my mouth, took my first sip, and instantly winced.

Bitter. Rancid. To the point where my stomach lurched.

I gave the liquid in the glass another sniff and realized *this* blood wasn't the one giving off the marvelous smell. This smelled like plastic and copper pennies.

No, the delectable fragrance came from in front of me.

I lifted my gaze over the rim of the glass and eyed Harold.

This was the closest I'd come to a human since Vlad saved Lucy from me last night. His scent was like coming home to the sweet smell of fresh cinnamon buns. My eyes fluttered shut, and I drew in another deep breath.

Without warning, the monster within took hold.

Before I realized it, I dropped the glass to the ground and lunged.

Chaos erupted within the room. Shattering glass and a man screaming, but none of it mattered. My fingers locked around Harold's arms, and I rode his body down to the ground.

Distantly, I heard Vlad order me to stop, but his words were a muffled haze, lost to my bloodlust.

I descended without a thought and struck like a snake.

My fangs pierced Harold's throat, and blood gushed into my mouth.

Mm. Heaven.

Nothing like fresh blood direct from the tap to appease a hungry vamp tummy.

I'D BARELY TAKEN a few sips of blood when a pair of cold, strong hands clamped around my arms and hauled me backward. I felt Harold's flesh give, tearing beneath my fangs, and another splash of blood coated my tongue. An animalistic growl tore free of my throat as I mindlessly dashed after my meal. All I saw was red, and all I could taste was blood.

I needed more.

Something struck my shoulder, and I flew backward, colliding with the nearest bookshelf. Pain ricocheted through my head as I slumped to the ground. I blinked and shook my head, clearing away the haze.

The scent of blood still rode the air, teasing and taunting me, but with distance came a bit of clarity. My vision returned to normal, and I stared across the room. Vlad leaned over Harold, hand clamped to the human's throat, but his furious gaze blazed at me.

"Oh shit," I whispered, my hands rising to my blood-smeared mouth. What had I done? I'd injured poor Harold. Possibly killed him? I'd felt my fangs rip through his throat. "Is he okay? Vlad? Is he okay?"

"There's a first aid kit in the bathroom, under the sink. Get it. Now."

I didn't even think to argue. I scrambled to my feet, clapped a hand over my mouth and nose, and tore through the room like a dervish. The stairs whirred by in a blur, and I barely acknowledged grabbing the first aid kit before I returned to Vlad's office and dropped to my knees at Harold's side.

"Hold your breath," Vlad warned, though his voice was calmer now. "It'll keep you from scenting his blood."

I nodded.

"Open the kit. I need a needle and sutures. You'll see a small bottle of alcohol, pour it over the needle."

I did exactly as he commanded.

154

"I'll need both hands to close these wounds, so I'm going to remove my hand now. Harold, I need you to hold still. This will be painful. I apologize for that, old friend."

Instantly, Vlad removed his hand from the wound.

Harold's neck pulsed, and a fresh stream of blood began pouring out. I continued to hold my breath, knowing that scent was my worst enemy right now. The sight of it, though, was almost enough to undo me.

No. *No.* I had to have better control than this. I couldn't walk around ravaging every human I saw.

Vlad barely paid me any mind as he snatched the newly sterilized supplies from my hands and set to work. By the way he moved, I could tell he'd done this before. Made sense. He'd been around quite a long time. I was sure he'd picked up little bits of information and knowledge that most of us didn't have.

It didn't take long to sew Harold up, thanks to Vlad's quickened speed. Soon, Harold's neck was stitched and wrapped in gauze, the edges taped to the top and bottom of his throat.

"There," Vlad whispered, sitting back on his haunches. "You'll be all right."

I still didn't dare to breathe. Not with so much spilled blood.

"Anna, go wash up. Then wait for me in your room while I handle all this."

I nodded. I didn't dare meet Harold's gaze. I wasn't brave enough to face the accusation within. I shouldn't have attacked him, but I couldn't speak to apologize. Not without releasing my breath and sucking in a new one. It'd have to wait.

"Go," Vlad snapped.

I shot to my feet and retreated down the hallway and back up the stairs toward my room. I snatched up yesterday's clothes from beside my bed and ducked into the bathroom. With the lights still out, I gripped the sink and *finally* released my breath. My chest burned with relief, but I hadn't felt the need to breathe once while down there. Guess air was only needed for talking and using our senses.

I don't know why, but that hit me hard. Another nail in the coffin, pun intended.

I was dead. And now, I'd almost killed a man. His blood still stained my hands and pajamas.

Fighting back tears—because I swore I wouldn't cry ever again—I stripped, then lifted my head and stared into the mirror, only to be met with *nothing*. No reflection. Not a hint of the person I was or had been. Nothing but empty glass, as though the mirror was taunting me.

This was what I'd become. A monster with no reflection who fed off humans.

Those damn tears were welling in my eyes, but I refused to succumb.

Instead, I snapped the shower curtain back, turned on the water, then stepped under the spray. In the shower, I could pretend like everything was all right. I wasn't a vampire. I was just a normal woman. I gave myself ten minutes to wallow, then washed up and stepped out.

This was my situation now. Crying about it wouldn't change anything. And sobbing over Harold wouldn't change the past. I needed to learn from this and improve.

There was a reason the queen recommended a week of isolation.

I patted myself dry before tackling my wet hair— a new challenge considering I couldn't see myself in the mirror to line up my part—then brushed my teeth. I *needed* to get Harold's taste out of my mouth. I scrubbed my fangs until my bristles came away tinged with pink.

Only then did I dress and venture back into my room.

Vlad stood near the window, his hands clasped behind his back. "I should apologize again."

I startled. *Him?* Apologize?

"I wasn't thinking. I shouldn't have had you walk to me to receive your meal. I should have brought it to you. I was distracted and let you get too close to Harold. This was my fault."

"What?" I whispered. "Vlad, no. You didn't do anything—I screwed up. I attacked him. I—"

"*You* are a one-night-old vampire." He turned from the window to face me. "You don't understand how alluring humans can be. I do. It's my job as your sire to teach you and to protect those within my care. Including the humans."

I considered his words. "Of course I accept your apology, but I'm sorry too. I'm going to work on this. I need to be able to be around humans. I can't hide away for the next hundred years. So I'm willing to do whatever it takes. Even if it means drinking that dreadful bagged blood."

A whisper of a smile crossed Vlad's face. "Perhaps that wasn't the best way to start."

"I'm open to other options," I gently teased, remembering the rancid taste of that crap compared to a fresh human. "How is Harold?"

"He'll live. Thankfully. I've given him and my

staff the rest of the week off. I feel it might be safer for the time being."

I hated that such precautions were needed, but I'd rather that than me inadvertently killing someone. That was something I couldn't live with.

Vlad walked toward me. With every step, my breath hitched. The man was so beautiful up close. I'd never seen anyone's eyes so dark—like obsidian gems.

After a moment's pause, he lifted a hand and tucked a wet rope of hair behind my ear. "I've never done anything like this before." When I lifted a questioning brow, he clarified. "You're the first person I've ever sired."

"Really?"

"Yes, well, don't let it go to your head."

I laughed, grateful when my shoulders started to relax. "Well, we can learn together."

Vlad nodded. "I've reached out to a few friends I trust. They'll educate me on how we should proceed. In the meantime, here." He pushed his sleeve back and offered me his wrist.

My mouth pooled at the sight of it, and my eyes widened. "But I thought—"

"One more feeding won't hurt you. You must

feed, and I can't have you snacking on my employees."

A shiver rolled down my spine. Oh, I wanted this. Wanted *him* in my mouth. My chest quickened as I sucked in one breath after another. "Are you sure about this?"

"Yes."

I forgot about my fangs and bit my bottom lip. I winced when they punctured the soft flesh. Blood welled over, and Vlad's eyes flashed at the sight. I knew desire when I saw it. That was one emotion I'd always been able to easily read. Would it hurt to give him a little of my blood? From what I'd learned in his office, it didn't seem like my blood would do anything for him, other than provide a thrill.

His eyes were locked on my lips, so without warning, I eased up on my tiptoes and pressed my mouth to his.

Vlad hissed and jerked back, his expression wild. "What are you do—"

"Shh." I slid my hands over his shoulders and offered him a second taste. That the proposition included my mouth was a bonus.

"You shouldn't be so giving of your blood," he scolded. "You don't know—"

"Just shut up and enjoy the moment."

Apparently, I didn't need to tell him a third time. I watched his throat move as he swallowed in anticipation, then his hands found mine and he wrenched me against him. His mouth crashed against mine with a hungry growl, his tongue sweeping across my bleeding lip. Vlad groaned and tilted his head, deepening the angle as he fed from my mouth.

The instant our tongues touched, I gasped. Desire uncurled in my belly, like a cat waking from a nap, and spread through my body. I wound my arms around his neck and plunged my fingers into his hair. So soft and thick. It made me wonder about the rest of him. What would I find hidden away beneath his clothes, and when would I get the chance to find out? I wanted to unwrap him like a Christmas present, taking my time to appreciate the gift within.

Vlad's fingers dug into my hips, and he lost himself to my mouth, ravishing me with a single kiss. I quickly learned how talented a five-hundred-year-old man was—because *damn*. I felt his touch everywhere, even though his hands hadn't moved.

The man undoubtedly had skills, proven when he artfully pierced my tongue without my notice, taking from me what I'd soon be taking from him. I had to admit, I preferred his method to mine. The wrist seemed hardly as provocative now that I'd experienced this way of taking blood.

Vlad's fangs scraped my bottom lip as he slowly drew back. We both panted for breath, his cheeks flushed with my blood. I immediately touched a hand to my tingling mouth, too stunned and aroused to speak. I'd never experienced anything like that, and I was far from a nun. I'd had my share of boyfriends—all former now. But Vlad wasn't a boy. My exes paled in comparison to him.

"I—I...." I had absolutely no idea what to say. I sucked in a slow breath and shivered. "Damn."

Vlad clenched his jaw tight, as though afraid to speak. Instead, he held my gaze and offered me his wrist. Veins ran beneath his flesh, pulsing with excitement. My mouth watered at the sight. If our kiss was any indication, I was in far more danger than developing a minor blood addiction. That alone should have been reason enough to pull back, thank him, and find another blood bag to choke down. But I couldn't seem to walk away. I *wanted* to taste him again.

I shot him a questioning glance, and when he nodded, I cradled his arm in my hands and lifted it to my mouth. Damn, I wanted this so bad.

Correction. I wanted *him* so bad.

Crazy, right? I'd known the man for two nights! Well, three if you counted the night he turned me. Maybe this attraction was a vampire thing? A sire-apprentice connection? The forums last night had mentioned heightened emotions and raging hormones while our bodies adjusted. Was that all this was? Did my emotions include desire? Did I care?

These were all questions for another time.

I bowed over his wrist, then slowly bit, sinking my fangs into his flesh. His hissed breath made my own catch. But it was the taste of his honeyed blood that had my eyes fluttering shut. I needed to focus on the feeding and not the throbbing between my legs. So he was an attractive man. That didn't mean I needed to jump him. But my brain took off with the imagery and started wondering what sex between us would look like.

It took every ounce of self-restraint I possessed not to jump Vlad right then and there.

Cripes, I needed to get a hold of myself.

It didn't help that his fingers were running through my damp hair, pushing it off my neck. The darkest part of my fantasies imagined him biting the soft part of my throat while I fed from his wrist.

Oh man, this was bad.

I couldn't be attracted to my sire, right?

My five-hundred-year-old sire named Dracula.

Because that would be insane.

And yet, when I pulled back from his wrist and lifted my head, my dead heart stuttered at the sight of him watching me, his gaze practically searing.

Seemed I wasn't the only one in this predicament.

9

REALITY CAME CRASHING DOWN, and I jerked back. I'd just kissed Dracula. Vlad. The Count. Whatever. The man had more names than I did panties at the moment. Which, speaking of, I needed to phone Lucy and ask her to go shopping, since we'd only packed weekend bags.

But that was a different, easily solvable problem. Nothing like this. Kissing Dracula had to rate stupider than busting into a vampire club to expose illegal bloodletting, which turned out not to be illegal. Impulsive, remember?

This right here was proof. Two nights under this man's roof, and I was making out with him and swapping blood like we were lovers. Gah! I shouldn't have thought that. I didn't need the word "lovers" in my head right now. Not with him standing so close, eyes still blazing, and certainly not with my lady bits still waving their pom-poms and cheering me on.

Kissing Dracula was stupid, right?

Maybe?

Who the hell even knew anymore? "I, uh, should go."

Vlad inched toward me. "Go where? This is your room."

Right. My room. Because I'd just showered after *attacking* Harold. And here I was, getting my freak on with the Count himself. If he could just stop watching me like I was the cherry on top of a very delicious strawberry sundae, that would be greatly appreciated. I couldn't think with him standing there, all smoldering eyes and swollen lips.

The invitation was clear, as were his desires. I wasn't one of those women who was blind to the opposite sex. If I so much as gave the word, Vlad and I would tumble into that tiny bed next to us.

And damn, I was tempted.

On the one hand, I was a grown-ass woman, allowed to kiss whoever the hell she wanted. But on the other, this man was five hundred years older than me—which, *ick*—and a vampire. All right, maybe that last one was unfair, considering I was also a vampire. But if he'd never been turned, he would be rotting away in a grave right now. Then again, so would I. Not a very sexy thought. Why focus on the what ifs, though? He *had* been turned, and instead of a rotting corpse, he was a downright gorgeous beast of a man who I wanted to dry hump like a randy mutt. Decisions, decisions....

"Okay, then you need to go," I told him. "I, uh, need to be alone. Is that okay? I need to think. And I can't do that with you here."

Vlad inclined his head and blinked, the heat fizzling from his gaze. "Very well."

"Thank you."

"Of course. I'll be in my office, should you need anything."

A shiver rolled through my body. I could think of one thing I needed, but my last impulsive decision had gotten me killed. I really needed to start thinking things through. And since I wasn't allowed to go to a bar and get wasted—probably wouldn't even work anyway—there was only one other thing I could think to do and that was call Lucy.

Vlad took my hand and kissed my knuckles before exiting my room.

I slumped against the wall and blew out a

relieved breath. Man, he knew how to wind me up. And he hadn't even done anything. Just walked into my room. Was that all it took now to get my engine revving?

Plucking my phone from my back pocket, I ignored all the missed notifications from my family and dialed Lucy's number. Texting wouldn't do for this situation. I needed to hear her voice when she told me this was a stupid idea.

She answered on the third ring. "How are you?"

The sound of her voice brought a smile to my well-kissed mouth.

"Slaughtered half of New Orleans yet?" she asked, not waiting for my answer.

That smile slipped. "Har, har. Considering I'm not allowed to leave the house, I think New Orleans is safe."

"For now."

Her words stung. Until I remembered that I'd just assaulted Harold. And then made out with his employer. Geez! What was becoming a vampire doing to me? How could I go from savaging a poor man's neck to ravaging my sire's mouth all within an hour?

Clearly, I was losing my damn mind. And I

blamed the hot piece of ass I'd just booted from my room.

"I...." My words died. I, what? Nearly killed a man? Lucy wouldn't take that very well. Should I tell her I kissed Vlad? A fanger? Cripes, her mind might implode with that one. Which was the lesser of the two evils?

How much was I even willing to say? Vlad's office was only one level down, meaning he could hear everything we said. Did I care, though? A gentleman wouldn't pry, and based on my experiences with him, I had to believe he would refrain from listening in. Maybe it was a part of vampire etiquette? Thou shalt not eavesdrop? And if he did, well, that was his problem, not mine.

"Anna? What's wrong? Are you all right? Did he hurt you?" She fired off her questions like ping pong balls.

"No, nothing like that. I just.... Lucy, I did something."

She drew in a sharp breath, then released it. "Okay. It's okay. We'll get you through it. Do you know who it was? Do they have family?"

My brows knotted. "Huh?"

"Honestly, it's okay," Lucy repeated. "Just tell

me what happened. I was expecting this. So I'm prepared."

Prepared for what, exactly? For me kissing Vlad? What could have possibly given her that impression in the two minutes she'd seen us together? The one and only conversation I'd had with him in her presence had mostly involved Lucy and me fighting. Vlad had barely been involved.

I opened my mouth, about to confide in her the whole story, when that damn light bulb went off in my head again. Lucy's sympathetic voice, telling me she'd expected this. She hadn't been referring to me kissing Vlad.

No.

She thought I'd killed someone.

I wanted to be mad. Hurt even that she would suspect such a thing. But honestly, who was I to cast stones? I'd almost murdered Harold. Me. A newly bloodsucking fiend from beyond the grave. Eating humans sort of came with the territory. Was it really so surprising that she'd prepared herself for the worst-case scenario?

Maybe instead, I should be grateful that she was still willing to be my friend and listen to my confession—had I actually murdered someone.

"It's nothing like that, Lucy. Although, I did accidentally bite Vlad's butler. I lost control."

"But he's alive?"

"Yes. Vlad assures me Beauregard will be fine. Vlad also gave his staff the rest of the week off so there won't be anyone else for me to hurt."

"Oh, okay. I mean, great! Really. That's great."

I frowned. She sounded unsure. Like she was trying to convince herself more than me.

"Well, if you didn't kill someone, then what did you do? Or were you just referring to this Beauregard guy?"

Oh boy. Here we go. I couldn't put my finger on why I was so nervous. So Vlad and I kissed. Big deal, right? Besides, Lucy's disappointment was second nature to me. She constantly waggled her finger at me about this and that—her impulsive and irresponsible friend.

"Okay, so, here's the thing." I pinched my brow and mustered up the courage. *Just spit it out, girl.* I cupped my hand around the phone and quietly hissed, "I kissed Vlad."

Silence.

And then came more silence.

With my newly heightened senses, I could hear her mouth opening and closing even though no sound came out. Her small inhalations. Hell, I could practically hear the gears spinning in her head.

"I'm sorry. I thought I heard you say—"

"You did. I kissed Vlad," I whispered.

"Okaaay." Nervous laughter bubbled across the connection. "I gotta say, Anna, I really don't know how to react to that."

Better than her immediately scolding me.

"Did he force you to kiss him?"

"Cripes, Lucy! No, he didn't force me!"

"Well! I don't know!" Her voice rose. "I hardly know the man. All I know is he changed you into a vampire. That doesn't exactly give me a good feeling about him. For all I know, he's the kind of guy who extorts sexual favors! And if he is, you tell him I don't care who he is, I'll march down there, stake in hand, and stab him in his vampy ass."

I snorted back a laugh. "Oh wow, Lucy. There are so many things wrong with that statement. First, you can't stab a vampire in the ass with a stake. Well, that's not true. You *could*, but I think you'll only piss him off. Second, Vlad really isn't the type to force himself on anyone. I don't think he has that problem."

"Oh shit, girl. Are you falling for him?"

"What?" I sputtered. "No!"

"Good! You better not! Because we're going home, remember? To Perish. To your folks and my family. Besides, you *cannot* fall in love with the first vampire you meet. That's so cliché!"

"No one is falling in love, Lucy. You don't need to fall in love with someone to suck face with them."

"Ew, Anna! Suck face? Really?"

A teasing grin tugged at my lips. Knew she'd appreciate that one. "Well, there was some sucking. Some biting. Some bloodletting."

"Oh, gross!" Lucy feigned gagging. "That's disgusting. I don't want to know about your nasty vamp ways. It has to be impolite to discuss your new plasma-enriched diet."

"I'm sorry. My what now?"

"Well, it sounds better than drinking blood, doesn't it?"

"Whatever helps you sleep at night," I said, laughing.

"Okay, can we get back to the issue at hand here?"

"I don't know, can we?"

"Girlfriend, I can think of half a dozen reasons why getting involved with the man who turned you is a bad thing."

"Sire," I told her as I sat on the small chest

pressed up against my bed. I stared out the window, my gaze immediately leaping to the stars.

Holy shit.

I'd always loved astronomy as a human. To stare up at the stars and name the constellations, watch the planets rise and set, count shooting stars. I'd even gone to a planetarium once and saw Saturn through a telescope. Absolutely breathtaking seeing the planets in all their splendor.

But none of that compared to now. The stars were so much crisper. Hell, I could count the craters on the freaking moon. Utterly incredible.

"Anna?" Lucy's voice called through the line.

I blinked and tore my gaze away from the twinkling sky. I found it comforting to know the night would never be empty again. I could see for miles now, even through the thick veil of darkness.

"Sorry, got a bit distracted there."

"You okay?"

"Yes. I'm just starting to comprehend the changes my body is going through. Like, I can see things I've never seen before. Lucy, I can hear people talking a few miles away."

"That sounds... uncomfortable."

"Anyway. You were saying?"

"Yeah, I said that it doesn't seem wise to get emotionally involved with your sire."

"Okay. Reasons?" I needed to hear them.

"Well, he's older than you."

"So were your last two boyfriends."

She scoffed. "By like three years, Anna. I highly doubt that qualifies."

Fair point. "What else?"

"He's a more experienced vampire than you."

"Isn't that a good thing?" One would assume that would help me become the best vampire I could be.

"Maybe. Okay. Um, he's Dracula?"

"And? Are you saying I can't be with someone because he's famous?"

"No, of course not." She sighed. "I don't know. This just feels weird to me. And unwise."

I bit my lip, careful this time not to puncture the flesh. For some reason, I suspected he'd be able to smell my blood all the way downstairs, and the last thing I needed was another make-out fest with the man in question.

"There's something else you should know," I told her.

"Uh oh, I don't like the sound of that."

"Earlier, Vlad told me it's dangerous for a newborn vamp like me to take blood from an older vamp like him. Apparently, there's a bit of a power transfer when taking blood from an ancient vamp or whatever."

"I'm gonna need you to explain that a bit more."

I sighed. I really didn't feel like recapping all this, but I couldn't keep this a secret from Lucy. It was a part of my life now, and secrets were like cancerous tumors. "Younger vampires have been known to go mad if they ingest too much blood from an older, more powerful vampire."

"All right, and how old is Mr. Dracula?"

"He's over five hundred years old," I admitted. "And he has two of those special ability thingies."

"Anna," Lucy whispered. "I don't like the sound of that."

I nodded. I wanted to reassure her that everything was fine. But I already felt the pull from his blood.

"You drank from him last night," she continued. "Before I left."

"And the night before, seeing as how he changed me."

"Right." She exhaled. "Okay, so maybe—"

"And, um, tonight too," I said, interrupting her.

"Anna!"

"I know. It was after I hurt Beauregard. I needed

to feed. He said a few feedings wouldn't hurt me, but that we needed to be careful."

"Careful? Why? What happens if a vampire loses their mind?"

"I think you already know the answer to that."

Lucy groaned. "I hate this, Anna. So much. I hate it! You're dead."

"Undead," I repeated softly.

"Don't start that up again. Or I will literally come to Vlad's place just to slap you."

My lips twitched.

"My point is there's so much we don't know about this world. I know you read up on it a little last night, about what becoming a vampire means. But that doesn't tell us anything about the actual vampire world. Do you realize we don't know anything about this queen of theirs? Only that she signed a treaty with our president? But what about everything else? Are there laws you have to follow? Are you indebted to Vlad? Are you trapped with him forever now? Do you have to do as he says for the rest of your eternal life? Or obey the queen without question? We know *nothing*. Can you even go home to Perish?"

All fangtastic questions, ones I didn't have answers to.

"They have you isolating for a week. Then what?

Do they just toss you out into the wild to sink or swim? Will they teach you how to feed? What about employment? Can you still work? You can't *not* work. How will you survive? You still need housing and whatnot. Just because you don't need to buy food anymore doesn't mean you don't need other necessities."

"Lucy—"

"And what about your family? How are they going to react? Is there any sort of program in place to help them adjust and accept that their daughter is, in fact, undead?"

"Lucy—"

"Or your friends for that matter! Or do you just vanish into the good night and start your new vampy life over without us. Because I can't lose you, girl. I just experienced how that felt, and I'm really not eager to go through that again. But what if it isn't safe for you to return to human society? What if that's forbidden? There's so much we just don't know!"

"Lucy!"

She sucked in a shivering breath. Even through the phone, I could hear the sounds of her impending panic attack.

"Okay, take a breath, hun."

"I really hate this, Anna." Her voice grew thick with tears.

Guilt sucker-punched me. I hated that I couldn't be there to help her through this. "I know. Just take a deep breath for me, okay? And when you're ready, let it out." At the sound of her exhalation, I nodded. "Good. A few more times. In and out. Just keep doing that while I talk."

She didn't respond.

"I want you to listen to me when I tell you I'm not going anywhere. Ever again. Literally. I'm immortal now, which means you're stuck with me until you're wrinkled and gray with dementia, crowing about your best friend the vampire. All your questions are valid, and we're going to find the answers to them, I promise. But believe me when I tell you, no queen or otherwise will ever keep me from you. Take another breath."

She did as I commanded.

"Do you feel better?"

"No," she croaked.

"I love you. You know that, right?"

"Yes."

"Good. That's all that matters right now. We'll figure everything else out together. After tonight, there's only five more nights until we can see each other again. We'll both feel better after that."

"Sure."

"Hey, we got this. We're two strong, kick-ass women. Dead or alive, it doesn't matter. Nothing's gonna tear us apart."

"Okay, INXS," she teased, sounding a bit like her old self.

A bark of laughter slipped past my lips. "It's getting late. Why don't you go take a bath or something, stop worrying, then get some sleep? If you're up for it, feel free to go shopping tomorrow. We both could use some clothes."

"Yeah, I thought about that. I'll hit the stores tomorrow. You should call your mom, though. I told mine we were staying a few more days. But yours should hear it from you."

I nodded, even though she couldn't see it. I didn't love the idea of reaching out to my family. Not yet. My family wasn't exactly a happy one to begin with. Their divorce burst our happy little bubble. But I couldn't ignore them either. My mom was expecting us home earlier today, so our absence would be noted. Especially considering Sunday nights were her version of family night. The one night a week my brother and I were forced to go to her place for a fancy dinner and games.

"Yeah. I have a few missed calls from my mom already. Dad probably hasn't realized that I'm not even home right now. You know how oblivious he is when it comes to his *real* family. I didn't answer their calls. I'm not ready."

"You'll need to make something up. Lie to them about why you're unavailable during the day. Until you're willing to tell them the truth, that is."

Just another problem to handle. I knew my parents. They were both going to lose their shit. Lucy was already panicking, but my mother would slip into full-on hysteria. It certainly didn't help that my dad was the mayor of our town, or that both my parents were churchgoing people, even though they were divorced. Honestly, I wasn't sure if they'd even see me as their daughter anymore, and I wasn't eager to find out.

"I'll call them both," I said, glancing at the clock. A little before ten. Mom would be in bed, but she'd still answer her phone. She generally stayed up until eleven or so. Dad was a bit of a night owl, considering he had his business and the town to contend with. But I wasn't ready to face either of them yet, so I amended my statement with a "Tomorrow."

"Anna."

"I'll call them tomorrow, Lucy. I promise. I'm just not ready yet."

"Okay," her voice softened. "You know, I never got to say how sorry I am this happened to you."

"What?"

"Last night, I was really worked up and frightened. I hadn't seen you in three nights. I thought you were dead. My thoughts had gone to a very dark place. But I want you to know, I'm so sorry. I never should have agreed to go to that club with you. If I hadn't...."

"I would have gone alone," I admitted to her. "This is so not your fault."

"I know, but—"

"No buts. No what ifs. This is absolutely, unequivocally not your fault. The blame rests on me. I got myself into this situation, but I can handle it. It might just take a little time."

"Still," Lucy continued, "I want you to know that what I said last night, about me leaving, I didn't mean it. You know you're my bestie. I'm not going anywhere."

Relief eased my shoulders. "Good, because I'd

hate to have to bite your ass."

"Oh, there won't be any biting. I... I need to be upfront about this. What happened to you is about the worst thing I can imagine. I don't want to become a vampire. Ever. Okay? If something happens to me, and I'm dying, let me die."

"Lucy."

"No, Anna. I know you can handle this, because you're so strong. I'm not. I couldn't handle having to feed off people or living forever while all my loved ones passed on. I'm not religious, but I—I can't become that."

I tried not to let her words hurt me, but they truly felt like a knife in the gut. Not that I'd even considered turning Lucy. But to think of her dying while I lived on... that was true pain.

"Anna?"

"I hear you," I told her. "And I understand."

She blew out a relieved breath. "Good. Thank you. Try to have a good night. Don't maul anyone else, 'kay?"

"'Kay."

"Night, girl."

"Night." I disconnected the call, then lowered my phone into my lap and stared out the window, letting the emptiness creep in.

I SPENT the next couple nights thinking about my past, present, and future. Truthfully, I had nothing else to do except avoid any further inevitable hanky-panky. At least not yet. But OMG, was I borrred. Wasn't being a vampire supposed to be exciting or some shit? Becoming a creature of the night *sounded* majestic and mysterious. Stalking my prey through the shadows, thirsting for their blood, living a life ripe with tragedy, caught in an eternal struggle between light and darkness.

Guess those ideas were rooted in fiction.

The truth was far more mundane.

Four nights had passed since I'd first woken—two since I'd played tonsil hockey with Vlad. For those two nights, I'd done little more than aimlessly wander his mansion, looking for something— anything—that might entertain me, all while avoiding what I assumed was an inevitable conversation. Vlad kept eyeing me *that* way, as though he wanted to discuss our kiss, but I sure as hell wasn't ready for that. Nor was I ready to talk to my parents yet. I was avoiding that phone call like herpes.

On the upside, thanks to Lucy, I had new clothes. She'd dropped them off the night after our phone call, giving me enough to last until we returned home. It'd sucked donkey balls not being allowed to see or talk to her, but I'd obeyed Vlad's instructions for Lucy's sake.

I'd also mastered drinking blood from a bag. Believe me when I say it was absolutely disgusting. Nothing like chasing down your drink with the smell of burned microplastics. Vlad promised he'd teach me how to feed off humans after my week's isolation. He kept pushing me to start considering who I'd welcome into my harem. I couldn't think of a single soul who would willingly donate blood to me nightly. That wasn't something I'd ever thought about before.

I spent my time combing through the many, *many* websites about vampirism to suss out fact from fiction. My readings had resulted in a lot of peculiar tests. Ones that I think were driving Vlad to the brink of frustration. I had to admit, he was really patient with me, considering the stunts I'd pulled.

The night before last, he'd feigned a heart attack when I dropped from the ceiling to the floor beside him. Fact: Vampires could defy gravity by scaling walls and perching upside down on rafters like a bat. Guess I hadn't mastered enough stealth yet to sneak up on him. But he'd been a good sport about me messing up his papers.

Before "bed" this morning, I'd forced him to race me once around his house, just to see how fast we could run. He'd consented to the challenge, deciding it was best for me to learn these things before releasing me back into the wild. Unfortunately for my competitive soul, Vlad whooped me hard. Before I'd cleared half the distance, he'd done a full lap and was coming around for a second one. My own Captain America. Swoon.

Tonight, he'd found me in the kitchen, only to learn I'd cracked open every single jar of pickles, salsa, olives, you name it, just to test my strength. All because I *could.* No more grunting and cursing while struggling to open some obscure jar of food. Not that I'd need to open any jar ever again. But hey, I could totally open things for his human staff now. Huge win in my books.

His baffled expression had me doubled over with laughter.

Lock me up for a week and weird shit happens. I didn't know what else to tell him.

After that, he'd agreed to simply answer my questions instead of me destroying his house in the name of science. Which led us here, to his sitting room. Vlad eased onto his stupid fainting couch and faced me with a knowing smirk. I returned to my stool, but this time I had a notepad resting on my lap and a pen in hand, my mind buzzing with everything I'd recently read.

"Flying," I said, jumping right in.

"Fact."

My head snapped up. "Seriously?"

"Well, semi-fact? It's a power some vampires have developed."

Ah. Okay, so not fact for everyone. "Accelerated healing?"

"To save you the hassle of stabbing yourself to test that theory, that one is fact. I wouldn't wish to see you waste the blood."

I grinned. Less than a week together and he already knew me so well. I probably wouldn't stab myself, but there would have been some experiments. "Shapeshifting."

"Fact. But again, only as a power some vampires develop."

If I had a choice, that was the power I wanted. I would love nothing more than to romp through town as a stray dog. See the world through their eyes. "Running water."

"Fiction." He rolled his eyes. "I assure you, water running has never affected me in the slightest."

"Holy water, then?"

"Fact. It's a very unpleasant experience. I don't recommend it."

I nodded, then quickly jotted an X through it. "Crosses."

"Fact."

I raised a brow. "Care to elaborate?"

"There's not much more to say. Religious artifacts as a whole repel us. Being in the presence of a cross is as unpleasant to me as the first rays of sunrise."

"All religious artifacts?"

He considered that. "I've never had anyone throw a Star of David at me, but I'd imagine it would have the same effect, being religious and all."

"I'm an atheist," I told him. "I don't believe in religion or God at all."

He lifted a brow, as though that surprised him. Not sure why. Many people were atheists now. "I would imagine the artifacts would affect you similarly, but I can't say for sure. I've never tested the theory."

And I highly doubted he had a cross sitting around. So I moved on. "Entering a house without permission."

Vlad nodded. "Sadly, fact. We must be invited to enter a home."

Huh. Definitely needed to store that away for future information. "Silver."

"Has no effect on us. That's specifically a werewolf issue."

My jaw dropped. "Holy crap on a cracker! There are *werewolves*?"

"Fact." He rested his ankle on his knee. "I do not suggest seeking them out, though. Terribly ornery things. More bite than bark, and they have a distinct hatred for all things vampire."

"So *Underworld* was accurate then."

He lifted his hands, palms open, as though to say he didn't understand.

"It's a movie." I waved off his unspoken question. "Okay, hypnotism."

"Fiction. I can't think of a single vampire who has the power of compulsion."

Boooo. That would have been another cool power. Walk around flashing my eyes at everyone and telling them to do the chicken dance in the middle of the street until sunrise. Ah well, *c'est la vie*.

"Tell me about these so-called powers we develop."

Vlad chuckled. "I feel like I'm being interviewed."

He was, in a way. I gestured for him to speak. I was dying to know about this.

"As the centuries pass, you will begin to develop very specific abilities such as reading minds, telekinesis, flight, et cetera. There's no way to know which you will possess until it happens. As you already know, I, myself, have developed two."

"Is that normal?"

"For one of my age, yes. You must remember, even the queen is younger than I." Another person I had so many questions about. But I needed to pace myself. If I asked him every single question I had, we'd be here 'til the end of time.

"How many vampires are there your age?"

"A few. Some older still."

"Care to tell me about your abilities?"

He shrugged, then drummed his fingers against the sole of his fine Italian leather loafers. A girl could spot a good shoe a mile away, regardless of who wore them. "One of my abilities is the power to shapeshift."

I leaned forward on my stool, excitement lighting me up. "Really? That's the one I want! What can you turn into?"

"A bat and a wolf."

Oh man. I tried not to fangirl. But seriously, how *awesome* was that? "And the second?"

He seemed to grow uneasy with this one. His fingers continued to drum against his shoe, but the rhythm quickened. A case of nerves? But why would he be nervous about this last one?

"Let's move on."

I blinked. Just like that? What could it be? Something bad? But what kind of powers were considered bad? I wanted to press the conversation so badly. In the grand scheme, though, his second power had little relevance to our discussion. Not when there were so many other things I could ask.

I considered Lucy's many questions from last

night. Now was as good a time as any to get the answers. She'd definitely appreciate them. "What can you tell me about vampire society?"

"Vampire society," Vlad said, chuckling as though this phrase amused him. "What do you wish to know?"

"Well, there's the queen and her council. But what about below that? Is there a full monarchy? Does she have complete control over us all?"

Vlad shifted position on the couch. He dropped his foot to the floor and leaned forward, his expression amused. "Perhaps someone should write up a manual for new vampires. Especially for curious ones like you."

"Give me the answers, and I might do just that," I teased, then gasped when a new idea struck. "Or do a vlog on it!"

"You'll have to explain this vlog thing to me at some point."

Aww, I was touched he cared enough to ask. "Not a modern-day technology kind of guy, huh?"

"I like a quiet life, contrary to popular belief."

"Oh yes, fame and fortune can become so taxing." I laughed. "But seriously, how cool would it be if I created a vlog for all new vampires? A web series!" My mind started spinning. "Oh wow. This could be a really great idea. 'Welcome to The Undead Channel.'" I squealed and quickly began scribbling down notes. "I could provide them with *all* this information. This could be huge. It could be the hit I've been looking for to expand my reach."

"I don't know what any of that means, but I see a flaw in your logic."

My head lifted of its own accord, and I caught Vlad's gaze. "Huh?"

"You seem to have forgotten we have no reflection."

Crushing defeat crashed down on my shoulders. Shit. How had I not thought about that? I mean, there was so much going on, so much to acclimate to that things were guaranteed to be missed. But my lack of reflection was kind of a big one. Especially for someone who was seeking fame from her vlog.

"So I can't be recorded," I whispered. My mind flashed back to the video I'd taken of the vampires at Fallen. The playback had shown their clothes, but nothing else. Nothing recognizable. No faces to commit to memory. Fuck! How had I not connected the dots?

I pressed a hand to my lips and drew a deep breath. This ruined everything. And in so many ways. How the hell could I even continue my own personal vlog if I couldn't video myself? Everything I'd worked so hard to achieve was going up in flames right before my eyes.

"Anna?"

I blinked and gave Vlad a dead-eyed stare.

"Are you all right?"

"It's all ruined," I whispered.

"What is?"

"Me. Everything I've worked so hard for. Everything I've sacrificed. If I can't be seen on camera, all my hopes and dreams are over."

"I fail to see how this is that detrimental."

"You would," I whispered. "You don't even know what a vlog is."

"True, but—"

"I'm, uh, gonna go for a walk," I said, interrupting him. "Get a little fresh air."

"Are you sure you wouldn't like some company?"

"Oh, I'm sure." Deathly sure. I wanted a little peace and quiet to absorb this realization.

Man, becoming a vampire fucking sucked. Pun absolutely intended.

I CIRCLED Vlad's grounds a few times, stopping now and then to really absorb the changes in my body. Anything to distract myself from the knowledge that I'd never achieve my dreams.

The things I could hear now—birds chirping in the surrounding marshes, cars backfiring miles away, the buzz of New Orleans, even though Vlad's estate sat a good ten minutes outside the city.

I could even hear people nearby, chatting in their houses. Each residence sat on a good-sized portion of land, five or so acres. Vlad's seemed larger than the rest. I wasn't a professional surveyor, but it seemed like twenty or thirty acres to me. All surrounded by marshy wetlands and, from the sounds of it, many, *many* alligators. I *so* wasn't okay with that. Sharks and alligators were my two biggest fears. And one of those had no problem coming onto land. Where *I* lived. How inconvenient was that?

Thankfully, I could easily kill them if they strayed too close. Small consolation.

The sound of nearby bullfrogs and boars had me chomping at the bit to try out animal blood. They had to be better than tearing out a human throat, right? Vlad had promised to teach me how to safely feed, but I wasn't convinced I was ready, or ever would be.

What if I lost myself in the moment? Or started bathing in the blood of innocents? All right, maybe I'd read too many vampire novels recently, but those novels existed for a reason, right? Animal blood would weaken me, according to Vlad. Maybe that wasn't such a bad thing. Maybe it would keep me in check so I didn't hurt anyone else.

My mind flashed to the memory of Harold, sprawled on the ground, his face pale while blood gushed from his throat. I never wanted to experience that again. Perhaps animal blood was the answer. Considering how much I hated gators, I wouldn't mind putting a dent in their population.

I started toward the sound of the nearest beast, eager to test this theory, when I caught movement out of the corner of my eye. I glanced in that direction and scanned the perimeter. Hmm. Nothing. A figment of my imagination then? Probably just a random animal. Stray dog or something.

Back to the nearby gator... I braved another step when something streaked by me, as quick as lightning. My hand flew to my chest, and I sucked in a startled breath. Something was out here. Something moving across Vlad's property. And fast. Faster than both animal and human.

I inhaled and tasted the air, searching for a particular scent. But only magnolia and pine tickled my nose. My senses were still evolving, so I didn't quite know how to use them yet, how to fine-tune them into something useful.

Another flash of movement, so fast I barely saw it. Fear strangled me, my breath quickening as I scanned my surroundings.

"*Anna,*" a voice came, like a whisper carried on the breeze.

I choked on my breath, my hand still clutching at my shirt. I didn't respond—I knew better than that. Thanks to the plethora of horror films I'd watched as a teenager, I knew never to run upstairs, and never call back to a strange voice. The safest course of action was to get inside and tell Vlad what I saw.

"*An-naaa,*" that damn whispered voice came again, dragging my name out.

Something brushed the back of my neck, like fingers combing through my hair. I cried out and whirled around, slapping at empty air. Nothing. I stood alone in the middle of Vlad's back yard. Whoever it was, they were gone as quickly as they came.

A vampire then? Their movements were so

quick. But they knew my name. And the only vampire I knew was Vlad.

Was this all in my mind?

Was I imagining things?

No. I'd felt those fingers on the back of my neck, heard its voice in the darkness.

"So beautiful. So delicious. So very mine," it whispered.

Something brushed against my side an instant before cold fingers touched my cheek.

And me?

I fucking *screamed*.

11

Vlad materialized beside me with a gust of wind. I knew he couldn't fly in human form—that wasn't one of his powers—so he must have raced toward me the instant he heard my scream.

He stood in front of me with a pinched face. "What is it? What's wrong?" His hands cupped my cheeks, and he frowned. "You're shaking."

I gave a frantic nod. "There's someone out here." He opened his mouth, but I cut him off before he could jokingly tell me it was me. My mother used to do that when I told her I had something in my eye. She'd tease me and say, "Yeah, your finger." But I wasn't in the mood to be teased. "And I mean other than you and me."

Vlad held my gaze and cocked his head. For a moment, I thought he meant to contradict my statement, but then I realized he was *listening*. I could only imagine what his ears might pick up that mine had missed. I waited silently, my nerves jumping with anticipation. But the sight of his frown didn't instill me with confidence.

"Are you sure?" he finally asked.

"Of course I'm sure! I'm not insane. Something touched me. Called my name—"

"It called your name?" His face hardened.

"The voice said I belonged to him, called me delicious. Vlad...." I clutched his forearms, my fingers digging into his flesh.

"Him," Vlad repeated. "It was male?"

"I—I think so? The voice whispered, but yeah, yeah, I definitely got the feeling it was male." I forced myself to release Vlad, then took one giant step back. I needed space to think, to sort through everything. "I was standing right here, just listening to the sounds of nature. Considering trying to feed off an alligator—"

"What?"

I waved a hand. "Not important. Then out of nowhere, I started to see movement. Quick. Like a vampire."

Vlad's face turned thunderous. "A vampire?"

"I don't know, maybe? He was fast. Like you. When I screamed, you were here within seconds. This thing could move like that. Then he started whispering my name."

"Get inside."

"What? But—"

"Get inside, Anna. Go to my office and wait for me."

Oh, I didn't like the sound of this at all. First of all, I didn't want to be alone. Second of all, what if that thing, person, whatever, followed me into the house? That big, creepy mansion that I now realized was completely empty except for me and Vlad, since he'd given his staff the week off.

I gulped and glanced at his house. The lights were on, but literally no one was home. And the goose bumps running up my arms told me I *really* didn't like this idea.

When I didn't immediately move, Vlad's face softened, and he smoothed his hands down my arms, soothing the pebbled flesh. "Everything will be all right. Remember, no one can enter my house without permission. You'll be safe there."

Finally, I relented and hurried back to Vlad's house. I wasn't as quick as him, but that didn't surprise me. Once inside, I slammed the door behind me and shivered. Even the little hairs on the back of my neck stood up. I had to remind myself again that no one could enter without permission, but that didn't ease my fears. These new vampiric laws meant very little to me right now.

I bolted into Vlad's office, then took a seat in his chair and drew my knees to my chin. Now that I was inside, and safe and warm, I started to wonder if maybe I *had* imagined it all. Maybe the darkness had frightened me. Maybe it was a side effect of the change. My body was still evolving. Could have been my ears playing a trick on me.

I scoffed at myself. I'd felt those damn fingers on my cheek and neck. I hadn't imagined *that*. I needed to trust my instincts, and right now, they were screaming at me.

The minutes passed with only the sound of the flames in Vlad's fireplace crackling away. I turned in his chair to peer out the window, but I didn't see anything questionable. Nothing but the night growing long.

Eventually, a shadowed figure stepped out of the darkness, jacket fluttering in the breeze as he strode toward the house. My heart leapt at the sight, then settled when I realized it was only Vlad. He strolled across the land, stopping now and then to listen to his surroundings. Hopefully, he'd found something. That would put my mind at ease.

I listened as he made his way inside, his footsteps growing louder as he approached his office. He wasn't moving with liquid vamp speed, so maybe everything was fine.

But if it was, did that mean I *was* going insane?

Vlad eased into his office and shook his head. "I'm afraid I didn't find anything."

My hopes plummeted. What did that mean exactly?

"That doesn't mean there wasn't anything to find," he said. "If it was another vampire, he likely ran off when you screamed. It's one thing to face a newborn like you, but an entirely different situation when faced with someone like me."

"Someone has an ego," I mumbled.

Vlad's mouth twitched. "Ego has nothing to do with it. It's simply a fact. There are very few vampires out there who would willingly face me."

"Why? Are you some badass vamp with a penchant for murder?"

He held up his hands as though to say *well?*

All right. Fair enough. He was older than half a millennium. I suppose if it came down to it, I wouldn't want to provoke the infamous legend either.

"Vlad." I sighed and dropped my head back against the top of his chair. "He knew me. He knew my name. I swear, I didn't imagine that."

"I believe you. It's a strange process, becoming a vampire. But I've never known anyone to suffer hallucinations while transitioning."

I briefly closed my eyes. Vlad believed me. That shouldn't comfort me, but it did. Like his words validated everything. I needed to trust in my own instincts and not rely on his. But there was something powerful in being believed.

"Who do you think it was?" I asked. "Who all knows about me?"

"You were registered upon your undeath," Vlad told me. He crossed the room and perched against his desk, his hands gripping the edge. "The queen insists on this procedure. She feels it's the best way to keep tabs on her kingdom."

"Kingdom." I laughed under my breath. Apparently, becoming a vampire was the equivalent to time traveling. Never thought, as an American, that I'd fall under a queen's reign.

"Upon registration, your name is added to a database that she and her council arranged a decade or so ago. That database is accessible by every vampire in the world."

I squinted at Vlad. "Are you serious? What about privacy?"

"No such thing exists. We cannot have wild, rebellious vampires on the loose."

"Yeah, you mentioned that."

"And it's as true now as it was then. As one of the queen's subjects, it's my duty to abide by her laws. As it's now your responsibility."

Yeah, yeah, yeah, typical monarchy loyalty rubbish. "Except that means any vampire out there can access my name. What else does the registration include?"

"Location of death and sire."

"Perfect." I groaned and squeezed my eyes shut. "So, all it took was your name. You're one of the most infamous vampires out there. Everyone likely knows where you live. In other words, this vampire could be anyone."

"I don't believe that to be the case," Vlad said after a small pause.

"Hmm?" I opened my eyes and stared at him, enjoying the sight of him leaning so elegantly against his desk.

"You said he called you delicious?"

I shuddered. "Yeah."

"Anna."

My brows rose. "Vlad?"

"Only one other vampire has tasted you."

And just like that, my blood froze. "What?"

"I don't mean to frighten you, but we mustn't blind ourselves to a possible truth."

"You think...."

Vlad placed a comforting hand on my shoulder. "I've been waiting for a specific guest to arrive, one I made plans to meet with a few nights ago, if you recall. He should be arriving sometime tonight."

I remembered that phone call. The one before I attacked Harold. In all the commotion, I'd completely forgotten about it. "Who?"

Vlad rose from his desk and strode to his fireplace, holding his hands out toward the flames. "Queen Genevieve holds complete control over the vampire population. Her reign isn't the same as what you're accustomed to. Your kings and queens are more like figureheads. But Genevieve is absolute in her rule. She believes her laws should be unequivocally obeyed. To ensure that, she has placed what you would call sheriffs throughout different parts of the world. We call them reeves. These men and women are imbued with her trust.

She allows them to police their territories as they see fit, so long as they follow the letter of her law. Our reeve is a vampire by the name of John Johnson."

I blinked, a tiny smile playing at my lips. "I'm sorry. I thought you just said—"

"I did. John Johnson is his name."

I tried not to laugh. I wasn't eight years old anymore. But who the heck named their child John Johnson? Poor guy.

"John and I spoke a few nights ago. I asked him to pay us a visit, hoping you could pass along any information regarding the vampire who attacked you."

Right. "Then what?"

"Then we leave the rest in John's hands. It's up to him how he progresses."

"What if he decides that hunting this vampire down isn't worth it?"

Vlad glanced over his shoulder and grimaced. "There's a chance of that. But Queen Genevieve wouldn't appreciate a murderous vampire running amok in New Orleans. Not while she's trying to secure a peace treaty with your human president. I have faith John won't ignore this."

"Do you really think it was the same vampire?" I

whispered, my mind circling back to the current issue. "The one who attacked me at Fallen?"

"I can't say. I didn't see anyone out there. But the words you heard, calling you delicious and claiming you belong to him, make me wonder."

"I belong to no one," I snapped. "Least of all some murderous bastard."

"No one would question otherwise," Vlad assured me. He stepped away from the fire and crouched in front of me. When he took my hands, I relished in the heat from his palms. "Nor would I allow this vampire, or any other, to harm you."

"Because you're my sire?" I whispered.

Vlad hesitated, then after a moment offered me a small smile. "Of course."

AFTER VLAD's and my particularly disturbing conversation, I returned to my bedroom. I texted a bit with Lucy, then retreated into a book I'd stolen from Vlad's office, needing something to distract myself from tonight's events. The thought of that vampire hunting me down gave me more than chills. My entire stomach had become a nest for imaginary bats, all dive bombing my nerves. And the more thought I gave *that* night, the more I started to remember. Like the feel of my attacker's cold breath on my skin before he struck, and the feel of him feeding at my neck, lapping at my blood like a thirsty puppy.

So lost to my thoughts, I hardly remembered anything I'd read. As much as I wanted to turn off my brain, it seemed impossible. These memories haunted me and probably would for the rest of my life. I only hoped with time I could start looking at them objectively. But tonight wasn't that night, sadly.

A soft knock broke through my thoughts. I blinked and lifted my gaze only to find Vlad standing in my doorway. Seemed he'd changed his clothes in our time apart, and now he wore a tightly fitted Henley—black, of course—and dark slacks. Why wasn't I surprised? Twenty bucks said his entire wardrobe consisted of black clothing. He had a reputation to uphold, after all.

"Reeve Johnson is here and would like to speak with you," Vlad said.

I swallowed, then nodded and put down the book. I had to remind myself that this John was here to help. Hopefully. I'd done nothing wrong. Well, except infiltrate Fallen and bust in on a blood orgy, but I'd been human then. Surely vampire sheriffs couldn't hold me responsible for things done while human?

Knowing *my* luck, though, that was exactly what would happen.

I rose from the bed and approached Vlad. He offered a hand, one I immediately took. The feel of his fingers joining mine settled the bat cave. Vlad wouldn't knowingly endanger me. As my sire, he was duty bound to protect me. But I knew his dedication went deeper than that.

"John is a kind but resolute man," Vlad said as we headed downstairs. "He will hear what you have to say and decide on an appropriate course of action afterward."

Instead of entering his office, Vlad led me into the kitchen. I hadn't seen this room yet, and my eyes widened at the size and design of the room. Based on the rest of the house, I'd expected something Victorian in appearance, and mildly gaudy. Instead, the kitchen possessed a more modern feel. Gleaming stainless-steel appliances, a light-colored marble floor, even pale-toned walls. Eggshell, probably. The only splash of color came from the tiled backsplash behind the sink and stove—deep red, because of course it was.

A man sat on a nearby stool, his elbows and forearms braced atop the island's marble counter. A mug sat in front of him, steam curling up from inside.

I frowned, wondering what the heck was in there. "I thought we couldn't tolerate human food?"

Vlad's gaze followed mine, and a small smirk tugged at the corner of his mouth. "That's not coffee. John prefers his blood steaming-hot."

My stomach soured. Did he microwave it? I could barely tolerate microwaved food as a human—I doubt that'd change as a vampire.

"Evening," Vlad said, nodding once to John.

The man lifted his mug and held my gaze as he took a long sip. I fought to control my gag reflex. Bagged blood and I weren't pals. And the thought of super-heating it made me want to throw up. I couldn't wait for this week to be over. Vlad would teach me to hunt, and I would begin building my harem. And that sounded a hell of a lot more appetizing than overly processed blood.

"It's better when you spice it," this John fellow said in a slightly southern accent. His deep voice raised the hairs on my arms. He sounded like someone who'd smoked a pack of cigarettes a day before dying. "A bit of cinnamon does the trick for me."

My eyebrow jumped. "Cinnamon? But how...?"

"He mixes it into his blood. So his system doesn't reject it."

Interesting. Made me wonder what sorts of flavors I could add to mine. Anything had to be better than the plastic taste.

"So, you're Vlad's new gig."

"Gig?"

"My newborn, or apprentice, if you prefer," Vlad replied.

Oh, I *definitely* preferred apprentice. Newborn made it seem too familial, and considering our recent kiss, I really didn't want to picture Vlad as anything remotely father figure-ish.

"Well, let me have a look at you, darlin'," John rasped.

Vlad released my hand and gestured me forward. I stepped into the middle of the room and watched as John rose from his stool and circled me. "Hmm. She's pretty enough. Young, though. How old did you say she was?"

"I didn't," Vlad responded, his tone dry. "And since *she* is standing right there, perhaps you should simply ask her yourself."

I bit back a smile. Five points to Vlad for treating

me like a person instead of a possession. "I'm twenty-four."

"Quite young."

"My age has nothing to do with this," I retorted.

"Wrong." John circled around and came to a stop in front of me. His gaze narrowed as he took all of me in. "Blonde hair. Brown eyes."

"Hazel," I corrected.

He lifted a brow.

"My driver's license has it listed as hazel."

"Brown will suffice," he replied. "Slim. Almost no curves whatsoever."

"More than enough for me, thank you. And absolutely none for you." I fought back the urge to grab my chest and show him exactly what curves I possessed. Two minutes in this John Johnson's presence and I already didn't like the guy. What was the point of this little assessment?

His mouth quirked. "Fiery. That mouth, though. Did you say somethin' to piss someone off, lil' darlin'?"

I was about to flip him off when Vlad stepped forward and rested a hand on my shoulder. "Are you intentionally trying to provoke us?"

Us. This time, I did grin.

"No. And I apologize if I am." John dipped his

head respectfully. "My intention here is to build a profile. Blonde, dark-eyed female, young, slim. Murdered outside Fallen, you said?"

I shuddered at the word. After days of convincing myself I was undead, *murdered* seemed so final.

"In the back alley," Vlad commented. "I found her discarded alongside the garbage bins."

"Then the vamp in question didn't mean for her to survive."

"I think not," Vlad said. "If I hadn't found her when I did, she would have truly died."

"Hmm." John stood back and assessed me once more. "Well, let's have it then."

I shot him a startled glance. Have what?

"Your story, darlin'." John waved a hand at me. "I'll take your statement, and we'll go from there."

It took me a few seconds to decide where to begin. I wasn't sure how much to reveal. Would I be punished for snooping around the club? I couldn't avoid it, though. This so-called reeve needed to know where I was when abducted.

So, I started at the very beginning. It didn't take long to regale him with my story. But I left Lucy out. I didn't need anyone else knowing about her involvement, just in case. Once I reached the back-alley part, John held up a hand.

"Tell me about him."

"Who?"

"The vamp. You said you got a good look at him. Describe him to me."

I closed my eyes and recalled his memory. I grimaced the instant he filled my mind. That was a face I never wanted to see again. "Four or five inches taller than me," I said, remembering how he towered over me. "He wasn't thin, but he wasn't big either. Medium-sized. He had dark hair, blue eyes, angular face. And he had a mole on his chin. I remember that very distinctly. It was quite large and located here." I tapped the side of my chin.

John's gaze leapt to Vlad's. The two didn't speak, but I sensed the tension rising between them.

"What's wrong? Do you know this vamp?"

John carded a hand through his hair and returned to the island where his mug of blood awaited. "His name is Petrik Kamen."

I shot Vlad a curious look, only to find his expression completely shuttered. As though he feared giving something away.

"You know him too?"

A single nod.

Their reactions weren't very encouraging. "Okay, and why do you both look like the shit just hit the fan?"

John sighed and took a sip, then met my gaze. "He's the queen's sire."

12

My ATTENTION BOUNCED between the two men. Clearly, this Petrik was a big deal. I couldn't believe he'd sired the queen. If he had the queen's ear, why was he at Fallen? And why attack me?

Vlad's and John's expressions told me everything I needed to know. Petrik was bad news. Like, *whoops, I'm pregnant* bad news.

John cupped his mug and lifted it to his lips, breathing in the aroma. His gaze lifted to mine over the rim. "Hate to tell you this, darlin', but you've attracted the attention of the oldest vampire I've ever met."

My lungs squeezed out my breath. Older than Vlad? Crap on a cracker, that *was* bad news.

I turned to Vlad and cringed at his sympathetic expression. "You too?"

He sighed, then nodded. "Petrik dates back to William the Conqueror. He was one of William's many soldiers."

My jaw gaped. Growing up, I'd hated history class, but William the Conqueror was a well-known name across the entire world. If I remembered correctly, he'd conquered England sometime in the eleventh century, making Petrik nearly a thousand years old.

"Holy shit," I wheezed.

I reached for the nearest stool, my hand trembling as I pulled it close. I needed to sit. My damn legs had turned to jelly.

"That is, of course, if Petrik is indeed the one you saw," Vlad said. "We mustn't jump to conclusions until we know for sure. There are many vampires out there with moles on their faces."

My eyes fluttered shut, and I thought back to *that* moment, the one where my murderer had clutched my throat and leered over me. I remembered staring into his face, drinking in every last detail.

"He, uh... had a small scar," I said, my voice frail. "Right above his upper lip. I remember because the streetlights emphasized it." I traced the location, above my lip leading up to my nose. "Jagged. Like he'd taken a piece of glass to his face."

John's shoulders sagged, and he cursed under his breath. "Yeah, that's Petrik. No doubt about it."

Panic bubbled beneath the surface like molten lava just ready to explode. "Okay, okay. This is bad. Really bad."

Panic gripped my insides and twisted. I leaned against the island and dropped my head into my palms, cursing myself out over and over. I never should have left Perish. I never should have gone to Fallen. My ex-boyfriend had warned me this would happen. He'd straight up told me I'd die if I followed through with my plan. And I'd responded by dumping him. Thankfully, I didn't regret that part. He'd pissed me off by trying to forbid me from coming to New Orleans. No thank you. But he'd been right—for fuck's sake. Like that wasn't ironic enough, now I had a thousand-year-old vampire possibly hunting me.

"Vlad," I croaked into my palms. "Tell him about tonight." Because I sure as hell couldn't.

"Anna was exploring my grounds when she was graced by another vampire's presence. I believe it was Petrik. He seems to have staked a claim on her. Called her his and told her she was delicious."

"Delicious," John repeated.

I groaned and dropped my head onto the counter. This was ridiculous. What happened to my happy-go-lucky life? Blood, death, vampires, I didn't want any of it. What was the saying? It was all fun and games until someone lost an eye? Well, I hadn't lost an eye, but I think my lost life definitely fit the bill.

"Sounds like he wants another taste of her blood," John said.

"Thank you, Captain Obvious," I muttered. I lifted my head with a glare. "I'd like to state for the record that I do not consent to this Petrik so much as touching me. I'd also like it stated that if he comes near me again, I'm gonna do whatever the hell I can to murder *his* stupid ass."

John's lips twitched. "She's a cute one."

I growled under my breath, my lip curling up to reveal my fangs.

"Oh, just adorable," John said, laughing. "Darlin', let me drop a few what you kids call 'truth bombs.' You don't stand a friggin' chance against Petrik. Hell, I don't stand a chance against him. And I'd bet every last dollar of my wealthy estate against dear ole Drac here too. Petrik has five hundred years on him, and seven on me. You wouldn't be able to harm a hair on his head, lil' one."

I ground my back teeth together. "I'm not useless. Stake, beheading, fire, sunlight. There's more than one way to skin an undead cat, and believe me, I'm looking to do some skinning."

John chuckled. "I see why you changed her."

"No, you don't" was all Vlad said.

I blinked at Vlad but chose not to inquire further, not with present company.

John cast me another curious glance. "You look like one solid gust of wind would knock you down, darlin'. Petrik was a soldier. He's been fighting in wars since before you were a twinkle in your great-times-twenty-grandma's eye."

"I've taken self-defense classes," I muttered.

John burst out laughing. "Against vampires?"

"Well, no. But how hard can it be to drive a wooden stake into a vampire's heart, for crying out loud?"

"All right. Stand up, kitten."

"Do *not* call me kitten."

"Darlin', whatever. Up, up, let's go."

I slapped my hands on the counter and rose. This guy wanted a fight? Good, because I was hankering to do a little damage right now too. He made me feel weak and useless. Like I was some fragile little woman who needed the strong manly men to protect me.

"Anna, might I suggest refraining from this little demonstration?" Vlad implored.

I ignored him and held up my hands like I'd been taught in self-defense.

John snickered, then without warning blew past me and snagged me by the throat, his other arm like a vice across my shoulders. "See, darlin'? If you can't handle me, a mere three-hundred-year-old, how are you gonna handle someone of Petrik's pedigree?"

I caught Vlad's gaze, then winked. John might have bested me, but his position was sloppy. He thought he had me beat. His frame was loose and his grip relaxed. So, instead of wrenching away from him, I pushed backward until our bodies were flush, further loosening his arm at my shoulders. Then I spun around, wincing when his nails caught the flesh at my throat.

Now face-to-face, I had a second to catch John's surprised expression before I snapped my knee up and landed a solid blow to his boys below the belt.

John instantly howled and dropped. Once he finished rolling back and forth, mewling about his "damn balls," I kneeled next to him and pushed a lock of hair off his sweaty forehead.

"I may not be some ancient vampire, but I'm not useless either. Women have been dealing with this sort of abuse since the beginning of time. We have our tricks. Believe me when I tell you that Petrik will rue the day he attacked me."

"For the love of all that's tender, woman..." John rolled to the side, then rose to his knees, his hands still cupping his bits. "Back off and give me a moment to breathe."

"You're a vampire. You don't need to breathe," I quipped.

He chuckled, then slowly pushed to his feet, still rubbing his afflicted area. "I wish I could say I like you, but my balls might disagree. And I'm rather attached to them. Tell you what, darlin', I'll put in a grievance report to the queen, tellin' her all about her precious sire and what he's been up to. Whether she hears me out or agrees to let me handle this situation my way is hard to tell." He coughed into his hand, then repositioned himself below the equator. "In the meantime, Drac, might I suggest calling in a few friends. The more vamps surrounding your precious cargo here, the less inclined Petrik might be to take another bite."

"Noted," Vlad agreed.

"And that's it?" I frowned at John. "You submit a grievance? This guy almost murdered me. Or did, depending on your point of view. Who's to say how many other women he's killed?"

"I'll be lookin' into that. Missin' women aren't exactly a rare thing down here. Sadly, the human authorities have a lot of trouble in that regard. All the surroundin' gators, if you catch my drift."

I shuddered, pretty sure he was implying that these abducted women were killed then fed to the local wildlife. I knew I hated alligators for a reason.

"I'll see if I can rummage up a pattern and hopefully track our boy down."

"I thought all vampires were registered?"

"Sure, but that doesn't mean much for an ancient like Petrik. And it ain't like we put trackin' devices in everyone. If he doesn't wanna be found, there ain't much we can do about it."

Sarcastic laughter rushed past my lips. "Are you kidding me?"

"Now isn't the time for this discussion," Vlad said, finally speaking up. "The sun approaches. I need to get Anna into her coffin before retiring myself. John, if you feel you can't make it home in time, I keep a few spare coffins in the small mausoleum out back. It secures from the inside."

"Mighty grateful. I'll definitely take you up on that offer. This conversation took longer than I'd anticipated." He grimaced and tugged at the inseam of his pants again.

"Very well. Tomorrow, I'll summon those loyal to me, but I expect to hear from you regarding the grievance immediately."

"You got it, Drac."

Vlad rolled his eyes, then held his hand out to me. I instinctively took it, only afterward noticing how John's attention zeroed in on our embrace. Still, I didn't pull away, even as Vlad led me out of the kitchen and up to the attic. Vlad's touch soothed me, and right now, I needed as much comfort as possible.

Once next to our coffins, he released my hand and sighed. "There's something I wish to discuss before we retire for the day. You asked me about my second gift."

I nodded, sparing the inside of my coffin a dreaded glance.

"In light of all this new information, Petrik's identity and whatnot, I feel I should tell you what it is."

Curiosity lit within me, and I gave Vlad my full attention.

"Do you remember how I told you I heard your name in my head?"

"Of course." That wasn't something a girl forgot.

"I have the gift of foresight," he finally said. "Visions of the future, if you will."

"What?"

He inclined his head. "That night at Fallen, I *knew* I was looking for you, because I'd seen you in my dreams many years ago. In my dream, someone whispered your name to me. I knew then that we were fated to meet that night. But my gift is flawed, as it's still developing. I hardly ever receive all the pieces of the puzzle. I never saw Petrik or what would happen. Nor have I seen what's yet to come."

"Okay." I couldn't wrap my head around this. We were *fated* to meet that night? Did that mean I was also fated to become a vampire?

Shit, I didn't believe in fate! I'd always believed a girl made her own path, her own choices.

"I'm telling you this, because I need you to understand me when I tell you I will *not* let Petrik lay another finger on you." Vlad cupped my cheek, then leaned in and brushed a chaste kiss against my mouth. "We are fated to mean so much more to each other than this. I know you're conflicted about what you may or may not be feeling for me, but remember that I've had more time to prepare. I first saw you in my dreams fifty years ago."

My breath rushed past my lips, and I stared at him, dumbfounded.

"I've been waiting for you for half a century. And now that I've found you, I refuse to let anything ruin what we have the chance of becoming."

With a small smile, Vlad took my hand and assisted me into my coffin.

I slipped in without complaint, my mind whirling with everything he'd just told me.

Fifty years, fated to meet... I just... couldn't comprehend this at all.

My thoughts were deafening as he slid the coffin into place. But not so deafening that I didn't catch his soft "sleep well" before he climbed into his own coffin.

Thankfully, the sun rose, silencing my thoughts for the rest of the day.

I HAD SO many questions when I woke the next night. Almost like my stupid brain had refused to switch off even though my body sure as hell had. My thoughts kept going 'round and 'round, to the point where it felt as though I hadn't rested at all. My first night with Vlad, I'd asked him how he'd known where to find me. Yes, he'd been elusive, but he'd eventually mentioned hearing my name in his head. At the time, I'd assumed he meant he could read minds. He'd corrected me, but he hadn't been too forthcoming with the details afterward.

But foresight as his second gift? What did that even mean? I couldn't wrap my head around any of it, especially the whole waiting for my arrival for the last fifty years.

I absolutely did not believe in God, religion, or predestination. The thought that two people were fated to cross paths, that the world aligned specifically to bring them together, was too mind-boggling for me. Hell, it downright terrified me. I'd always believed I marched to the beat of my own drum, cut my own path through life, and that my choices—and consequences—were my own to bear. Now, here came Vlad with evidence to the contrary. How could he have possibly seen me in his dreams twenty-five-ish years before I was even born? And who was on the *other* end controlling our destinies? Who had woven the threads of our lives together?

Mythology had always intrigued me, so I knew all about the Greek Fates, the Norse Nornir, even the Egyptian god, Shai, but I'd never considered that any of those entities may have actually existed at some point. Or perhaps still did. Cripes, it was like someone had set a bomb off in my life, destroying everything I ever thought I knew, then leaving me to pick up the shattered pieces.

Okay. Time for a deep—albeit unnecessary—breath.

Here were the facts.

Número Uno: I was a vampire. Check.

Número Dos: *Señor* Vlad was my sire.

Número Tres: We were connected.

Those were three facts I could live with. So long as no one went around talking about fate and destiny, I could handle that.

Ugh, this was far too much to consider at seven-thirty in the evening. I hadn't even had a sip of blood yet and was already contemplating philosophy, which, side note, was a perfect example of hell. My brain wasn't awake enough to handle this kind of heavy thinking. And I certainly couldn't hide in my coffin all night, as much as I wanted to.

I stretched the kinks out of my body, then pushed my coffin lid back and climbed out with less fanfare than the last few nights. Even though I was *dead* during the day, I was exhausted.

I still yearned for a bed too. Something I could stretch out on and snuggle up to some pillows. But with everything hanging over us, it was doubtful that would happen anytime soon. We had a baby vampire to train—me, I was the baby vamp—and a villainous monster with tight connections to the queen to track down.

Boy, all that sounded about as fun as a trip to the gynecologist.

Damn, I really wished I could go back in time and slap myself upside the head before entering Fallen. Give myself a solid kick in the ass and point me home, tell myself to smarten up. All this in search of fame and fortune, and where had it landed me? Dead and completely unremarkable. I couldn't even host my vlog anymore, thanks to the whole no reflection thing.

Sighing, I smoothed a hand down my pajamas, then beat a quick path to my bathroom one floor down. Though I was hankering for a nice sip of AB+, I also felt the desperate need for a shower. Was I avoiding Vlad? You betcha. I so wasn't ready to face —or discuss—the truth bombs he'd set off in my life early this morning. Nor was I ready to contemplate what it all meant.

Could this whole "fated to meet" thing explain why I was so attracted to him? Was there some sort of deity out there getting her jollies by pairing me with Vlad? If so, I bet she was getting one hell of a laugh out of all this. Shit, I *hoped* she was. Someone ought to be laughing somewhere.

I reached for the shower taps, about to turn them, when I heard movement downstairs. Unfamiliar voices greeting Vlad like old friends. All right, so I might have perked an ear and eavesdropped a little.

But it didn't take long for me to realize the voices belonged to his allies. The ones he'd mentioned calling on tonight. And since he woke a good hour or so before me, it sounded as though he'd already summoned them. They must have lived nearby, to be here so soon. Probably in New Orleans.

I wouldn't learn anything more though until I showered and dressed. So, instead of asking myself unanswerable questions, I turned on the taps, then ducked under the spray and quickly scrubbed. If showering was an Olympic sport, I would have won gold. Once finished, I climbed out, only to scream at the sight of an unfamiliar woman sitting on my toilet.

"Sweet baby Zeus!" I shrieked, clutching my towel to my chest. "Who the fuck are you?"

The dark-haired beauty slowly raised a brow. "You really are a baby, aren't you?"

Holy shit—her voice was like liquid butter. "Excuse you, I'm twenty-four."

Her lips parted, and I caught sight of her shiny fangs before musical laughter rose from her throat. "I mean a baby vampire, you naïve little dolt."

Holy guacamole, I could listen to her talk all day. Her voice was pleasantly pitched—a bit lower than most women—but it flowed with the cadence of a professional singer.

But then I blinked. Had she just called me a dolt? Wasn't that something kids called each other in grade school? And did that mean we were about to get in some sort of hair-pulling fight? I hoped not. I liked my hair right where it was, attached to my skull.

"You let the water dull your senses," she said before slowly standing and rising to her full height, a good few inches taller than me. Whoa, I wasn't used to looking up at other women.

Damn, this woman was absolutely breathtaking. Her golden-brown skin shone like the sun on Mediterranean sand, and her dark eyes sparkled with humor. She looked like an Egyptian goddess, even while dressed in a modern loose cable-knit sweater, black tights, and thigh-high boots.

"Who are you?" I demanded.

A small smirk tugged on her pale rose-petal lips, so perfectly painted that I had to wonder how she'd done it without a mirror. "My name is Camilla."

I waited for her to offer a little more information —like maybe a last name and why she was here— then sighed when she gave me nothing else.

"And why are you in my bathroom, Camilla?" I asked politely.

"To meet you, of course. To introduce myself to the woman who finally stole Vlad's attention."

Oh shit. I didn't like the sound of that. Was Camilla some past lover of his? Did she intend to stake her claim on him or something? Because I *so* wasn't interested in getting into a pissing match with a former lover.

"Calm down," she said, her lilting voice rising in a chuckle. "I'm not here to fight."

Phew. That was a relief. "Then do you mind if I get dressed?"

She lifted a delicately stenciled brow, her dark gaze assessing me. "If you wish, though I'd prefer you didn't if you're offering me a choice."

I bobbed my head, then froze. What?

Her suggestive smile and wink raised even more questions. "Um, okay. I'm going to get dressed then. My room is—"

"I know which room is yours, little vamp."

"Right. Then I'm just gonna...." I clutched my towel tightly and practically bolted out of the bathroom into mine.

I grabbed the first things I could find, then paused. Vlad had invited his allies here to help protect me. Logic dictated Camilla was one of those allies. And based on her appearance, I couldn't just throw on sweats and a T-shirt. If I'd learned *anything* from all the vampire fiction out there, it was that they took their appearances seriously. Vlad himself never dressed down, though that might have more to do with his personality. But even Camilla looked like a living goddess. Perhaps it was time to give my wardrobe the same consideration. Unfortunately, I didn't have much to play with. Lucy had bought enough to last me the rest of the week, but nothing fancy. She knew my style. I was a jeans-for-life type girl.

Thankfully, she did understand my penchant for shoes. So, I slipped on a pair of ripped skinny jeans paired with knock-off Gucci heels—because who could afford the real thing?—and a black sleeveless shirt, topped with a leather jacket. Fuck, I loved my bestie. She always seemed to know exactly what I needed.

Afterward, I towel-dried my hair—le gasp, I know—and considered a style. My usual one was a low messy bun. But I had a feeling these vamps wouldn't appreciate the look. Not to mention, walking around with my neck exposed felt like a giant *come bite me* sign. Especially with Petrik out there. Instead, I grabbed some mousse, finger-tousled my locks, then scrunched them up as best I could.

Whether that gave me the beach waves I was going for, I had no idea. And I really didn't feel comfortable asking Camilla for her opinion. So, regardless of my final appearance, I was going to own it. Walk out there in my knockoffs and strut my stuff, like I belonged here with the rest of them.

But before I could reach for my door, it opened, and in Camilla strode.

Her eyes widened a fraction before a tiny smile played across her lips. If I had to guess, I'd impressed her, at least. Hard to say, considering I didn't know her.

"It's Anna, right?" she asked.

I nodded.

She circled me like a shark, the sound of her leather boots soft against the floor.

"Does Vlad know you're up here?" I asked.

Her laughter sent a shiver up my spine. "Sweetie, he's a vampire. Of course he knows I'm up here."

Right. Just like how I'd heard them arrive, he would have heard her come upstairs. I attempted a different tactic. "Is there something you want from me?"

"Not yet," she mused. "I just wanted to meet you. It isn't every day someone catches the eye of the infamous Dracula. In fact, you're the first he's ever paid a lick of attention to, other than his darling Mina."

My heart sank like a stone. "Mina?"

"Mm. His precious wife."

And just like that, everything within me shattered into a million pieces. "His wife," I rasped. He'd never mentioned a wife. But I'd never asked. And why did this bother me so much? Yes, we'd kissed. Once. It didn't mean anything, right? And maybe he'd dreamed about me fifty years ago, but that didn't *mean* anything either.

Yet, I burned. With anger, with hurt, with heartbreak.

"Oh, sweetie." Camilla gave a twinkling laugh. "Mina was his *human* wife, before he was turned. She died years before he did."

I frowned. "Then why mention her?"

"To see how you reacted." She shrugged, then flounced over to my bed and flopped against the pillows. "Oh, I always loved Vlad's guest beds. That man definitely knows comfort."

"I... don't understand. What game are you playing?"

"Game?" A wicked smile spread her lips, and she

patted the bed next to her. "Sweetie, if you want to play a game, I'm all for it."

"What? No. Why mention his dead wife? Why test my reaction? What do you want from me?"

Her face sobered, the vampire within peeking out. "Vlad is one of my dearest friends. I've known him for more than three centuries. When he called me this evening, I was stunned to learn that he'd sired a new vampire. A young woman. One who has apparently caught the eye of dear Petrik."

I winced. *Dear* Petrik? There was nothing dear about that monster. My hand instinctively rose to my neck.

"I have agreed to help protect you," Camilla continued, once again studying my reaction. "But I want to know what you two mean to each other before I involve myself. Petrik is the queen's sire, as I'm sure you know."

I gave a jerky nod.

"Then you should know any harm done to him will come back on us twice-fold. The queen is not so forgiving when it comes to the people she loves. And she loves Petrik dearly."

"Well, maybe she should have kept an eye on her *beloved* then, considering the dude is walking around murdering innocent women."

Camilla's brow shot upward. "You're hardly innocent in all this."

Oh no, she did *not* just go there. Maybe there would be a catfight after all. Twenty bucks said all that beautiful hair of hers were extensions. I could easily rip those out. "Excuse me?"

"My sweet summer child, ignorance is not an attractive trait. Vlad has already told us your intentions at Fallen. To expose the blood orgies."

"Yeah, so? How does that make it okay for someone to murder me?"

"You're far from dead."

"Not this again. Look, Petrik intended to kill me. It was just luck that Vlad came across me."

"Luck. Yes, I suppose you would consider it that."

I blinked. "What?"

Instead of answering, Camilla rose from my bed and crossed my room. When she reached the door, she paused and crooked her head toward the hallway. "Well?"

This time, I raised my brow. "Well what?"

"Your audience awaits. Come tell us your woeful story about the nosy reporter who dug too deep and now has to live with the consequences."

My gaze narrowed. "You know, I don't think I like you."

Her mouth grew into a fangy smile. "A shame."

Shaking my head, I trailed after Camilla, my gaze unabashedly dropping to her swaying hips as she prowled through Vlad's hallways. Damn, the woman could move. She reminded me of a lioness stalking her prey, while I looked like... well, remember? The drunk gazelle? I loved wearing heels. Loved the shape they lent my legs, *loved* the sound of them clicking against the floor, but I was horrid at walking in them. Lucy always teased me about it, how I looked like Bambi on stilts. With luck, tonight, I'd manage something halfway between a sashay and faceplanting.

Once we reached the stairs, snippets of conversation began trickling in. I immediately recognized the deep timbre of Vlad's voice and had to stave off a shiver.

"My, you *do* have it bad," Camilla teased, glancing back at me.

"What?"

She tapped her nose and threw me a salacious wink. "Our sense of smell is our strongest ally. It doesn't develop immediately, but soon, you'll be able to pick up on anything. Including"—she waggled her brows at me—"people's emotions and desires."

My cheeks flamed. Sweet mother of all things bloody, was she trying to suggest that she could smell how I felt for Vlad? That wasn't possible, right? Surely desire didn't have a scent?

But the sight of her waggling brows told me otherwise.

"Oh my God," I lamented.

Camilla immediately shrank back, and her lip curled up—a monstrous caricature of her previous playful face. "Don't utter that name in my presence."

"What name?"

Her jaw tightened. "*That* name. I won't repeat it. You know what you said."

"Oh, you mean G—uh, the big G upstairs?"

"Have you no manners?" she snapped. "What is Vlad teaching you?" She sighed and came to a stop on the stairs, her hands perched on her narrow hips. "Listen closely, little vampire. *That* name is not spoken among us. It's an offense to our existence."

I frowned. "Okay."

"Maybe you new millennial vampires"—she rolled her eyes—"don't see a problem uttering that name, but those of us who have been around for more than a few nights take great offense to it. If you don't want some older vampire taking yet another chunk out of you, I suggest you refrain from speaking it again."

This time, I rolled my eyes. "I get it, thank you. Let's move on."

She scoffed. "Newborns, I tell you. Absolutely no couth or gratefulness for the life they're given. You're not the first new vampire I've met this week, and I must say, so far, I'm not impressed."

"Yeah, yeah, you're the big bad. You used to walk to school uphill both ways in the snow. I get it."

"I beg your pardon?"

The stark confusion in her expression made me laugh. "It's a saying. Something our grandparents used to say to us when we were children and whining about something they never had the pleasure of experiencing. They'd tell us we didn't have it hard, that we didn't know what hard even meant, because when they were our age, blah, blah, blah."

Camilla huffed under her breath. "Ungrateful wretch."

"Undead fossil," I retorted.

"Undead what?" Anger morphed her features into something almost ugly.

"Fossil. Dinosaur? Ugh, it isn't funny if you make me explain it."

Camilla gaped at me. "I can't believe I'm having this conversation. You're like a five-year-old."

"I'm rubber, you're glue," I needled. I wish I could say I regretted the comment, but I didn't. She was just too fun to piss off. And clearly my comments were lost on her.

"Just... get in his office," she muttered. Camilla smoothed down her hair, as though I'd frazzled her to the point of giving her split ends—my new goal in life —then continued down the rest of the stairs.

I chuckled and followed her into Vlad's office, where from the sounds of it, other vampires awaited.

Oh boy.

My phone buzzed the second I stepped into Vlad's office. It had to be Lucy. Even though both my parents were likely still awake, it was beyond what either of them considered an acceptable hour for phone calls. They were the sort who believed any interruptions an hour past dinner was rude. But as much as I wanted to take Lucy's call—and tell her all about my new "friend" Camilla—I knew now wasn't the right moment. Not while four strange vampires were staring me down like I was nothing more than an insect meant to be squashed.

"Anna." Vlad strode toward me and extended his hand.

I instinctively took it, clinging to the one ally I

had in this room. Camilla had sought me out upstairs, eager to meet Vlad's new apprentice, but I had a feeling she wasn't quite as interested in being besties now. Nor did any of the others look at all welcoming. Good first impressions and all that.

"I see you've already met Camilla," Vlad said, gesturing to the goddess on his left.

She stood closest to the door, her hand on the knob as though she meant to bail on us. The smile she wore reminded me of all the teachers in my life who had sent me to the principal's office. That eager, knowing grin that told me I was about to get my ass chewed out by Mr. Penuckle.

"This here is Eli," Vlad continued, drawing my attention to the man standing closest to Camilla. He reminded me of a young Idris Elba, with his dark, flawless skin, broad shoulders, and tapered waist.

Eli's eyes narrowed on me, and if I wasn't mistaken, there was a flare of annoyance in them, as though he'd already decided to blame me for this entire mess. *Welcome to the club, kid.*

"You didn't tell us how young she is," Eli muttered, his lip curling up over his fangs.

Oh yeah, we were going to be great friends—*not*.

Vlad tensed but ignored Eli's comment, then

politely gestured to the vampire standing at his right. "Breccan O'Connor."

I bit back a smile at his clearly Irish name. Breccan seemed more at ease in my presence, even going so far as to crack a grin at me. The tension eased from my shoulders, and I grinned back. There was something so likable about him. Maybe it was his warm brown eyes or his mussed sandy blond hair that gave me the impression of a careless teenager. Whatever it was, his friendliness put me at ease. Of course, sharks could grin too, so I knew not to take his kindness as reassurance that he wouldn't kill me.

"The infamous Anna," he commented in a brogue thicker than his eyebrows.

"And this is Rebecca." Vlad gestured to the fourth vampire.

Rebecca stood alone across Vlad's office, perusing his bookshelves, much like I had a few nights ago. Except, she seemed rather impressed by his collection. With her back to me, I couldn't make out more than the long curtain of shiny black hair that fell to her waist. When she finally turned, I gaped at the sight of her beautifully sculpted face. If I thought Camilla gorgeous, she was nothing compared to Aphrodite here. Geez, didn't Vlad know any ugly vampires? Or was that a statistical impossibility? Were all vampires drop-dead gorgeous? Emphasis on dead.

"Evening," she said, her soft voice somehow carrying across the entire room.

I offered a smile, hoping it was enough. I really didn't know what more to say. I'd never been the sort to envy another woman's appearance. Self-assurance wasn't something I lacked. I was attractive, sure. But compared to Camilla, Rebecca, and even Lucy, I looked like someone's awkward little sister. And for the first time ever, I felt it, a tiny prick of jealousy.

"Anna, I've already filled them in on our little problem—"

"Her," Eli interrupted. "*Her* problem, Vlad. None of this has anything to do with you."

Vlad growled, a terrifying deep sound that raised the hairs on the back of my neck. He took a step toward Eli, then stopped and drew a deep breath. "I am her sire."

"Yes, well, we all know that doesn't always work out. You could walk away from her right now. There's no need to endanger yourself like this. Petrik will eviscerate the lot of us if we go against him. And if by some miracle we survive and Petrik doesn't, the queen will pike us so that everyone else can see what happens to bad little vampires who betray her."

"We aren't betraying Genevieve," Camilla chimed in, surprising me. I honestly hadn't expected her to side with me. "We're handling her rogue sire who has been stirring the pot for some time now. Are we to be blamed for solving a problem the queen should have handled long ago?"

"Of course you would see things that way," Eli snapped. "Your loyalty only runs as deep as your cunt."

I gasped, but before I could even think of a response, Camilla shot across the room, snatched Eli by this throat, then heaved him through the air. He sailed clear across Vlad's office and slammed into one of the bookcases before crumpling to the ground.

Vlad stood next to me, anger radiating down his body. He stared at Eli with a terrifyingly murderous expression, hands fisted at his sides and fangs peeking out from beneath his upper lip. Seemed Camilla wasn't the only one angered by Eli's rude outburst.

"If you don't wish to involve yourself, then see yourself out," Vlad uttered, his voice as dark as the surrounding night. "But if you choose to stay, you will conduct yourself appropriately. If I hear one more disparaging remark from you, I'll feed you your guts before piking you myself."

Eli picked himself up from the floor and dusted off his jacket before nodding curtly at Camilla. "I apologize."

She sneered and turned away—not that I blamed her. Why did men always go after a woman's sexuality in order to shame them? As though it was the only way they knew how to control a woman? In my opinion, he was lucky Camilla had merely tossed him around a little. I might have gone for something a little more permanent, like turning him into a eunuch.

My phone buzzed again, disrupting the uncomfortable silence rooted in the room. I grimaced, then reached into my pocket to silence it once more. Lucy would just have to wait until this meeting concluded.

Vlad turned to face the other three vampires, purposely giving Eli his back. Perhaps Vlad was comfortable with this display of dominance, but I sure as hell wasn't. So I positioned myself to keep an eye on the temperamental vamp.

"All I ask is that you remain in my mansion for the next few weeks until I can resolve this matter with Petrik. I will provide you all a harem to feed from. Reeve John is petitioning the queen as we speak. He's also submitting a formal grievance on

Anna's behalf, explaining the details surrounding her attempted murder. I'm not asking anyone to hunt Petrik down. That matter will remain between me and the queen. I'm merely asking you to help me keep Anna safe until the queen has contained her sire."

"Of course," Rebecca said, her icy-blue gaze cutting to me. "We all understand the protective nature between a sire and apprentice. I'll remain to assist, regardless of how long it takes."

"As will I," Camilla chirped, flashing me a wink.

"I'm here for ya, mate. I'm sure we'll have a whale of a time with Anna here. I wouldn't abandon ya in your time of need."

Vlad nodded at the three of them, then turned to Eli. "And you?"

Eli cut me a scathing glare, as though I'd personally offended him, when I had yet to speak. I think it had to be a new record for me. Must have hated my face or something.

"Fine," he muttered. "But under protest."

"Coward," Camilla scoffed.

Clearly, there was no love lost between these two, and I made a mental note to steer clear of them during their time here. I really didn't feel like cleaning up body parts for the next few nights.

I cleared my throat, then winced when all five vampires turned to face me. Phew, this was almost as bad as speaking publicly in front of my classmates.

"I, uh, also want to thank you." My gaze bounced between them all. "You guys don't know me, so this means a great deal to me—"

"We're not doing this for you," Eli grumbled.

I blinked at him. "Got it—you're the dickhead of the group."

"Watch it," he snarled.

"I just call it as I see it." I shrugged. "If you don't want to be known as a dickhead, don't be a dickhead."

Camilla chuckled under her breath. "Told you I'd like her."

Vlad's hand came to rest on the small of my back, a movement the other four seemed to instantly take notice of. Heat rushed through my body, responding to his touch. I arched into him, and my eyes fluttered shut when a strangely erotic scent teased my nose. I'd never smelled anything like it before. Heady, hot, and intoxicating. And I wanted more.

My words ran dry, and instead, I inhaled, savoring the potent aroma.

"What is that...?" I stumbled over my question.

Vlad cleared his throat. "Let's return to business, shall we?"

I shook my head, hoping to clear away my muddled thoughts. There was something entirely too distracting about this scent. It reminded me of chocolate-covered strawberries, and champagne.

"Anna?" I distantly heard Vlad's voice calling to me. His hands cupped my cheeks, and he caught my gaze. "Anna."

It took me a few moments to snap out of the trance. When I did, I came to only to find the room silent again except for the incessant ringing in my back pocket.

"Perhaps you should answer that," Vlad suggested.

Answer what? Thankfully, the scent was gone now, and I still had no idea where it'd come from. I gazed up at Vlad, wondering if it might have come from him. He'd been the only one standing near me, and it'd happened when he'd touched me.

"Anna." Vlad's voice came out sharper this time.

I gave my head another small shake. "Sorry. Distracted, I think? What happened?"

"We'll discuss it later." He gestured to my backside. "I think it might be best to answer that. It won't stop ringing."

Right. My phone. That was the chirping I kept hearing.

"It's just Lucy," I said. "She can wait 'til we're done."

"You're sure?"

I nodded. "We were discussing the plan?"

"Were we?" Vlad asked, his mouth quirking.

"Well, that was my intention before I was interrupted." I shot Eli a scowl. "I meant to ask if you had a plan other than sitting here waiting for Petrik to show up."

Vlad nodded, then addressed the entire room. "Reeve John has agreed to investigate Anna's case. However, I feel we'd be remiss if we didn't take some matters into our own hands."

"Like?" Camilla asked.

"Due to the extreme nature of these circumstances, I believe we should accelerate Anna's training. I intend to teach her how to feed starting tonight."

"What?" I gasped. "What about the rules? The weeklong isolation and all that?"

"Your circumstances differ from most newborn vampires." Vlad gave me a reassuring smile but was careful not to touch me again. "If something *does* happen, and we're separated or worse, I need to know you can take care of yourself. Learning to feed is the most important lesson I can impart upon you. Hopefully, you will never need to use it."

I bit my bottom lip, careful not to puncture it with my fangs.

"Camilla, I called on you because I would like for you to teach Anna to fight. She may need to know how to defend herself in the coming days."

Camilla's grin broadened. "Gladly."

Wait, fight? This was spiraling out of control so fast.

"Rebecca, Eli, Breccan, you three will be responsible for keeping an eye on the grounds. Petrik knows Anna is here. We could move her, but he's proven able to track her. I think instead we should focus on security."

Rebecca and Breccan bowed their heads, but Eli stood by like a sullen child.

My wide gaze darted between the five of them. "This is your plan?"

"Do you have a better one?" Vlad asked.

"Weapons? Police? I don't know, werewolves even?"

Vlad laughed under his breath. "I assure you, such extremes won't be necessary. More than likely, John will convince the queen to undertake Petrik's punishment. And he'll be out of our hair without another glimpse of him."

Hmm. Why didn't I believe that?

Before I could probe any deeper into Vlad's plan, my damn phone went off *again*. This time, I sighed and dug it out of my back pocket. The second I lit up the screen, a flutter of *something* passed through my chest.

I had eight missed calls—three from Lucy, five from my parents, all spanning from a few hours before I woke until now. Then there were a dozen text messages from Lucy and my brother—which was beyond disconcerting, considering my brother and I never texted—and tons of notifications on social media, along with quite a few Google alerts.

Something was wrong.

But before I could read any of the texts or listen to the many voicemails, my phone lit up again. *Mom* flashed across my screen with a silent urgency even I could feel. I shot Vlad a startled glance and noted the concern in his eyes.

With a deep breath, I answered the call, only to be met with the sound of my mother's panicked voice.

"ANNA?" My mother's sharp voice rang across the line. "Anna, answer me!"

"Mom?"

Her relieved sigh carried like the wind through my phone. "Thank God. Oh my God. Thank God."

I didn't wince, but the five other vampires in the room did, as though my mother's prayers were like hot pokers under their skin. I don't know why the word *God* didn't bother me. Maybe because I didn't believe in him? My parents did, though. Absolutely. They still went to Church twice a week and prayed with all their friends. My father called himself a God-fearing man. They'd always hated how I rejected all religion and turned my back on their precious Lord. More than once, they'd told me I was going to hell—huh. Guess they were right. Welp, no point belaboring on that.

"Are you alright?" my mother demanded, her tone rising with every word.

I cradled the phone against my ear and stalked across Vlad's office in search of a little privacy. "I'm fine, Mom. What's wrong? Are *you* okay?"

"No, I am *not* okay. Anna Marie Perish, tell me you aren't dead!"

I froze, my breath forming a lump in my throat. "Of course I'm not dead. I'm talking to you, aren't I? What a silly question."

"Don't play dumb with me, young lady!"

"Mom, come on. I'm not a teenager—"

"Well, you damn well—sorry—darn well act like one."

Whoa, my mom never cursed. "Um. Okay? What is it I'm supposed to have done this time?"

She released another aggravated breath. Before she could respond, another incoming call chirped in my ear. I quickly glanced at the screen and noted Lucy's name once more. Frowning, I returned the phone to my ear, not that I necessarily needed it.

"I saw... pictures," my mother hissed. "Of you in that godforsaken club."

Oh. Shit. My hand shot to my mouth. "I can explain."

"Really?" Hysterical laughter rang through the phone. "You can explain why you and Lucy went to a monster bar? How you ended up *dead*?"

Did Lucy rat me out? Was that why she was calling? What the hell was going on? "Mom, I'm not dead. Listen to me."

"You're one of them!" she shrieked, her hysterics ramping up another notch. "Aren't you? I saw the pictures, Anna! Of you being turned!"

I winced. My chest grew cold, as though it'd frozen into a block of ice. "What pictures?"

"What pictures? You expect me to believe you haven't seen them? They're all over the internet! Your brother and I were in *church* when this was brought to our attention. The entire town is talking about it. Anna! What have you done?"

Fuck. Fuck. Fuck!

"I haven't seen any photos, Mom." I cradled my head and closed my eyes. This was bad. Like *nuclear war* bad. So much for maintaining a little anonymity.

"Tell me it isn't true! *Tell me* you're not some... some... *vampire*." Utter revulsion dripped from her words.

My mouth opened, but nothing came out. What

could I even say? I refused to lie about this, because when I returned home, she'd see the truth for herself. But I hadn't imagined my "coming out" like this.

"Anna," my mother moaned. "Tell me this isn't true."

I swallowed and forced out the words I never wanted to say. "It's true."

The scream that tore across the line deafened me. I cringed away from my cell, my ears ringing from the assault. But before I could reassure her that I was fine, my mother succumbed to deep nerve-wracking sobs.

Tears pricked my own eyes but I quickly blinked them away. No, I wouldn't cry about this. And I couldn't let my mother's hysterics drag me down.

A heavy hand came down on my shoulder, and I glanced up to find Vlad standing behind me, his eyes warm with sympathy. "We'll be outside. Give you some privacy."

I nodded, then mouthed "Thank you." I had a feeling this call was going to take some time.

Vlad and the others left, leaving me alone with my emotional mother. Listening to her heart-wrenching cries was difficult, but I let her sob in peace, knowing she'd calm down once she was finished. In the meantime, I sat in front of Vlad's fireplace and warmed my now frozen body.

This wasn't how I'd imagined this playing out. I'd planned on waiting a few months if possible, until things between the vampire and human communities settled, until people were more forgiving and welcoming of us fangers. Then I'd intended to take my parents to dinner—separately, of course—and explain everything there. By then, they'd see I hadn't changed, because I would have been there in person with them for a few months. They would have accepted the change more gracefully. Not devolved into a hysteric mess.

"Anna!" my mother wailed.

"I'm here, Mom."

"Come home. Right now."

The ice in my chest fractured. Honestly, I'd feared her rejecting me entirely. Telling me to never step foot in Perish again. Telling me I wasn't welcome there anymore.

"I can't right now, but I'll be home soon."

"Why?" she demanded. "I want you here, now. I want to see my daughter."

My eyes fluttered shut. She wasn't going to like my answer, but in for a penny, in for a pound, right? Might as well tell her everything and let her adjust all at once. "Because it isn't safe for me to leave right now."

"Safe?" she shrieked. "Why isn't it safe? What's going on?"

"Where's Caleb?" I asked.

"Your brother didn't want to be here for this conversation."

Another nod. Of course he didn't. Because Caleb avoided anything that made him unhappy. Ignorance was bliss in his perfect little world. My brother was the type who'd gone to college on a football scholarship. He'd never made it into the NFL, but he'd come close enough to be considered a star in our little town. People had compared the two of us our whole lives. Troublesome Anna and perfect little Caleb. Well, now they had something else to gossip about.

My mother blew her nose, then sniffled. "Tell me what happened."

"Are you sure, Mom? This isn't pleasant conversation."

She whimpered. "I—I need to know. I need to know what happened to you."

Sighing, I crossed my legs and rested my elbows on my knees. How much should I tell her? I couldn't imagine the truth would help matters. But if someone out there had scooped the story, I knew better than to lie. The truth might be painful, but lying was worse.

So, I told her everything. From infiltrating Fallen to Petrik's attack to Vlad saving me. When I mentioned he was Dracula, my mother just about fainted.

"I can't handle this, Anna," she whispered into the phone. "You're dead. My daughter is dead."

"I'm not dead, Mom. I'm right here. You're talking to me."

"You're one of *them*, though."

"This doesn't need to be an *us* versus *them* situation."

"Anna, you're a fucking vampire!" my mother screamed.

I winced. I could recall on one hand the number the times I'd heard my mother swear and so far, she'd cursed twice in this conversation. She was a southern belle, through and through, unlike her daughter. A church-going, debutante ball, dress-wearing, tea-drinking southern belle. Guess the apple really did fall far from the tree.

"This isn't how I wanted you to find out," I said. "I was going to tell you myself."

"Just another thing you screwed up," she snapped.

Oh. I felt that one.

"I—I'm sorry," she mumbled. "I didn't mean that."

Yes, she did. My mother had always considered me a fuck-up. Because I hadn't followed in her footsteps. I'd chosen my own path—and look where it'd landed me.

"Mom, I should go. I'm needed elsewhere."

"Elsewhere? Where the heck could you possibly need to be right now?"

I didn't mention that Vlad wanted to teach me how to feed. That wouldn't soothe her already broken psyche. Nor did I mention that Petrik was still hunting me. That was vampire business and none of hers.

"I'll call you in a few nights, okay?"

"Anna, don't you dare hang up on me—"

I hung up and dropped my cell into my lap. Even now, my phone was blowing up. Notifications from every social media site, along with countless text messages pouring in.

I'd officially been outed as Perish's first vampire.

Lucky me.

AFTER SCOURING ALL the posts about me, I texted Lucy that I'd call her later, then turned off my phone. I hadn't bothered reaching out to my father or brother. It seemed pointless now. My mom could pass along what I'd told her. In the meantime, I needed to stay off the web.

I'd always longed for fame, but not like this.

I held my cell in my hand and attempted to digest everything I'd just read. Apparently, a tabloid reporter had spotted me and Vlad in the alleyway and had snapped a few quick pictures. She'd caught herself a big-time story—a vampire changing a human. Even though Vlad wasn't visible in the photo —other than his clothes, and let me tell you how *odd* that looked—I was. I looked dead in it, arms dangling at my sides and blood gushing from my neck. With Vlad unable to be photographed, no one knew his identity, but mine hadn't been hard to find, thanks to my online presence. And that was all it'd taken to spark this piece into something larger.

The reporter had gone to my hometown and interviewed my friends and my damn ex-boyfriend. She'd dug up everything she could on me, including how Lucy and I had left for New Orleans in search of illegal bloodletting. My weasel of an ex had gone on and on in the article about how he warned me not to go, how I left determined to get myself killed.

Then it'd circled back to Lucy. She'd been "unavailable for comment," but this same damn reporter had photographed Lucy coming and going from "Dracula's mansion," leading them to believe that I had indeed been turned. There was even a "Where is she now?" article, speculating that I was hiding in Vlad's estate, mourning the loss of my human life.

Kaboom. Instant infamy.

I couldn't focus on this right now, though. Not with Petrik still in play. After the dust settled, I'd worry about the photos and the articles. Maybe with luck, the story will have petered out by then. Some new celebrity story to steal the attention from me.

"Anna?" Vlad rapped his knuckles against his office door. "Is everything all right?"

I honestly couldn't say. It was all so fresh still, and I felt a little numb. Fame was my life's dream. For everyone to know my name. And now, I just wanted to curl up and die. Again.

"Everything's fine," I finally said. "Just a small hiccup. Apparently, someone took a photo of us outside Fallen."

Vlad stepped into his office and closed the door behind him. "I fail to see why that's so upsetting."

"You would. They can't see you. All they see are your damn clothes, for crying out loud. Me? They can see everything. Just what I wanted, for the whole world to witness my death. The stupid reporter posted these photos everywhere. And now everyone knows I'm a vampire."

"Ah." Vlad crossed the room and came to a stop in front of me. He slipped his arms around my waist and drew me into his chest. I went willingly, hungry for some comfort right now.

"Will this get us in trouble?" I whispered, my head resting against the swell of his chest.

"From whom?"

"The queen? Seeing a photo like that, with me being turned into a vampire when she's in the middle of peace talks with the president... isn't this bad?"

Vlad didn't answer immediately, so I tipped my head back and stared up at him. A flicker of something darted behind his eyes. Concern, maybe?

"John would have already notified her about Petrik and the developing situation. She may not like how public this has apparently become, but I can't see why she would punish us."

"Um, she can punish us?"

"It's within her rights as the queen." He smoothed my hair back from my face. "But don't fret over things that aren't in our control. We must focus on the issue at hand, yes?"

I groaned. "I had a quiet life before this—and I hated it. Now, I would give anything to have it back."

"I admit, I'm not as well versed in the internet as you, but I imagine it'll pass. As all things eventually do."

I nodded.

"In the meantime, we need to focus our attention on other matters."

"Like apparently teaching me to feed."

Vlad gave me a small smile. "And teaching you how to be a vampire."

"And then what?"

"Hmm?"

I flicked my tongue against one of my fangs, a stark reminder of my future and all it entailed. "I just... what happens to me after you're done teaching me how to be a vampire? After I'm self-sufficient. After I establish my harem. Am I expected to leave?"

Vlad frowned down at me. "Leave to go where?"

"Anywhere. Do I go home? Do I strike out on my own, away from you? And what about you? Do you move on to greener pastures? Move on to someone else?"

Vlad's expression cleared the second I uttered those two final words. "Ah, I see."

"What? What do you see?"

"Allow me to ease your worries."

Without another word, he leaned down and claimed my mouth. I sucked in a surprised breath, then moaned when he took advantage of my parted lips to deepen the kiss. His hands pressed into my lower back, holding me in place—not that I minded. I melted into him, eager to taste all he had to offer.

I'd had a few days to think about our first kiss, whether or not I regretted it. And I knew now, without a doubt, I most certainly did not. Vlad was unlike anyone I'd ever met before. His touch made me burn, made me ache, made me *want*. It was like he awoke something within me I'd never experienced before. This *need* for someone else, like he completed me in a way none of my previous boyfriends had. Almost as though we were made for each other.

That thought terrified me.

He'd dreamed of me fifty years ago. He'd saved me, then literally changed me by turning me into a vampire. But with him, everything felt right. Like nothing in the world could touch us. With him, I felt invincible.

I nipped at Vlad's mouth, then groaned when my fangs pierced the plump part of his lip. The taste of his blood blinded and inflamed me. I slipped my arms around his neck, then sighed contentedly when he cupped my ass. One small hop, and I was in his arms, my core pressed against his stomach. I didn't even care that there were four other vampires in the house with extremely sensitive hearing. I wanted Vlad. Right now.

He broke from the kiss and pressed his forehead against mine. "Careful. You haven't fed tonight. And you shouldn't feed from me again."

Shouldn't. Not couldn't.

I licked my lips, my eyes drifting to his throat. I cupped his neck and ran my thumb along the vein. That strange scent from before returned, so warm and inviting yet delicate. Desire, I realized. That was what I scented earlier when Vlad touched me in front of the others. Whether it was his or mine, I had no idea, but I knew the smell now. And I reveled in it.

"Shh," Vlad whispered. "It's difficult to separate passion from hunger at first."

"I know the difference," I told him. "When you touch me, I come alive."

Vlad's throat bobbed as he forced himself to swallow. "That's just your bloodlust talking."

"No, it's a different part of my body talking," I teased. "The one pressed against you right now. And it's *starving*."

The shadows lifted from Vlad's face when he chuckled. "You're incorrigible."

"I know." I stole another kiss, swiping my tongue across his. Yup, I could do this forever. The feel of him pressed against me was addicting. And all I could think about was pinning him to his bookcases and ravishing him.

"We can't," Vlad rasped, pulling back from my kiss. "Not right now. Not with the others in hearing distance."

"Aren't all vampires always in hearing range?" I teased, nipping at his jaw.

Vlad's fingers gripped my ass, as though he was struggling to maintain control. I loved it.

"Anna, stop. I can't believe I'm saying that right now." He groaned and shook his head. "There are things we need to do tonight."

"Yup—each other."

He gave a breathy laugh. "What am I going to do with you?"

"With me? Or to me?" I waggled my brows.

With a sorrowful sigh, he lowered me to my feet and stepped back. "Our first time will not be in my office while my allies are in listening distance."

"Aww. Party pooper."

He blinked at me, then chuckled and strode toward the door. "Come. Let's get you dressed and teach you about vampire dining etiquette."

"Don't think I'm not onto you," I called after him. "You still haven't answered any of my questions."

He turned and lifted a brow. "Haven't I?"

Hmm. Pretty sure he'd avoided answering them. But that was okay. Just meant I could pester him some more. And if that resulted in more schmexy times, I was game.

THE "BIG EASY" was anything but. The sights and smells—*especially* the smells—were nearly enough to undo me the instant we stepped foot in the city. I'd visited New Orleans many times throughout my life, particularly during Mardi Gras, and I'd always noticed how badly the city stunk. But it was so much worse now as a vampire. There was an acrid mixture of body odor combined with stale food and the bitter tang of what I assumed was sex and alcohol that made my nose crinkle.

Live music poured out of every building and off each street corner, and the hum of the city lights nearly gave me a headache. It was all incredibly overwhelming. And so very intriguing at the same time. Things I hadn't seen as a human were now overtly visible. Like the fine craftsmanship of the buildings and the beauty of the entire city.

Crescent City was alive and pulsing with humanity, but Vlad and I stood in the shadows, like creepy little stalkers. After my recent debut on the internet, the last thing I wanted was for someone to spot me.

"The most important thing to remember when feeding is not to drain the human completely," Vlad said. "Unless you intend to turn them, of course. But I would counsel against such a decision until you've aged a few centuries."

His hand brushed against mine, and I glanced down in time to watch as our fingers joined together. Vlad followed my gaze and offered his own little smile at the sight. Nothing like a midnight rendezvous in the middle of New Orleans to get a girl's blood pumping. Considering we were getting a meal, I decided to call this a date.

"A vampire's bite can be sensual when done correctly. Humans tend to think they've engaged in a little foreplay. They remember more the 'necking' part and less the 'biting' part. So take care to leave them with good memories."

"How often do you need to feed?"

"Once a night, but I haven't dined out in a long, long time."

"What?" I stared up at him. "Why not?"

"I have no need. My harem feeds me."

"Then why bother teaching me this? Why can't I just use a harem?"

Vlad sighed. "Not all vampires can afford to keep one. It's expensive to house and feed humans. If you cannot own a harem, you'll need to know how and where to properly feed. I refuse to unleash an uneducated vampire on society."

Right. And since I was a former twenty-four-year-old human with very little money to my name, it seemed unlikely that I would possess a harem any time soon. Why hadn't I gone to college for something a tad more lucrative, like medicine or law? Nope. I had to shoot for the stars, aim for fame, and all that nonsense. Well, where did that leave me? Penniless and undead. Score one for me.

"Okay. So, what's the game plan here?"

"Come."

Vlad's hand tightened around mine, and the next thing I knew, we were jogging through the streets. The feel of the residual heat from the day and the nighttime breeze against my face made me smile.

After five days of isolation, I'd been about ready to climb the walls... more than I already had.

Vlad led me through the French Quarter, past Marie Laveau's House of Voodoo, to a quaint little shop. I'd heard of Boutique Du Vampyre before, but I'd never visited it, seeing as I wasn't one for the touristy gimmicks.

"What are we doing here?" I asked as he pulled me inside.

He led me through the store, pausing only to catch the eye of the storekeeper, then guided me to the back. We approached a velvet-framed door where Vlad lifted his hand and gave a rhythmic knock. Without delay, the door swung open, and the strong scent of incense and blood wafted out.

I gasped, overcome by the delicious notes floating through the air.

"Hold your breath if needed," Vlad counseled. "You'll adjust in time. But the scent of blood to a newborn can be a bit much."

I fought the urge to plug my nose, then followed him inside.

The door slammed shut behind us, but Vlad didn't seem to care. Instead, he slipped the doorman a crisp fifty-dollar bill, then approached a booth near the back. Once seated, a human server approached and untied a silk ribbon fixed to the wall. A curtain slipped free and closed us off in our own private nook.

"What is this place?" I whispered.

"The Vampire Lounge. It's a private club owned by the Voodoo Queen."

My jaw gaped. "The Voodoo Queen? You mean Marie Laveau?"

"Shh." Vlad patted my thigh. "It's an unwritten rule that we don't speak of her. She hasn't been seen or heard from in decades, so we allow her some privacy."

"Decades? But she died over a hundred years ago."

Vlad gave me a look, the kind that suggested I was being naïve.

"Her people opened this lounge a few years ago, but it's always been a well-kept secret. I imagine business will spike now, thanks to the treaty. Here, we can order our meal. All the humans are consenting, which makes it far easier for us, since we now can no longer drink without permission."

"Wait, *this* is what you meant when you said you wanted to teach me to feed?"

Vlad lifted a brow. "What did you expect?"

"I don't know, some wild frat party where we feed off drunken humans—"

"Illegal."

"Okay, catching some would-be murderer and exacting some vengeance—"

"Illegal."

I blew out a breath. "Okay... um, luring in some young stud and—"

"Illegal, Anna. All of that is illegal now. The classic vampire ways are now dead, thanks to Genevieve. She's brought us into the twenty-first century so we can feed openly."

"Geez, talk about taking all the fun out of being a vampire."

"You think it would be fun to murder people?"

"No!" I scoffed. "Who said anything about murder? Whatever, just show me how this all works."

Right on time, the curtain fluttered open and our server appeared. "Good evening. My name is Rainn, and I'll be your server tonight." She lifted her head, then gave a dramatic gasp. "Oh! Dracula. Wow. It's an honor, sir."

I stifled a stunned laugh. Of course Vlad would be recognized. No wonder the man chose to feed off a harem.

Rainn's gaze swung to me, and she blinked. "And holy shit—sorry, I didn't mean to curse—but you're Anna! Anna Perish!"

If I'd thought myself stunned before, it was nothing compared to now. "Um...."

"I saw your photos online! Everyone's been wondering where you are. But you're here! And you're a vampire! By the blood, you *have* to tell me what it was like. Being turned, I mean. I am like your *biggest* fan. Ah! To think, you're here. You're really here! Oh my G—sorry, no, I won't say that. I'm just so excited! I didn't think it was possible. Did Dracula turn you? Was he the one in the photo turning you? My G—" She slapped a hand over her mouth, her wide, unblinking eyes boring into mine.

Holy. Shit.

Was this what it was like to be famous?

"Um...." That was all I could think to say. This was all so new to me, and completely unwelcome. Yes, I wanted fame. But I'd wanted it on my terms. Not accidentally. Not because someone had taken a few photos of me on the worst night of my life. I mean, sure, I could turn lemons into lemonade, but I really wasn't ready for that kind of sickening positivity yet.

"AB+ please," Vlad commented, his tone lacking all warmth.

"Right. I'm so sorry. This is only my second night on the job, and I wasn't expecting to meet you two, like ever. Man, you are a beautiful couple. Has anyone told you that before? Did you two know each other before Anna became a vampire?" She gasped loudly, her hand clutching at her tattooed neck. "Oh wow, are you two in love? So you turned her? To spend eternity together?"

Vlad and I were deathly silent. When it was clear she had no intentions of leaving, Vlad slowly exhaled and answered. "I assure you, I would never turn someone I loved in the middle of a dark alleyway unless there were no other options. I was providing Ms. Perish a service. Otherwise, she would have succumbed to her injuries."

Rainn practically melted on the spot. "You saved her life? How romantic."

Wow, she and I were on completely different wavelengths here. I appreciated what Vlad had done for me, absolutely. But romantic? No. Not even a little.

"Our order?" Vlad implored.

"Right. Gosh, I'm so sorry. AB+ for the Count, and for you, Anna?" Yet another gasp. Rainn needed to calm down before she started hiccupping. "Or would that make you the Countess now?"

Before I could correct her, Vlad held up his hand, and said, "O+ should be fine."

Rainn practically curtsied before fleeing our secluded booth.

I exhaled and slumped against the seat. "That was...."

"You'll get used to it," Vlad said. "Yet another reason why I keep a harem."

"How did she even know who you are? I get me. My picture's been slapped all over the web, including the damn vamp gossip sites. But you?"

"There are a few portraits of me here." Vlad waved his hand dismissively. "I let Marie talk me into sitting for a series about a hundred years ago. I'd forgotten what I'd looked like, so I'd agreed to them."

Oh wow. I needed to see those before we left.

We were barely alone for a minute before the curtain fluttered open and Rainn returned. Two humans stood on either side of her, their expressions equally as gobsmacked.

"Wait, what is this?"

Vlad gestured to the open seats next to us. "Have a seat."

"Oh my gosh." One of the women sat next to me,

giggling with wide eyes. "You're her. Aren't you? When Rainn told me, I couldn't believe it."

"What's going on?" I shot Vlad a dark look. Was this some sort of creepy fan club?

"Our meals." He gestured to the woman who sat next to him. Hers was more of a silent wonderment, but I could see the stars in her eyes as she gazed up at Vlad.

"Enjoy," Rainn murmured, apparently trying to regain a little professionalism. She stepped out of the booth and fixed the curtain to ensure we had our privacy, then vanished.

Vlad's companion extended her arm, wrist facing up. I watched as he gently cradled her arm and brought it to his mouth. His eyes flicked to mine, then his mouth parted and he slowly bit down.

My breath caught at the scent of fresh blood welling over her skin, but something south of the border practically quivered with excitement at the sight of Vlad's mouth closing around the girl's wrist. His eyes closed, and he sank into the feeding. Sensual, he'd said. Yeah, I definitely could see that.

"Ready?" my meal asked.

I turned to her, my nerves fluttering anxiously. "I've never done this before."

"I know. I'll walk you through it."

"Do you feed a lot of vampires?"

A sweet smile brightened her face. "I'm here every week. We're not allowed to come too often. I consider it an honor to be your first meal."

Vlad had actually been given that honor. And I would cherish those memories for the rest of time. Especially the aftereffects. I just hoped I didn't respond to every meal like that. I liked to think there was something special between me and Vlad.

"What's your name?"

"Maybelle," she answered.

"Is that your real name?"

She winked. "No."

"Fair enough." I wouldn't want to give a bunch of strange vampires my real name either. "Well, Maybelle. Shall we give this the ole college try?"

She offered me her arm the same way Vlad's companion had. So I mimicked his movements. I cupped her forearm and lifted it to my mouth. Her scent practically smacked me in the face. So mouthwatering. My eyes fluttered shut, and I nearly lost myself. But then I remembered Harold. How horrible I'd felt after attacking him. I couldn't allow that to happen again, no matter how intoxicating her scent.

"Take your time," Maybelle cautioned. "Let your fangs do all the work. You don't need to bite hard."

I licked my lips, then pressed her wrist to my teeth and exerted the slightest amount of pressure. She was right, my fangs did all the work, sliding into her flesh with hardly any resistance. Her blood instantly flooded my mouth, and I bit back a groan, not wanting to frighten her. I needed to maintain complete control of the situation here. I would make Vlad and myself proud by not becoming a savage beast.

Maybelle sighed contentedly and leaned into me. Guess I'd done something right.

I drank deeply, reveling in the warmth that spread through my body. Maybelle's blood differed from Vlad's. Delicious, but hardly as exhilarating. There was something about his that excited me, whereas Maybelle's simply nourished me.

"Anna." Vlad's voice called to me through my feeding haze. "That's enough."

For a moment, I almost ignored him. The hunger within wasn't sated yet, but after a moment's hesitation, I regained my senses and gently pulled away from Maybelle's bleeding wrist.

My eyes fluttered open to find my companion leaning against the booth with a satisfied grin.

"You did really well," she breathed, almost as though she'd enjoyed my bite a little *too much*.

I shot Vlad an anxious glance, but he seemed unperturbed. In fact, his companion had practically melted into her seat, her eyes closed while she hummed to herself. Rainn magically appeared and led our meals away as though she'd been watching.

"Very good, Anna," Vlad said. "How do you feel?"

I released a shivering breath, then catalogued my emotions. My hunger was abated, but there was a different craving rising beneath the surface, one that I was fairly sure only Vlad could satiate.

That same sweet scent from his office rose between us, and Vlad's eyes widened. He chuckled and cupped my cheek, rubbing his thumb along my lower lip. I nearly pounced on him right there.

"Feeding can be sensual for both parties. You'll learn to separate it in the coming days."

"She didn't taste like you," I whispered.

"No human ever will."

I dampened my lips with my tongue, then caught Vlad's finger with my teeth, careful not to split his skin. I wouldn't be able to handle that right now. So many thoughts ran through my mind, all more deafening than the last. I'd bitten Vlad's wrist more than once, and now Maybelle's. But how did it feel to feed from the neck?

"What does it feel like?" I finally braved asking. "To be bitten by someone who cares for you? I mean, you sort of tasted me when we first kissed..." Blood warmed my cheeks. "But I've only really been bitten by...." I couldn't say his name. I didn't want to ruin this moment by even thinking about him, but I couldn't stop myself.

A shudder swept through Vlad's body. He leaned forward and rested his forehead against mine. "Would you like to experience it?"

Heat flushed my entire body, and I shuddered. I hadn't realized it was something I wanted until right now.

"Mm. I'll take that as a yes."

I wanted Vlad's teeth in my throat, if only to erase the memory of Petrik's. I wanted to experience what Maybelle just went through. What Vlad had experienced when I'd bitten him. I wanted to experience it all.

"My neck," I said.

Vlad drew back and met my gaze. "Are you sure?"

I gave another jerky nod.

"I know that's where Petrik bit you. I'd

understand if you aren't ready to share such an intimate thing with me so soon after his attack."

"I trust you," I whispered. I *yearned* for this, more than I'd ever yearned for anything before.

"Anna—"

"Vlad, please. I want this. You. Everything."

His eyes fluttered shut, but I caught the sight of a soft smile. "And I you."

He shifted his weight and leaned into me, pressing his mouth against my neck. I shivered against him, my hands sliding up his thighs. Maybe this wasn't the right place for this, but the curtain was drawn, secluding us from sight. His mansion had four other vampires present. But here, it felt like it was just the two of us.

"Anna... I—" Vlad's teeth found their mark, interrupting whatever he'd meant to say.

The slight pressure made me squirm, but the instant his fangs slipped into my flesh, my entire world imploded.

I CERTAINLY WASN'T AS calm and collected as Maybelle—far from it. The second Vlad's teeth made their mark, I had to forcibly restrain myself from molesting the poor man. *Poor man*—yeah, right. I'm sure he wouldn't have minded a little molestation. But since his fangs were deeply imbedded in my neck, it seemed wiser to hold still. The reality was a bit more sexual though. Little moans escaped my throat, and I practically squirmed in my seat.

Vlad's hands seemed to have a mind of their own. One cupped my hip, locking me in place, and the other threaded in my hair, holding my head still. His lips were soft and warm against my skin, but his bite was erotic—the stark opposite of Petrik's. Vlad's intention was to pleasure, and boy, was he a master. Seconds into the bite, heat had already begun spiraling through my core and spreading through my limbs. Far faster than my vibrating boyfriend back home.

A girl could get used to this sort of thing. If I wasn't mistaken, he was seconds away from causing a massive eruption in my lady bits without even touching them.

"Vlad," I moaned.

His teeth slowly came free from my throat, and he leaned back, running his tongue over his lips. His skin was just as flushed as mine. Apparently, it'd been just as good for him.

I watched him visibly swallow and shivered. How did he make that look erotic?

"I think we should leave," he murmured.

My head jerked. Oh yeah. We needed to leave. Now. Stat. Pronto. Because someone—namely Vlad —had awakened the horny little beast within me, and it was desperate for more.

Vlad cleared his throat and blinked. "You need more blood first."

"I do?"

"I just fed from you."

"Can I feed from you?"

He shook his head. "I'd fear the ramifications right now if you did."

Yeah, me too. If I had my mouth on him, I had a feeling The Vampire Lounge would be catching more of a show than they'd bargained for.

Vlad stuck his hand outside the curtain, which seemed to summon Rainn. She appeared a few seconds later, her grin telling me she'd seen more than I would have liked. Curtain or not, guess we hadn't been entirely discreet.

"More blood?" Rainn asked me.

"Can it come from Maybelle again?"

Rainn nodded. "She has a few more feeds in her tonight. I'll grab her."

"You liked her?" Vlad asked when Rainn left.

"She helped calm me, and right now, I think that's what I need."

Vlad gave a very knowing and manly chuckle.

It didn't take long for Rainn to return with Maybelle. She slid into our booth and, with a soft smile, offered her other arm. "Glad to be of service."

So formal. It was quicker this time, and certainly easier. I knew how to hold her arm, how to bite, and when to pull back. Maybelle left for a second time, her hand cupped over her wrist. But she was still standing, alive, and happy. That was all that mattered.

Vlad dropped a few bills on the table, then grabbed my hand and started to guide me out of the Lounge. I hurried behind him, my body pressed against his, chuckling under my breath. Guess I wasn't the only eager one. I just hoped we made it home before either of us lost our patience. Twenty bucks said it would be me who caved and jumped him first.

Distracted by the feel of Vlad's back against my chest, I didn't realize his hand had tightened into a bruising grip until he shoved me completely behind him, shielding me with his body.

"What—"

"Petrik," Vlad growled. "What the hell are you doing here?"

Ice ran through my veins. Petrik was here? Right now? I released Vlad's hand in case he needed it and gripped the waist of his pants, holding on for dear life. I pressed my forehead against his back and closed my eyes.

This wasn't happening.

This wasn't happening!

"Vlad," Petrik drawled in a faint English accent. "How wonderful to see you here, old friend."

"We're hardly friends," Vlad spat.

"Such animosity. To what do I owe the honor?"

Vlad sucked a breath in through his teeth but didn't respond.

"I smell our mutual friend. I would know that scent anywhere. You needn't hide her."

Tension zipped through Vlad's body, and I hugged him even tighter. Terror coursed through my freshly fed veins. A part of me knew I wouldn't be able to handle seeing Petrik, or even speaking to him. The memories of that night returned in full force, blinding me to everything else. It was like I could feel the cold fence against my back and his fingers gripping my throat, choking me. I gasped and buried my head against Vlad's back. I hated feeling this weak and cowardly. But Petrik downright terrified me.

"Stay away from her," Vlad growled. "John and I have already petitioned the queen for your punishment."

Petrik scoffed under his breath. "Such a waste of bureaucratic time. You and I both know the queen will do nothing of the sort. If you feel I've slighted you, then let's handle this now."

My gaze caught sight of Vlad's hands tightening

into fists at his side. "What exactly do you think a duel would accomplish?"

"For you, absolutely nothing. For me, it'll remove the one thing currently standing in my way."

Vlad, I realized. Petrik was referring to him.

"Ask yourself this, Count. Is she worth your life?"

"A thousand times."

I froze, Vlad's response startling me. I knew he cared for me, but enough to die for me?

"Your affections for the girl run deeper than a sire's," Petrik mused. "How adorable. You've convinced yourself you love her."

My fingers tightened on the edge of his pants.

"Leave," Vlad snapped. "And if I catch you sniffing around my house again—"

"You'll what?" Petrik laughed, and the sound lifted every last one of my hairs. "Let me remind you, boy. You're nothing but a name. You may be famous, but fame means nothing. I'm five hundred years older than you and can destroy you in the blink of an eye. So don't push me. Give me what I want, and you'll live to see another night."

The thought of Vlad facing Petrik made me sick to my stomach. All that fresh blood was about to come rising up. I couldn't let him do this for me. I needed to be able to stand on my own two feet. Be the vampire Vlad wanted me to be. I'd told John I could handle Petrik, but here I was, cowering behind Vlad like some child.

I drew a deep breath, ignoring my trembling bottom lip, and stepped out from behind him.

Petrik's cold gaze instantly latched onto me, and his cruel mouth curled into a malicious smile. "There she is. Tired of hiding behind your sire, are we?"

Emboldened by the fact that we stood in a public place, I braved a step forward and jabbed a shaking finger into his chest. Petrik's eyes widened with amusement.

"Leave me the hell alone," I growled, though it sounded more like a meek puppy than a vicious wolf. "If you ever come near me again, I'll consider it a threat. And I don't give two shits about the laws or your precious queen. My face will be the last thing you see."

Petrik's mouth split into a wide grin, exposing his fangs. "How adorable—Ms. Perish, is it? I never did catch your name."

My hand curled into a fist. "Keep pushing me, you misogynistic asshole."

"Anna," Vlad warned.

"No. I'm not going to stand here and listen to his

threats, and I certainly won't let him terrorize me. I may not be a thousand years old, but I will *not* let you threaten me or those I care about. Maybe it's you who should be watching *your* back, Petrik. Because fire burns us all. And while you're a fucking mummy from ancient times, I'm not. I have people who would *love* to set your ass on fire during the day."

"Anna!" Vlad snapped.

Petrik's face darkened, and his frosty gaze narrowed on me. "Oh, Ms. Perish, I think you're going to be a fun little toy to break."

I swallowed but managed to maintain my bravado. "Try it, old man. Let's see who dies first."

"That's enough!" Vlad grabbed my hand and yanked me away from the developing scene.

"I'll be seeing you again soon, Ms. Perish," Petrik called behind me.

Vlad cursed under his breath and rushed me out the front door, muttering something about me being a foolish newborn. Guess he hadn't appreciated my little show.

No one had spoken in a good ten minutes. I was pretty sure no one had moved either. Supernaturally freaky. Not a single eyelash batted, or even a twitchy finger. All five vampires simply sat in Vlad's office, staring at... well, me. And it was fucking unnerving. I wanted to clap my hands in their faces, slap their cheeks, anything to get them moving again. But they sat as still as statues.

"Okay, fine." I tossed my hands in the air. "Maybe I was reckless. But that guy absolutely terrifies me."

"Another fine reason to keep your mouth shut," Vlad suggested.

My brows shot upward. "Excuse me?"

Vlad sighed and dropped his head into his open palms. "I apologize. I didn't mean it that way. I just wish you hadn't spoken to Petrik."

"Why? What's the big deal?"

"The big deal?" Camilla rose from her seat and stalked toward me. "You really don't understand the first thing about vampires, do you?"

"Considering I've been one for like five minutes, no, I can honestly say I don't."

"Allow me to break it down for you then." Camilla spun on her heel and stalked the length of Vlad's office, ticking things off on her fingers as she spoke. "First of all, addressing Petrik in any manner will present itself as a challenge to him. The man is a predator, and his prey just made itself ten times more intriguing by giving in to his provocations."

"Oh, for crying out loud, are you actually suggesting I should ignore him so he'll go away?"

"There's truth to that idiom. Second of all, you threatened his life, which now gives him further reason to want you dead."

"So what? He *killed* me, reason enough for *me* to want to see *him* dead."

"*Third* of all"—Camilla scowled at me—"you mentioned your human friends *and* threatened him with *them*. Which now gives him cause to hunt down and massacre pretty much everyone close to you."

This one caught my breath. "What?"

"In other words, you're a fucking idiot," Eli snapped.

I rolled my eyes when he rose from his seat. He was the very last person I needed to hear from right now.

"Vlad could have handled it," Eli scolded.

"I'm not saying he couldn't or wasn't. I just didn't like hiding behind him like some coward."

"As you pointed out," Camilla interrupted. "You're freshly turned. What can you possibly bring to the table to inspire fear in Petrik? Your little threats did absolutely nothing except make you a much more interesting target. So, congratulations. You just made this ten times harder for us all."

My gaze leapt between the five of them. Vlad still cradled his head, like I'd done the worst thing imaginable. Eli glowered at me like I was little more than a stain on his life. Rebecca pitied me, but that didn't endear her to me at all. And Breccan appeared amused more than anything. He even chuckled under his breath and whipped his hand through his tousled brown hair.

"You guys don't understand," I whispered. "He *terrifies* me. I can't just stand there and let someone else fight this battle for me."

"Why not?" Vlad questioned.

"Because how would I live with myself? Knowing that I was such a coward that I put someone I care about at risk? Petrik is twice your age. He's as dangerous to you as he is to me. I can't just let you take my place."

"That wasn't my intention either." Vlad rose from his seat and approached me. When he took my hands, my nerves settled. "I was attempting to diffuse the situation."

"It wasn't working," I whispered.

"It might have, if you hadn't jumped in with your threats and taunts."

I blinked and shook my head. They didn't understand. And how could they? They hadn't been powerless like this for ages.

"I suggest we bring her friend here to stay with us," Rebecca finally chimed in. "One less target for Petrik to go after."

"Lucy?" I shook my head. "No, I don't want her anywhere near this."

"Too bad," Eli said. "You brought her into this when you made your threats. If you want her safe, she needs to be here where we can keep an eye on her."

I caught Vlad's gaze, who nodded. "Call her."

Sighing, I reached for my phone and sent Lucy a text, then faced the rag-tag group of vampires surrounding me.

"I'm sorry if I made things more difficult. But I refuse to hide."

"Good, because that's not an option anymore," Camilla said, storming back over to me. "Vlad brought me here to teach you to fight. So, guess what, sweetheart? We start tomorrow. And I will not go easy on you. You just brought down a whole world of trouble on all of us, so now you need to learn how to fight for yourself."

"Perfect." I lifted my chin and met her stare. "I don't want you to go easy on me."

Camilla's mouth twisted. "Believe me, you're going to wish Petrik killed you."

I squared my shoulders. I refused to let Camilla cow me. I didn't care if I was a walking bruise for the next month. I would show them all that I could handle this.

Or die trying.

18

"Come on, Anna! Put some damn effort into it!" Camilla shouted. "Show me you've learned *something*."

I doubled over and drew a deep breath. Maybe I didn't need air to function—except to speak and smell—but it was a habit. Comforting. Reminded me that once upon a time, I'd been something other than this walking zombie.

Two weeks had passed since the "night of the pathetic taunts," as I'd come to call it. The night Vlad and I had run into Petrik at the Vampire Lounge. Camilla hadn't been kidding when she'd said she was going to make me regret surviving, and damn, had she delivered on that promise. Since I was technically dead, I didn't bruise. But I sure as hell *felt* them. Every inch of me ached in some form or another. She'd broken my limbs, snapped my neck, paralyzed me, unleashed every physical torment she could think of, all in the name of defense. Every night, I woke healed, only for her to put me through the wringer once again.

Needless to say, my last two weeks had *sucked*.

Camilla pushed me, trained me, broke me. Every few nights, she tagged in Eli. Those nights were my least favorite. Whereas Camilla sometimes pulled her punches, Eli refused. In fact, I was pretty sure he got off on abusing me.

What few glimpses I caught of Vlad, he seemed equally tormented by my training. More than once, he'd pulled Camilla off to the side. I'd caught snippets, thanks to my improved senses, him imploring her to ease up, but Camilla had just laughed off his concerns. "What doesn't kill her makes her stronger," she'd said. And since I was a vampire, that pretty much left everything except stakes, fire, and beheading.

This was what my life had become.

Worse, Lucy barely spoke to me. She was angry with me. Her first night here, I'd explained the situation, and the moment I'd told her Petrik wanted me dead—again—she'd lost her shit on me. Accused me of throwing away my life and reminded me that I'd promised I wouldn't seek him out. She'd refused to listen when I'd tried to explain how he'd found us. We hadn't really spoken since.

What fleeting moments of peace Camilla offered, I spent them with Vlad, though nothing fun ever came of them. He often appraised my broken body, then shook his head and fetched me blood.

On the upside, I was far too exhausted to care that the house teemed with humans again. Harold and the rest of the staff had returned along with a new harem for Vlad's guests and me. I'd become a pro at feeding, or so a few of the walking Happy Meals told me. I hadn't had the chance to learn their names yet. Their blood was the only thing that kept me going, but I was too focused on feeding and healing to learn anything else.

"Are you listening to me?" Camilla demanded. "Get your arms up. Defend yourself."

My arms? The ones she'd practically snapped in half a few minutes ago? I could barely lift them, let alone use them to block her attacks.

Gritting my teeth, I ignored the agonizing pain and lifted my broken limbs.

Camilla rushed forward and unleashed another

KINSLEY ADAMS

series of attacks I could barely follow. I managed a few blocks before her leg swept out and took me down. I crashed to the mats, a torturous jolt zipping up my arms and ringing in my head. My vision dimmed, and I gasped. How the hell was I supposed to defend myself when I couldn't move?

"Get up!" she shrieked. "For crying out loud, it's like you haven't learned anything! What the hell are we here for if you're not even going to try?"

Rage simmered in the pit of my stomach. I *hated* this—hated *her*. I was so sick of the insults, sick of the complaints, sick of *everything*. I was especially sick of training. She was right. I hadn't learned anything. And why? Because two weeks wasn't enough time to master a skill like fighting. People trained for years to learn how to do this shit. What did they expect from me?

"Get up!" Camilla shouted again.

"Shut the fuck up," I rasped.

"Excuse me?"

"I said shut up!" I shrieked.

The simmering rage exploded within me like an erupting volcano. Heat spilled through my limbs, and with a deafening battle cry, I launched off the ground and retaliated. My movements were liquid fast, so much so that I couldn't even follow them. I simply let my instincts take over and attacked. Everything Camilla had beaten into me for the last two weeks came rushing out of me.

"Yes!" Camilla cried out, fending off my blows.

I growled and launched a fresh attack. I didn't want her blocking me. I wanted her broken and bleeding on the floor. I wanted her unconscious. I just wanted this to *stop*.

My fist grazed the side of Camilla's shoulder and set her off balance. While she fought to correct herself, I darted around her and pounced on her back. Then, without thought, I struck like a snake, my mouth zeroing in on her pale throat.

The instant my fangs pierced her golden flesh, she shrieked.

Her sweet blood filled my mouth, and my eyes fluttered shut, even as she whipped us around. Her hands clawed at my shoulders and neck, but I held on for dear life, draining her of blood. It was the only way I knew how to win the fight.

"Anna!" a deep, commanding voice boomed through the room.

My eyes snapped open to find Vlad standing across the room, his face twisted with horror.

"Get off me!" Camilla screamed.

Her blood helped me regain a sense of myself,

and I scrambled off with a sharp gasp. "I—I'm sorry. I don't know what happened."

I backed away from Camilla, my trembling hand touching the blood droplets clinging to my bottom lip. I fought not to lick it off, knowing it might insult her.

Camilla glared at me with all the anger she could muster.

"I'm so sorry," I mumbled around my fingers. "I wasn't thinking. I just reacted."

She heaved a sigh, then touched her neck. The holes had already sealed over. "It's not the most orthodox method, but I suppose it works. I don't recommend trying that again though. Petrik is older than all of us combined. Who knows the effect his blood would have on you."

I gave a frantic nod. Even Camilla's blood, rich with age, had me craving more. She wasn't as old as Vlad, but she was close enough. I needed to be careful. Drinking from older vampires was addicting, Vlad had warned me of that. And I'd likely ingested more ancient blood than any other newborn out there.

"A break might be prudent," Vlad suggested.

Camilla nodded. "I'll find a quick meal to top me back up, then we'll get back at it. Before you bit me,

Anna, you were onto something. You were attacking instead of defending. Your hits were solid and strong. Definite improvement. I don't want to lose the momentum. Meet me back here in twenty minutes."

I finally licked my lips, then nodded. Thanks to Camilla's blood, I didn't need to seek out a harem member for once. I glanced at my arms to find them already healed. Amazing, the things blood could do for a vampire. In fact, I felt better than I had in two weeks. Her blood was just the pick me up I'd needed.

"You must be cautious, Anna," Vlad said as he approached. "Consuming our blood—"

"I know," I whispered. "I honestly don't know what came over me. I was just so angry and in pain, and I wanted it to stop."

Vlad sighed, then slipped his arms around my back and drew me into his chest. "I hate seeing you like this, but Camilla will do right by you. She'll make you strong, and should there come a day when I can't protect you—"

"Hey." I lifted my head and gazed up at him. "It's not your job to protect me."

"It is. I'm your sire. It's in the job description."

My smile wavered. Was that the only reason he cared?

As though sensing my concerns, Vlad leaned down and kissed me. It was the first one we'd shared in weeks, and my body reacted instantly. Flushed with fresh blood, the feel of his mouth against mine shattered all my defenses. I stretched up on my tiptoes and ravaged his mouth, devouring him until we both came apart, breathless and, for lack of a better word, randy.

"I miss you," he murmured, his hands sliding up my back and into my hair. "And Lucy doesn't care for my presence." He gave a haughty laugh. "I think she's the first person to reject me. Most fawn over me."

I winced. "You know that's not why I like you, right? The fact that you're Dracula means nothing to me."

"I'm well aware," Vlad teased, brushing his lips across the tip of my nose. "I believe Lucy is lonely, though. I feel it's important the two of you spend some time together tonight before we retire. I'll have Camilla end your training a few hours early."

I brightened inside. "Really?"

Vlad nodded. "It's my understanding that 'girl time' is equally as important as training."

"Lucy said that, didn't she?" I started laughing.

"Among other things. She's not afraid to express

her opinion."

"She really isn't." I cupped the back of his head and brought our mouths together, showing him with my tongue how appreciative I was of this small schedule change.

Lucy and I desperately needed some bonding time. She was still mad at me, but I knew she was going stir crazy. Much like I had during my first week. It was worse for her, though. No one to talk to or hang out with other than the stuffy humans Vlad had hired to feed us. I highly doubted Lucy had connected with any of them.

"I also feel a little 'us time' is imperative too," Vlad murmured against my mouth. "I want to take you out tomorrow evening, before you resume your training. Would you like that?"

"What do you think?"

Vlad offered me a small smile, then with a final kiss, left me to continue sparring. Camilla wouldn't return for another ten minutes or so, but in the meantime, I could pound the salt out of the Petrik-shaped dummy she'd designed for me. If there was anything that would help me blow off steam, it was that rubber atrocity.

THE SMELL of wafting popcorn led me to my bedroom. I'd told Lucy to make use of the space however she liked, since I was too busy to enjoy it myself, and from the smells of it, she'd done exactly that. During the last two weeks, my senses had grown exponentially, and my nose was no exception. With this many humans in the house, I would have preferred that one remained dull, but alas, it was something all vampires had to endure. I was slowly learning how to tune certain things out, such as the sound and scent of someone relieving themselves, and focus on other things, aka: popcorn.

I slipped into the bedroom and chuckled at the sight of Lucy sprawled on the bed, a giant bucket of popped kernels next to her, and the movie *Vamps* playing on her laptop in the background. Because of course it was. Lucy and I had watched this flick years ago. At the time, we'd found it downright hilarious. I wasn't sure what I'd think of it now, seeing as it hit a little closer to home.

Lucy rose from the bed with a tentative smile. "Hey."

"Hi." I closed the door behind me and leaned against it. "Um, thanks for getting me out of training for a few hours."

"Oh, of course!" Lucy scooted over and brushed

any lingering crumbs off the bedspread. "I figured you could use a small break."

I nodded, a little unsure of what to say. Things had been strained between us since Vlad had turned me. I understood her apprehension. It had to be hard having a vampire for a best friend. The lifestyle was so unlike anything we were used to. I'd gone from being a cherub-faced vlogger to a predator in the span of a single night. That wasn't something one just adjusted to.

"Come sit," Lucy patted the space next to her.

I couldn't help but smile. Her eagerness made me think nothing would ever truly separate us. Except death. And boy, did that thought kill the mood.

"What part are you at?" I asked as I perched on the edge of the bed.

Thankfully, I wasn't driven by the scent of blood anymore. And after gorging on Camilla, I was feeling pretty sated. But I didn't want to make Lucy nervous by sitting too close.

"The part where Stacy draws Goody so she can see what she looks like."

I slowly nodded. Man, that part made me nostalgic. We'd laughed the first time, and "aww'd" at their friendship. Now, I was wondering who would do that for me in two hundred years.

"So, how have things been going?" I asked.

"Eh." Lucy shrugged, then hit pause on the movie so we could chat. "It's boring here. Like *insanely* boring. I told Count Fangerton that he needs to update his place. I'd like to stream some shows without being confined to my room."

I chuckled. Yeah, Vlad's place was certainly outdated. The most modern thing he owned were the fireplaces. Not a single TV or radio in the house. No computers or laptops. Not even a single tablet. I'd even spotted an old accounting ledger on his desk that he used to keep track of his finances. Modern, Vlad was not. But what did we expect from a guy that old?

"What did he say to that?"

"He agreed. I think he had your needs more in mind than mine, though."

I shrugged. "I don't know. I haven't been feeling the need for modern technology lately. Staying *off* the Web is more my style these days."

Lucy pushed her laptop aside. "Have you been online at all in the last couple of weeks?"

I shook my head. It was best for my own sanity to stay incognito. I didn't want to read any more comments about how I'd brought my death on myself, how as a twenty-something-year-old woman, I should have known better than to endanger myself that way, that I was lucky Vlad had been there to save me. I'd seen it all, then shut it down. And honestly, my own self-worth had improved dramatically since. Odd how strangers' opinions could affect us.

"They... uh, they're calling you The Countess of Blood."

I winced. Of course they were. Ms. Rainn from The Vampire Lounge had been incredibly quick to tell everyone online her story about how she'd served the Count and the new Countess that night. She'd graciously left out the part about us necking in the booth, but people had latched onto my new nickname and run with it.

"Have you spoken to your mother recently?" Lucy asked.

Ugh, now there was a line of questioning I didn't want to answer. "Not since that first call. She's ignoring me."

Lucy's hand covered mine. "Give her time. Once she sees you're the same person, she'll reach out to you."

"She can't see that if she doesn't *let me* reach out

to her," I said.

"What about your dad?"

"Radio silence," I admitted. "Guess she hasn't told him yet. I don't know. And I don't have time to think about this. I have other more important concerns right now."

"Right. Like Petrik."

Yet another discussion I didn't want to have.

"Have you or Vlad heard from the reeve yet?"

"No. He's been eerily quiet about all this. I'm starting to wonder..."

"What?"

I met Lucy's gaze, then scraped my fangs across my bottom lip. I'd perfected the art of *not* biting myself, but that was one human tell I'd held onto. "I'm wondering if something happened to him. Vlad assures me not. That we'd know if the local reeve had gone missing. But two weeks is a long time not to hear anything, right?"

"Dunno. Guess it depends on how long it takes their queen to see him?"

"You'd think she'd make this a priority," I groused.

"Yeah. Her sire is going all bananas. That definitely seems like something a queen would wanna stamp out ASAP."

"From what Camilla's said, I'm not the first sign that he's been losing his marbles."

"Oh, even better. Let's just let a crazed, powerful vampire on the loose, hey? Wonder if our president knows about any of this. I can't imagine she would sign the treaty if she did."

"Let's forget about politics tonight," I said. "I'm sick to death of worrying about all this stuff. Tonight is supposed to be 'girls' night,' so what do you have planned?"

"Okay, okay." Lucy clapped her hands together and giggled. My eyes widened at the sound. I think the last time I'd heard her giggle was high school. "So I've been thinking."

"Oh, Lordt," I muttered. "What diabolical plans have you been concocting in that head of yours?"

"Hear me out first, 'kay?"

My eyes narrowed. "That depends."

"First, a pedicure." She scrambled off the bed and fished a foot spa out of the closet. "Since it's not safe for you to go out yet, this will have to do. I was thinking we could paint our nails, and if you're willing, I could give you some fresh highlights in your hair?"

"You know I hate pedicures," I growled.

"Yes, but you'll be doing all the work yourself!

No one touching your grody feet but you."

I mulled over that and finally consented. So long as no one else touched my feet, I could work with that.

Lucy brought her hands up to her mouth and bounced on her toes. "Then I was thinking... we record a vlog!"

Every bit of me shut right down. "No."

"Anna, hear me out—"

"No, Lucy."

Lucy sighed and threw her hands down. "Would you just listen? You're popular right now. Like, incredibly popular. All of your previous vlogs have millions of views now! You've made it big, baby. Just like you always wanted."

"Yeah, because of this!" I tapped my fangs.

"I know. So, let's use that to our advantage."

"Vlad said the queen has every vampire under a hush order right now."

Lucy waved a dismissive hand. "Who cares? The people want to hear from *you*. They're clamoring to get your take on everything."

"Lucy." I shook my head. This was a bad idea just waiting to happen.

"Look, I know you don't have a reflection anymore. But they'll still be able to see your clothes, right? So let's slap some massive sunglasses over those bloodshot eyes of yours, a hat to cover up that dire situation called your hair, wrap a scarf around your scarred neck, and boom, the Invisible Woman on camera."

I couldn't help but chuckle at the image she painted. "You've got to be kidding me."

"It could work! I think people would love it. And you'd be the first vampire on camera, the first to give an interview, the first to do *anything* modern. You could welcome vampires into the twenty-first century."

Her idea was engaging, but I knew it couldn't happen. At least, not right now. And I told her exactly that. "Petrik is literally chomping at the bit to kill me right now. I really don't need to give the queen *another* reason to hate me. I love your enthusiasm and the idea, but we can't, okay? Not right now, anyway. Let's wait until the dust has settled."

Lucy clucked her tongue, then slumped onto the bed next to me. "Yeah, I guess it wouldn't be smart to broadcast you to the world when there's some psycho out there gunning for you." She cast me an anxious glance. "What are you going to do about him?"

I glanced at the closed door, then leaned over

and started the movie before cranking the volume. The house was too full of sensitive ears to have this discussion without any sort of precaution.

Once the movie was blaring at full blast, I leaned into Lucy and whispered, "Easy. Kill him first."

"Anna—"

"No. I know what I promised you, but everything's different now. I'm not going to sit around like some daft heroine and wait for him to attack me. You know who does that?"

"Smart people?" she hissed.

"Cowards. I won't live my unlife in fear of this vampire. He wants to break me, kill me, whatever. Well, I say let's kill him first."

"And how do you plan to accomplish that?"

"Find his daytime resting place and light it on fire."

"What? How the hell do you think you can manage that?"

I eyed her with raised brows. Funny how quickly she clued in.

"Anna, no! Are you trying to get me killed?"

"You won't be in any danger," I assured her. "We're dead to the world during the day. You sneak in, set him on fire, and get out. Simple as that."

"There's nothing simple about your plan!" Lucy

expelled a heavy breath. "What does Vlad think about that?"

I folded my hands in my lap to keep from twisting my fingers. "Vlad doesn't know yet. But I plan on talking to him about it. I think we'll need his help. I don't intend to rush into anything or do something that puts you at risk. If he doesn't agree, we won't do it. Simple as that. But the question is, what do you think?"

Lucy eyed me, her mouth a grim slash. "A lot of this hinges on me."

"We'd help you as much as we could. We'll send in a team of humans—I don't know. I wouldn't ask if I didn't think you could handle it."

"And fire kills them? You?"

"Him, and yes. I'd prefer it if you kept the flames away from me, as an FYI."

Lucy gave a weak chuckle. "Okay, fine. I'll do it. But only cuz it's you, and I love you. And only if Count Fangerton agrees to help. We can't do this alone."

"Definitely." I slung an arm around Lucy's shoulders and grinned triumphantly when she didn't cringe away from me. We were getting there. One night at a time. Soon, it'd be me and my best friend against the world once more.

19

NEW ORLEANS WAS beautiful at night. The city skyline combined with the twinkling stars lent the world a magical ambience. I hadn't been able to experience much of NOLA since my dramatic foray into the vampire world, but Vlad seemed determined to fix that tonight. Which was why we now stood on the City Park docks, ready to board a cute gondola.

"Are you sure this is okay?" I took Vlad's extended hand and let him help me into the boat.

"It's a short ride, less than an hour. Hardly enough time for you to cause trouble."

"I dunno about that."

I took a seat in the passenger cabin and noted the fancy bucket with two miniature wine-shaped bottles of blood in it. My gaze flew to the gondolier, but he seemed entirely nonplussed about the whole thing. I guess when you lived in New Orleans, *real* vampires weren't exactly a startling revelation. It'd almost been a month since vampires had made their stunning debut. Plenty of time for people to adjust, I suppose.

"What if Petrik makes another appearance?" I asked.

Vlad settled into his own plush seat, then nodded to the gondolier, who started rowing. "I highly doubt Petrik will know to look for us on a boat in the middle of a lake."

"Trouble seems to follow me everywhere lately," I surmised, thinking back to Lucy's and my discussion. Before retiring to my coffin this morning, I'd dared to read the posts Lucy had mentioned. And sure enough, Rainn had taken it upon herself to announce to the *entire* online vampire community that I'd risen as a vampire and visited her place of work. Rainn had outed Vlad as my sire and had innocuously dubbed me The Countess of Blood. Welp, that name had stuck. I'd finally turned my phone off when my brother's text message came rolling in at a bright and early six a.m., accusing me of destroying the family name.

Best family ever. A mother who wouldn't take my calls—angry that I'd hung up on her—a father who hadn't even called to check up on me, and a brother who blamed me for everything. Made a girl realize who her true family was. And the Perishes weren't it.

"Yes, but you're worth the trouble." Vlad took my hand and lifted it to his mouth, brushing a light kiss across my knuckles. I'll admit that I had to clench my thighs. There was something about Vlad's gentlemanly, aristocratic demeanor that set my hormones aflame. But we were in public. And even though we were safe from photographers, I really didn't need our home boy gondolier here selling his experience with us to the tabloids. Especially a naughty experience. My reputation had taken enough of a hit as it was without adding "vampy slut" to the mix.

"Your life can't be wholly comprised of training," Vlad continued. "Everyone needs a break now and then to stop and smell the roses."

The roses, really? I nudged his shoulder. "Is this your way of telling me that *you* needed a break?"

Vlad cracked a rueful grin. "If I have to listen to any more of Eli's obnoxious complaints, I may tear his throat out myself just to shut him up."

I burst out laughing. "I think that's the most impolite thing I've ever heard you say."

"I do have my moments, I'm afraid," he said with a small, panty-melting wink. "We both desperately needed a respite. So I thought this might be a nice chance for us to spend a few minutes alone while enjoying some wonderful scenery, fresh air, and fresh blood."

"Fresh?"

He reached for the two bottles and handed one to me. "Businesses have been popping up all over the city, including those who wish to provide blood for us fangers, as they've started calling us."

Sigh. Yeah, I used to be one of them. Funny how I really didn't like the word now.

I cracked open the bottle, took a whiff, then moaned at the delicious scent. "Has anyone checked to make sure they aren't poisoned or something?"

Vlad shrugged. "Poison wouldn't harm us to begin with, so I don't believe anyone cares."

Fair point. "How are they getting the blood? I mean, I know The Vampire Lounge has humans employed to serve us on the spot, but how does this bottled stuff work?"

"Similarly to The Vampire Lounge, except these are ordered to go. I had one of my employees pick them up tonight and deliver it here for us to enjoy."

"No illegal stuff? Like people stealing humans and draining them into bottles for profit?"

Vlad gave a slow blink. "Your mind goes to some truly dark places."

"That's my job."

"Is it? I was led to believe you've had some doubts as to whether you should continue your vlog."

I lifted an eyebrow. "Eavesdropping on me and Lucy, are we? Hasn't anyone ever told you how rude that is?"

"If you didn't wish to be overheard, you shouldn't have had the conversation in the house."

I chuckled and nodded. That was why I'd cranked the volume up last night before discussing my *burning Petrik alive* idea. I hadn't wanted anyone else to overhear that particular part of the conversation.

"I honestly don't know what I want yet," I confessed. "My vlog was a part of my life—my human life. But I'm not human anymore."

"Perhaps not, but it's still a part of who you are."

This time, I was the one blinking. "Wait, you *want* me to continue my vlog?"

"While I don't approve of it right this moment, I

do believe you should continue with the things you love. Once this entire Petrik matter is handled and the queen has lifted the hush order, perhaps you can revisit the idea. I know you had a few ideas you wanted to explore, such as a channel for newborn vampires. I think that might be helpful—if I'm understanding this vlog concept."

"You're such an old fart," I teased.

Vlad grinned and leaned in. "Young enough to still teach you a thing or two."

I rolled my eyes playfully. "So, where are we going on this thing?"

"Absolutely nowhere." Vlad slid his arm around my waist and drew me flush against his side.

I couldn't help but rest my head against the swell of his chest and just listen to the sound of the local wildlife and the boat cutting through the water. I could hear the hustle and bustle of New Orleans, but I was learning to tune out the less important things and focus on what mattered. Like right now, I wanted to focus on the boat ride and Vlad. Nothing else.

"Hard for Petrik to find us if we're literally nowhere," I jested.

Vlad's arm tightened around me. "I just wanted a few minutes alone with you."

"Well, we're hardly alone." I pointed at the gondolier.

"He knows what he's doing. I paid him extra for the illusion of privacy."

I chuckled under my breath. Of course Vlad had gone that extra mile. He didn't seem the sort to half-ass anything. As a boyfriend, he was quite attentive.

Boyfriend? Huh. Was that what he was to me? We'd shared a few heated kisses with a definite desire for more, but did that mean we were "together?" Could someone even date Dracula? The concept seemed a tad laughable. The man had more years under his belt than most people did spare money. But what else could I call him? Boyfriend was legitimately the only applicable word I could think of. And it made me laugh aloud.

"What's so funny?"

"Nothing." I snickered. "Just a random thought I had."

"Oh?"

"I thought of you as my boyfriend. Funny, right?"

Vlad huffed. "I fail to see the humor in that."

"Because it's *you*. Dracula. I highly doubt anyone would describe you as a boyfriend."

"Hmm."

For a moment, I wondered if I'd offended him. I

glanced up and found his gaze locked in the distance and could practically hear the gears spinning.

"I suppose there isn't a better word," he mused. "We aren't lovers. Yet."

My whole body warmed at the thought. If we weren't in public right now, I'd rectify that issue. Immediately.

"But you mean far more to me than simply a 'girlfriend.'"

Ah, damn this man. He knew how to make a girl melt.

"We aren't married, so I can't address you as my wife."

Ignoring the terrified implosion in my head at the sound of the word "wife," I meandered a wee bit off topic. "You were married once though, weren't you?"

"A very long time ago. Before I even knew vampires existed, let alone became one."

"Mina?" I whispered. "Right? That was her name?"

"I see Camilla has been running her mouth."

I shrugged. "She wanted to test me, I think."

"Yes, she would. That woman is infamous for sticking her nose where it's unwelcome. Such as my private life."

"If it bothers you to speak of Mina, we don't—"

"Why would it bother me?" Vlad repositioned himself so I could straighten and meet his gaze.

"She was your wife, and she died—"

"A long, long time ago. Believe me, I'm not still pining for her. This is not a fresh injury. Nor do I miss her. Not anymore. I did once, of course. She was my wife, and I loved her dearly. But her memory hardly stands in the way of me finding love with someone new."

I was *so* not ready to be dropping the L-word. So I rushed onward, completely ignoring that particular line of discussion. Returning to the original discussion seemed safer. "I suppose we could simply say we're dating."

"Dating." Vlad's fangs peeked out when he laughed. "How modern."

"I can only imagine the tabloids now. Who's Dating Dracula Now?" I snorted with laughter. "Then they can call us The Count and Countess of Blood."

"The what?"

"Oh." I waved a dismissive hand. "That's what they've dubbed me online, thanks to Rainn. The Countess of Blood."

Vlad groaned. "That does not paint an inviting image."

"Yeah, I'm not a fan of it either."

He slid his arm around my back once more and tucked me close before laying a gentle kiss against the top of my head. "Perhaps we don't need to assign a word to us."

"Is there not some fancy vampiric term?"

"We were once human, so we tend to use the same words. But for those in our situation, most would call themselves mates."

My brain jumped back to the information I'd read from the council. How vampire mates were rare and the bond unbreakable. That was some pretty heavy stuff.

"The term runs deeper than partners and spouses," Vlad continued. "A mate is someone you are destined to meet and fall in love with. You spend your eternal lives together."

Ah, stupid destiny again. Okay, this conversation was taking a path that scared the bejesus outta me. A lot of four-letter words were being thrown around. And if I couldn't handle the ones that started with L and W, what the heck made him think I could handle this new M-one?

"You dreamed about me." My voice trembled as I recalled how he'd mentioned we were destined to meet. I cleared my throat. "Does that mean we are, uh, mated? Mates? However that word is used."

Vlad chuckled. "Don't have an embolism on me now."

Nervous laughter rose from my throat. "Can vampires even have those?"

"Of course not." He sighed and shifted his weight, throwing the boat a little off-kilter. "Are you sure you want to have this discussion?"

"Nope. Not in the least. But I mean, don't I *need* to have it? To be aware of what's going on? Instead of blindly trudging through the swamps?"

"It's merely a word, Anna. It means two who are destined to be together. Nothing except death will part them."

Well, when he put it like that, I definitely got some warm, tingly feelings. But then I remembered that was the exact same thing people said in their marriage vows—'til death do us part and all that nonsense.

"Who decides all this? Who's pulling the strings on the other end?"

Vlad raised a brow. "Destiny. Fate. Choose whichever word you prefer."

"But *who* is that?"

He laughed. "I don't have an answer for that. I imagine few would."

"You understand how mind-boggling this is for me, right? For cripes' sake, I'm twenty-four. And you're sitting here telling me that I'm your mate and destined to be with you for the rest of our undying lives."

"I never said that. You inferred."

"Oh, don't get cute," I groused.

"Does knowing you're my mate frighten you?" he asked.

"Hell yes." I canted my head to the side. "And also, no. It's a terrifying concept but also reassuring. My head is a very confusing place to be."

Vlad chuckled, then leaned in and kissed me. I wanted to pull back and tell him how unfair that was, using his wicked mouth to distract and disarm me. But that would mean I had to stop kissing him, and that seemed like a crime. The man was a pro with his tongue, and it would be shameful to ignore his talents.

With a soft moan, I practically climbed into his lap and melted against him. There was something about Vlad that called to me like a moth to a flame. His heat and passion stoked the embers of my own inner fire, whipping it into an inferno that only he could extinguish—with his dick, if that wasn't clear.

"Anna," Vlad murmured. "Not here."

"I know." I sighed and leaned back, ignoring the gondolier's bemused expression. "Sorry. Just getting a tad impatient."

"As am I." Vlad touched his forehead to mine and breathed me in. "Soon, it'll just be the two of us, and we can enjoy each other's body without anyone listening in."

I shuddered. Yeah, the thought of his four vampire buddies listening to us during our first time did not inspire romantical thoughts. At least Lucy's hearing was as dull as a human's, but we wouldn't be so lucky with the others.

"It's getting a bit hard," I admitted.

"Mm." Vlad nipped my earlobe, then whispered, "It is."

It took a few seconds for me to realize his joke, and when I did, I burst out laughing and slid off his lap.

"Feel better?" he asked.

"Yeah, that mouth of yours has magical powers. Makes me forget everything else that's going on around us."

"I did notice that."

"Oh, shut up." I laughed. "Don't make me destroy that ego of yours."

Vlad clasped my hand and tucked it against his chest. He then gestured toward the gondolier, who started rowing us back toward the docks.

"We should return," Vlad said. "I imagine Camilla is eager to resume your training. She's quite pleased with your progress, by the way."

I scoffed. "Thank goodness all it takes to heal me is a little blood. Otherwise, I'd be dead right now."

Darkness shuttered his face. "Yes, there are certain upsides to vampirism."

We fell into a comfortable silence, with me resting against Vlad's side and his fingers idly playing with mine. When we arrived at the docks, he slipped the gondolier a tip, then helped me disembark.

"As important as I know your training is, I wish we didn't have to return tonight. There are so many other things I long to be doing with you right now."

"You and me both, big guy," I told him. "But really, just the *one* thing." When he raised his brows, I wiggled mine, and said, "Like the horizontal tango, doing the nasty, shag like the devil, hump our brains out."

I swear he blushed. And I'd never seen anything

more endearing than Dracula blushing in the streetlights.

"The things you say." He sounded almost impressed by my urban lingo.

I stretched up and brushed my mouth against his. "You love it."

"Mm. Indeed."

I refrained from teasing him about his stilted *indeed* and, instead, led the way back to his town car. I still had a long night of being brutalized to look forward to, after all.

THERE WAS no warm welcome awaiting us when we returned to Vlad's home. No happy greetings, no friendly nods. Instead, it was like a grim funeral. Everyone stood gathered in his entryway, their faces as bleak as a dark winter night.

"Oh, this is encouraging," I muttered as I slowly stepped inside.

Camilla and Rebecca stood in the front with Eli and Breccan in the back. And in the center stood Reeve John Johnson. Even Lucy hovered on the stairs, her anxious expression telling enough. Something bad had happened.

You know, I was getting a little tired of this. Becoming a vampire had done nothing but introduce a hell of a lot of melodrama into my life. There always seemed to be one catastrophe after another. Couldn't we have one night of peace? One night that didn't end with me broken and bleeding on the floor or worrying about my incredibly long future?

"Alright." I kicked off my shoes and nudged them up alongside the wall. I was the only one who did this. Everyone else wore their shoes inside, but there was something about socked feet on linoleum, or marble in this case, that I just loved. "Let's have it. What happened?"

"John." Vlad stepped forward and greeted the reeve with a polite nod. "I've been waiting to hear from you. It's been a while."

"Let's talk in your office," John said by way of greeting. "I brought some files to share with you."

Joy of joys.

Vlad's eyes narrowed on the reeve, but eventually he nodded and gestured everyone onward. Seemed this was to be a group affair then.

I hung back and waited for Lucy. Once the vampires had left the room, she skittered down the stairs and clutched my hand.

"What's going on?" I whispered.

"I don't know. He arrived about half an hour ago. And since then, everyone's been incredibly tense.

Especially Camilla. Did you have fun with Vlad at least?"

I nodded. "It was nice to get out of the house for a bit. I did learn one interesting thing."

"Oh yeah? What's that?"

"Apparently, I'm Vlad's mate." I didn't go into further detail.

Lucy stared at me like I'd lost my mind, before finally hissing, "What does that mean?"

"I have no idea," I said, laughing. "Something about how we're destined to be together. Soulmates type thing."

She reared back from me, eyes wide with shock. "Seriously?"

"I'm still figuring this stuff out myself. Shall we join the others? See what has John Johnson's panties all in a twist?"

Lucy bit her lip. "I mean, we won't learn anything out here."

"You are correct, madam," I teased, then led her into Vlad's den.

All six vampires had spread out, giving us a false sense of security as we entered. I felt for Lucy. It had to be hard being surrounded by a group of blood drinkers. Thankfully, everyone here had mastered their appetites, and I was even more grateful that I could now be included in that list. I no longer lost my mind when I caught the scent of a nearby human.

"You have the floor, John," Vlad said. He sat in his office chair with the air of a noble, his gaze intent on the sheriff.

A sheriff who looked quite perturbed.

"Let me start from two weeks ago." He rubbed his face, as though attempting to wake himself. Come to think of it, he looked downright exhausted. Harried, even. A word I'd learned from Vlad. "First, I approached Queen Genevieve with Anna's grievance. I detailed how Petrik abducted her from Fallen and attempted to murder her in the alley. I explained how Drac saved her, thereby saving the queen the hassle of explaining to the human president why one of his Americans had been murdered by a vampire no less than one week after the signing of the peace treaty."

We all nodded. We knew the story. Intimately.

John eyed each of us, then carded a hand through his hair. "The queen didn't care."

"Excuse me?" Vlad's voice had deepened with unmitigated anger. He rose from his seat, his body practically vibrating with rage. "The queen didn't care?"

I released Lucy's hand and slowly made my way

to Vlad's side, quickly taking his hand. His fingers clenched mine almost painfully, but I didn't ask him to let up.

John sighed, and his body practically deflated, as though he himself had given up. "I don't know what to tell you, Drac. She was entirely unfazed by the situation. Said Petrik was within his rights to feed on whoever he wanted."

"But that's against the law!" Lucy suddenly shouted from the back of the room.

Every vampire turned toward her, and she cringed backward, clearly regretting her outburst.

"She's right." I drew their attention back to me. Except, my voice was oddly calm. Almost frighteningly so. "It *is* against the law."

"How can Genevieve not care?" Rebecca demanded. She took a spin around the room, her face knotted with concern. "We are her people. Anna is now one of hers. She signed a peace treaty with the president and agreed to outlaw all vampires who feed on nonconsenting humans. She is literally breaking her own treaty."

"Petrik has always held a special place in the queen's heart," Eli grumbled. "It's why I didn't care for this plan to begin with."

"Yeah, yeah, shut up," Camilla snapped. "Like you're so smart."

When Eli opened his mouth to retort, Vlad straightened and glared at them both. Without uttering a single word, the two fell into an uncomfortable silence. I definitely needed to learn that trick. But right now, I was more focused on the developing situation.

"So, Genevieve essentially pardoned him," I mused aloud. "He's been given free rein to do as he pleases."

"This is where it gets worse." John stalked over to Vlad's desk and tapped a pile of folders. "These are files I found on other victims."

"Other victims?" I released Vlad's hand and approached the precariously teetering stack. "What other victims?"

John swallowed, then met my gaze. "Petrik's victims. It took a bit to track them all down, which is what took me so long to report back here. I had to check with the different morgues and request photos so I could measure the bite radius and confirm they were his kills."

"How many?" I whispered.

John sighed. "Thirty-four that I've found so far."

The room fell deathly silent, and I felt the

world start closing in on me. My vision tunneled on the folder, and I reached out to flip the first one open.

"I wouldn't recommend that," John said.

But I ignored him. Because of course I did. Who wouldn't?

I lifted the file with trembling hands and leafed through the papers. "Blonde, dark eyes, average build, twenty-three years old." I dropped that file and moved on to the next. "Blonde, dark eyes, average build, twenty-five years old." Then the next. And the next. And the next. Until I'd gone through the entire pile. Tears burned my eyes, but I *still* refused to let them fall. Instead, I glanced at Vlad. "They all match my description."

"Or rather, you match theirs," John said. "You didn't start this. You ended it."

"What do you mean?" I whispered.

"You were his last, or rather, his latest victim."

I blinked away the tears. Now wasn't the time. "He hasn't killed anyone else since me?"

"Not yet."

"Why? What's he waiting for?"

"You," Lucy murmured from her spot against the bookcase.

I turned to face her. I must have looked as

confused as I felt, because she continued without anyone asking her to.

"You survived, in a manner of speaking. All the other women are dead?"

John nodded.

Lucy's face broke, but she swallowed and pressed on. "It sounds like this Petrik is a bit of a serial killer. But you're the one victim who got away. You survived. What did he say to you when you ran into him at The Vampire Lounge?"

"That he would have fun breaking me," I whispered.

Lucy quickly closed the distance between us and took my hands. "He hasn't killed anyone else yet, because he hasn't *finished* with you. By surviving, you upped the ante. Made the game more exciting for him."

"And the queen doesn't care that this monster is roaming the streets?" I asked.

"Genevieve and Petrik have a long history." Vlad rested a hand on my shoulder. "We haven't had time to get into Genevieve's history yet. But you should know, she was born with a different name. One I'm sure you'll recognize."

Lucy and I shared a concerned frown.

"Genevieve's birth name was Maria Antonia, better known as Marie—"

"Antoinette," I whispered. "What? How? But she...."

"Petrik saved her from execution. The night before her scheduled death, he replaced her with a prostitute named Nicole who looked eerily similar to Marie. The world believed Marie was beheaded, when in truth..."

"Nicole died in her stead, and Marie was turned into a vampire," I surmised, utterly stunned by this revelation.

"The queen is intimately fond of Petrik. Even though she's found herself a vampire husband, she and Petrik have been known to indulge in each other over the centuries."

"Holy shit... Marie Antoinette is the vampire queen?" I just couldn't wrap my head around that. Talk about history coming to life.

"You mustn't ever mention that name in her presence," Vlad urged. "That name is dead to her. She had to choose a new one, because her former name is as infamous as mine."

I nodded, completely understanding. It wasn't like she could rule the vampires while using a name renowned for inciting the French Revolution.

"Back to the problem at hand," John said. "The queen has denied Anna's grievance and refused to punish Petrik. Nor will she publicly admit to his crimes."

"Once a bad queen, always a bad queen," I mumbled.

"Talk like that will get you killed," Eli warned.

I waved off his complaints yet again. I didn't have time for his whining. "Maybe Petrik has lost interest? It's been two weeks without any word from him, and I haven't seen him."

"You haven't seen him, because you've been locked up here training with Camilla," Lucy commented.

"She's right," Rebecca chimed in. "I've had a few of my own allies keeping an eye out for him in town, and Petrik's been spotted every single night."

"He lives here. Of course he's been spotted."

Camilla gave me a reproaching look. "My sweet summer child, Petrik doesn't live in New Orleans."

"Then why is he even in town?" Then it clicked. "The blood orgy. He was partaking in it that night, wasn't he?"

"Vampires come from all over for those events. They travel clear across the world for them, since they're only permitted in certain locations," Camilla said.

"Just my luck to stumble across a serial killer with a penchant for blondes."

Vlad's hand came to rest at the small of my back, and I took comfort in his touch. "I told you, this was all preordained."

"Meaning I was destined to run into Petrik that night."

"Fate will always find a way. It isn't always pleasant, but nothing will keep it from happening."

I pressed the heels of my hands against my eyes and groaned. I hated this. All of it. It felt like I had zero control over my life. For fifty years, Vlad had known we would find each other. And then fate, like a bitch, threw me into Petrik's path and ensured Vlad was nearby to save me. Had I no choices in life? Was it all dictated by some higher being who may or may not even exist? It was too much to wrap my brain around and made me feel small and inconsequential.

"Do the human authorities know about the other victims? That they're vampire kills?"

John shook his head. "We know how to cover something like this up. And it's incredibly important that it remains that way right now. We can't do anything that might disrupt Genevieve's negotiations with the president."

"So, what do we do?" I asked, needing to focus on something other than the unraveling of my life. "I refuse to stand around and wait for Petrik to make his move."

"Then we don't," Lucy said, gripping my hands tighter. "Tell them."

"Tell us what?" Vlad immediately demanded.

When I didn't speak up, Lucy repositioned her grip and squeezed, offering me silent encouragement. She was right. I needed to tell Vlad my plan. But it needed to be in private. I hadn't intended on discussing Petrik's *murder* in front of five other vamps, one of which was the local reeve.

I turned to Vlad and attempted to convey the need for privacy through some form of mental communication neither of us possessed. I guess I was just hoping he would read my discomfort and understand what I needed. Silly, right?

Well, color me surprised when Vlad cleared his throat and asked his vampire companions to leave.

Huh. Maybe there was something to this mate craziness. We couldn't speak telepathically, but he certainly knew how to read my facial nuances and mood.

Vlad crossed the room and flicked on a record player, which, if the mood weren't so grim, would have had me laughing. Of course he had a record player. The man didn't own anything modern.

Jazz music filled the room, loud enough to hopefully keep anyone from listening into my murderous scheme. Ugh. This wasn't going to be easy.

I grimaced, then took his seat and hung my head in my hands. How the hell was I going to approach this topic with him? *Oh hey, I thought maybe we'd commit a little murder? Kill him before he kills me?* That would go over about as well as a fart in church.

"I know what you're thinking," Vlad said.

"Doubtful."

"I was there, remember? I heard the threats you cast at Petrik. Only one made sense."

"And let me guess—you think it's a stupid idea."

"I think it's a reckless, dangerous idea."

"That's me," I mumbled. "The reckless one. The one who doesn't think things through. Who stumbles into a vamp club, only to find herself on the business end of a serial killer's fangs. What are the chances? And don't talk to me about fate and destiny. I've had about as much of that as I can take."

"I can't pretend any of this is easy," Vlad said, his voice softening as he crouched in front of me.

I lifted my head and found myself caught by his somber gaze. "So, what do we do then? If burning him alive isn't an option?"

"I never said it wasn't an option."

My eyes widened. "What?"

"I said you had one idea that made sense. Setting him aflame while he is trapped in his coffin is likely the only idea that would work. He's far too old for either of us to attack directly. Perhaps even too old for all of us to handle together."

I clutched Vlad's hands. "You agree to this? You want to help me burn Petrik? Kill him before he can get his hands on me?"

"If I must choose between you and Petrik, I choose you. Always. Forever."

My undead heart shivered with affection. "Even if that means angering the queen?"

Vlad's steadfast gaze never wavered. With a smile, he leaned in and kissed me. "What is it you Americans say? Duh?"

This time, I lost the battle, and the tears spilled over. But at least they were happy ones, and I couldn't stop them even if I tried.

21

Vᴌᴀᴅ ʀᴇᴀᴄʜᴇᴅ ʙᴇʜɪɴᴅ ʜɪᴍ, snatched a tissue off his desk, then returned to quickly wipe my cheeks. I gave a watery laugh and sniffled. I must have looked quite the sight. One of those sad clowns with red makeup running down their cheeks.

Once the waterworks finished, I clutched Vlad's hand in mine and squeezed. I couldn't believe my luck to have found someone like him. He was nothing like the fictional Dracula I'd grown up reading about. The man didn't possess a single cruel bone in his body. I realized in that moment I didn't care that fate had forced us together—I wanted him in my life.

I also wanted him in a dirtier, schmexier way, but

alas, we had evil plans to machinate and a villainous vampire to kill.

"So, how do we do this?" Lucy asked, drawing my attention back to the matter at hand. "Does anyone even know where Petrik lives?"

"Camilla has a contact who's been keeping an eye on him. I believe she knows his resting location."

Hmm. I wasn't sure how I felt about bringing the others into my plan. When plotting and scheming nefarious acts, less was certainly best. Spread the word too far, and wham-o! No longer a sneak attack.

"What about the vampire registry?" I asked. "Could we learn his location that way?"

Vlad shook his head. "When John checked, Petrik still had his European address listed."

"Great. And I don't suppose there's any other way of finding his local address?"

Lucy gave a haughty laugh. "Not unless he uses the internet so we can track his IP address."

"You've seen too many movies, my friend," I teased.

"Well, sorry, Little Miss Smarty-Pants. It's not like I go around planning murders in my spare time."

I brought a finger to my lip but still chuckled. "All right. Then we ask Camilla. Maybe make it sound more like we're hoping to talk to him to resolve things peacefully."

"Because that's believable," Lucy grumbled.

"Girl!" I threw Lucy some shade. "Can I go two minutes without comments from the peanut gallery?"

"I'd like to say yes, but...."

"Yeah, chances are slim."

When I glanced at Vlad, I found him chuckling softly into his hand. "You two are quite the interesting pair. Have you ever...?" He flicked his finger back and forth between us.

"Ever...?" I let the word hang like he did.

"Had naked sleepovers?" Lucy chimed in.

"Lucy!" I scolded.

"What? We both know that's what he's asking!"

"You're incorrigible, seriously."

"I learned from the best, sweetie. The best meaning you, in case you didn't piece that together."

"Yeah, I did," I snapped.

"Ah, good. Because we all know you're not the smartest tool in the shed."

"Sharpest!" I bit out, my cheeks flaming. Lucy knew how much I hated when she mixed up her idioms.

"I know, but I wanted to really make sure you got it." She tapped her head.

I unleashed a playful growl. "Keep it up, Juicy Lucy, and I'll literally bite you."

"Oh, you did *not* just go there, Anna Banana."

"If we could return to the topic at hand?" Vlad interjected.

I threw Lucy a final glare before exhaling. "Right. What were we talking about again?"

Vlad pushed to his feet and clasped his hands behind his back. He strode toward his desk, then opened the top drawer and pulled out what looked like a cellphone.

"Ohmigosh." I practically tripped over my words, then my feet, when I darted to his side. "You *do* have a phone! I didn't think that was possible."

"I'm not completely out of touch with modern technology."

"Says the guy using a record player."

"I prefer the sound. It's deeper. Less synthesized."

And also a tad grating on the ears, but who was I to judge his musical preferences? I watched his fingers fly across the keyboard as he—le gasp—texted Camilla, asking her to join us in his war room, I mean office. Color me surprised. The man knew how to text. Why the hell did I find that so hot? Ugh. I definitely had some problems.

It only took a few moments for Camilla to push open the door and stride in. She cast a disparaging glance at the record player, then closed the door behind her. "You summoned?"

I snickered. I couldn't imagine anyone summoning Camilla or ordering her to do anything. She certainly was her own... vampiress? Ooh, I liked that. Maybe that was the word I'd use from now on.

"If you wouldn't mind, could you find Petrik's address for me, please."

Camilla didn't even bat an eye. She simply pulled out her phone, typed out yet another message, then glanced up at Vlad. "Planning to go a-murdering, are we?"

"What?" I choked. "No! That would be illegal, wouldn't it? We're just going to talk to him."

"Sweetie, please." Camilla's laughter rang through the room. "No one goes to *talk* to Petrik. And technically, we vampires don't abide by a set of laws. The queen's rule is absolute. If she determines you've done something reprehensible, she calls for your death. It's as simple as that. Since most don't wish to be hunted down by every single vampire known to her, they behave themselves."

"That's insane," Lucy said. "Your society is fucked up."

"A conversation for another time," Vlad commented. "The address?"

Camilla stole a peek at her phone, then read out his location. If my memory and knowledge of New Orleans and the surrounding area served me right, Petrik lived about an hour away from us.

"So, what's the plan, boys and girls?" Camilla demanded. She crossed her arms over her chest and stared each of us down. "Attack en force?"

"I appreciate the offer and your loyalty, Camilla, but no. Your part in this is done."

"The hell it is." She closed the distance between us and slung an arm around my shoulders. I was tall. Camilla was taller. Unnerving to say the least. I was used to being the most vertically blessed woman in the room, but she towered over me. "Our girl is in danger. I'm here to help."

"Our?" Vlad rumbled. "There is no 'our' here, Camilla. I will not share Anna, not even with you."

"Share? Whoa." I held my hands up. "Nobody is sharing anything."

"Precisely." Vlad returned his phone to his desk drawer, then faced us, his gaze locked on Camilla.

"Can't blame me for trying." She snickered, then

released me and practically danced over to Lucy. "What about you, sweetie. You digging this?"

Lucy's eyes grew comically wide. "Um, I prefer to drive stick."

Camilla threw her head back and laughed. "You and me both, sister. But sometimes it's nice to enjoy the fairer sex."

For one brief second, I thought I caught a whiff of intrigue from Lucy, but she shook her head and took a step back from Camilla.

"No fun." Camilla sighed. "I'm still here to help, though. I won't abandon you or yours in a time of need, Vlad."

"You know what this means, right? If Queen Genevieve ever learns that you were involved...."

"I know. She'll hunt us all down like the dogs we are."

Fear tweaked my nerves. "No, we should think of a different plan then. Something that doesn't paint a target on your backs."

Vlad took my hand and pulled me up against him. "Petrik won't stop until you're dead. You saw the files as well as I. His victims are numerous. And if the queen refuses to see the truth, then we must deal with it. Her treaty with the president depends on *all* vampires obeying the word of this new law."

"But you guys just said vampires don't have laws."

"Times are changing. We do as our queen orders. Most of us, anyway. She has ordered a peace treaty with the humans, and Petrik has already disobeyed. Our queen is blinded by her affections for him. So, we must step up and rid the world of him."

"Gee, Drac, you almost sound altruistic," Camilla teased. "And here I thought you were just doing this for a hot piece of ass."

"Camilla," Vlad growled, his chest vibrating against me.

She waved a dismissive hand, then sat in the only free chair in the room. "If you guys are serious about this, then we need to establish a plan. One that's well thought out. I assume, since little miss human is here, that your plan is for her to set Petrik's house on fire?"

Vlad nodded.

My stomach twisted. This was my idea, but I hated the thought of putting Lucy's life at risk.

"Then we need a solid plan," Camilla continued. "Taking Petrik's age in consideration, he likely rises before dusk. How early, I can't say. But I think it's best to assume he'll be awake by late afternoon."

"Then whatever we do, it has to be before that."

"Midday is best," Vlad offered. "Based on my

own sleep habits, it seems safe to assume that he can also remain conscious longer after sunrise too. The sun currently rises around six-thirty in the morning. To keep Lucy as safe as possible, I would suggest between eleven and one, when the sun is at its zenith."

"Oh, sure. Just go set a house on fire in the middle of the freaking day," Lucy grumbled. "It's not like I'll have other humans or police to worry about."

"You can't set his house on fire from the outside," Camilla said. "We must be smarter than that. Simply setting his place ablaze risks him surviving. Fire is a definitive way to kill us, but what if the fire doesn't reach his coffin before the authorities arrive and put out the flames? You will need to enter his house and start with the coffin."

"You're freaking kidding me, right?" Lucy shot the three of us a terrified stare. "You want me to enter Petrik's house, alone, and set his coffin on fire, then escape before I, myself, burn to death?"

"And what about servants?" I asked. "This place, as an example, is never quiet. Vlad has a human harem."

"Petrik doesn't," Camilla informed us. "I've been inquiring about his living arrangements since we put him under surveillance. It seems our boy prefers hunting for his meal."

"Evidenced by my neck," I groused.

Camilla inclined her head. "If my information is accurate, he lives alone, and much like us, his coffin is kept in the boarded-up attic. He leaves upon waking to track down a meal, then spends the rest of the night at The Vampire Lounge or getting his jollies off at Fallen."

I shuddered. That was one night club I'd never go back to.

"So, if Lucy can sneak into his place, she could, in theory, be able to open his coffin, set him on fire, and escape before the flames spread."

"That would be the ideal plan." Camilla rose and stretched out her shoulders. "Things rarely go as planned, though."

"Then what do you suggest?" Vlad asked.

"I don't believe Lucy should go alone."

"Agreed." Vlad's arms tightened around my waist. "Who do you have in mind?"

"Now, hear me out before saying no."

"Oh, I look forward to this."

"I think it'd be wise to send her in with Samuel."

I felt Vlad tense even before the stern "No" left his lips.

Camilla spun in the chair and glared at Vlad, her arms once again crossed over her chest. A power pose, if ever I saw one. She clucked her tongue and rolled her eyes. "You and I both know that Lucy will need some muscle in there. But more than that, Samuel will help her find Petrik's coffin faster. And he'll be able to help steer her clear of any human authorities."

"I'm sorry." I lifted my hand. "Who's Samuel?"

Vlad cursed under his breath, and I startled. It was the first time I'd heard him swear.

"Samuel is the brother to one of *my* harem members," Camilla told me. "Dear ole Drac here doesn't like him, because he's a—"

"His nature has nothing to do with why I dislike him," Vlad snapped.

I stepped out of Vlad's embrace and tiptoed toward Lucy. If a fight was about to break out, I really wanted nothing to do with it. Nor did I want to be near either of them when the shit hit the fan.

"Vlad, you need to get over this—"

"He *urinated* on my coffin, Camilla!"

I bit back a sudden laugh. "I'm sorry, he what?"

Camilla sighed. "What do you expect? He's a—"

"I expect your guests to be better trained than that."

"Better trained? He's not a damn house dog!"

Vlad held up his hands as though to say *well*? "It wasn't just my coffin, Camilla. He also relieved himself in Harold's quarters. Not to mention his hair. It took the cleaners months to get it all up. He sheds more than any mutt I've ever met."

"He was younger then, Vlad. Come on. You can't hold those transgressions against him."

"Can't I?"

I shot Lucy a startled glance. "Do you think we're talking about an actual dog here?"

"I have *absolutely* no idea, but I'm freaking riveted right now. Want to take bets?"

"Pomeranian," I said. "Twenty bucks."

"No way. Not if he's shedding that much. My money's on Bernese Mountain Dog."

Vlad unleashed a glare on us, and I pantomimed zipping my lips. No need to anger my sweet Count any more than necessary.

"Look, you won't even know he's here. He'll meet Lucy during the day, and they'll leave together for Petrik's."

"He's coming to me?" Lucy whispered. "Must be well-trained. Wonder if I'll need a leash."

"Dunno. Maybe a muzzle, just to be safe?"

"For crying out loud, he's not a dog!" Camilla

barked. "Samuel is a werewolf. And Drac here is a little... prejudiced against the shifter-kind."

"Not even close," Vlad muttered. "Just him."

I couldn't say I blamed him. I couldn't imagine befriending someone who'd peed on my coffin. I burst out laughing the second a new thought crossed my mind. "He was marking his territory."

"What?" Lucy asked.

"He's a werewolf. In a vampire house. He was marking his territory."

Vlad's stony expression darkened. Apparently, he didn't see the humor like I did.

I cleared my throat and wiped the smile from my face. Guess this was all a sensitive topic for Vlad. "Honestly, I would prefer someone go with Lucy. And who better than a werewolf? I assume he's preternaturally strong like us? And quick? He does more than pee and shed hair, right?"

Lucy pressed her lips together to keep from laughing.

"Yes," Camilla said, clearly exasperated with our antics. "He'll keep your darling best friend safe and help her handle the job."

"Then I'm all for it." I commented, unleashing upon Vlad what my mother had always called "those darn puppy eyes."

It seemed he wasn't immune to them either. He worked out his jaw, then grumbled a harsh, "Fine. Take the damn werewolf with you. But don't blame me if he starts humping Lucy's leg."

I lost the battle and started laughing. "Could you imagine? Lucy trying to beat him off with a rolled-up newspaper!"

"Hey! Different expression, please." Though, even Lucy was laughing. "I'm not beating anybody off with anything. Especially not some wolfman."

"Werewolf," Camilla corrected.

"What's the difference?" Lucy asked.

"Absolutely nothing." Vlad shook his head. "When should we do this?"

I flicked a glance between Camilla and Lucy. Really, the plan hinged on the two of them. One had to fetch this Samuel—and yes, I giggled at the word fetch—and the other had to start the fire.

"Immediately," Camilla said. "The sooner, the better. The last thing we need is for Petrik to catch wind of our plan somehow."

"Agreed. This afternoon." Vlad' s jaw tightened. "Is that enough time to send for Samuel?"

"Plenty."

"Wait, so soon?" Lucy whispered. "I mean...

that's *soon*, guys. I've never murdered someone before, you know? Can't I have a few days?"

Camilla, Vlad, and I all shared a glance. This entire plan hinged on Lucy. I suppose we could just send in Samuel, but I didn't like the idea of resting my future on a stranger's shoulders. Especially one known for peeing on vampire coffins. Still, I wouldn't force Lucy to do anything she wasn't comfortable with.

"We can wait a few days," Camilla hedged. "But the risk factor increases."

"No one here is going to go blabbing about our plan, right?"

"Right. But he could leave town. He could murder another woman. He could somehow learn about our plan. There are many uncontrollable factors at play."

Lucy took a deep breath, then bent in half and rested her head against her knees. I could hear her pulse thrumming away like a hummingbird's. I'd seen this once before, when she'd tried to ask her crush to prom. Poor thing nearly had a panic attack right in the middle of the hallway. Only my quick thinking had saved her from reliving that embarrassing moment for the rest of her life.

I crossed the room and took her hands, softly

telling her to count to three. Lucy wasn't the impulsive one in our relationship, so this had to be difficult for her. Everything had to be planned with the utmost care before she willingly jumped into anything.

"We can take some time—"

"No," she rasped. "Camilla is right. The longer we wait, the greater the risk that Petrik finds out. She's right. We need to strike while the iron is hot. We know where he's staying in the city."

"Luce, you don't need to do this—"

"Who else will?" She gripped my hands so hard. "The wolfman? Do you trust him?"

I didn't answer. Her question was rhetorical anyway.

"I can do this." She sucked in a shuddering breath and rose to her full height. "I won't be alone, right?"

"Right."

"And this will save your life?"

"You are correct, my lady."

A tiny grin cracked through her panicked exterior, exactly as I'd hoped. "Then let's do this."

"You're sure?"

She blew out a trembling breath. "Not even

remotely. Think I can handle a thousand-year-old vampire?"

"Girl, you can handle anything."

"Okay. Summon the wolfman."

"Samuel," Camilla said, sighing.

"Him too."

"Thank you, Lucy," Vlad said. "I wish there was more I could do, but alas, we vampires are all slaves to the sun."

"I get it. I'd do anything for my sista here, and she knows it. But don't think I'm not gonna be calling in a million favors once this is finished."

I chuckled. "A million and one, just cuz I love you."

Camilla and Vlad excused themselves to finalize the plan and call the wolfman. Vlad brushed a light kiss against my cheek, patted Lucy's shoulder, then left.

Once alone, Lucy and I dissolved into nervous giggles.

"The wolfman? Seriously?" Lucy stage-whispered.

"You're not even a dog person at the best of times."

"I like dogs," she said with a shrug. "Just not enough

to own one. Or care for one. They're so much work. Plus, I'm allergic, so that sorta puts a damper on the whole cute, loveable part. It's hard to like something when you're practically dying whenever you get near one."

I bit my lip to keep from laughing. I'd seen Lucy's allergic reactions to dogs, and it wasn't pretty. Gasping, coughing, sneezing, hives... the whole kit and caboodle. Hopefully, this Samuel didn't set her off. I couldn't imagine how difficult it would be to set Petrik on fire while snotting and weeping all over herself. But what a sight.

I choked down a laugh, the sound coming out more like a snort. "This is a disaster waiting to happen."

"Tell me about it." She groaned and palmed her face. "It's a million and *two* favors now."

Slinging my arm over her shoulder, I pulled her into my chest and ruffled her hair. "Girl, you do this for me, and you can have as many favors as you want."

"I'm gonna hold you to that."

22

W‍ITH TWO HOURS UNTIL BEDTIME, my energy was
waning. I hadn't noticed it when I first woke as a
vampire, but I was keenly aware of it now. An
awareness I possessed that told me the sun was on
the rise. It was like I possessed this internal clock
tasked with reminding me every few minutes that my
daily death approached.

Such a strange feeling.

Thankfully, the rest of the night had gone by
peacefully enough. Lucy had gone to bed around
two a.m., determined to get a good night's sleep
before she went a-murdering in the morning.
Camilla had gone to fetch Samuel. Eli was off
sulking in his room or something—honestly, I didn't

care what he was doing. Vlad had retreated to his office. Rebecca was reading in the sitting room. And Breccan... well, he was off engaging in a little hanky-panky with one of the harem members.

And boy, was I glad Vlad insisted we wait to consummate our relationship. I'd overheard people having sex before. It's inevitable these days. But *nothing* compared to the sounds my vampire ears now picked up. The squishing, the moaning and grunting, the skin slapping... ugh. I'd snuck into Lucy's room and stolen her headphones just to block out the sounds of Breccan feasting on his human companion. One, because it was embarrassing to listen to. And two, because it was turning me on just a little. No way in hell could I have sex with Vlad though, knowing *everyone* was listening. Sure, I sometimes watched porn, but this was a whole new level of voyeurism I wasn't interested in. I wanted Vlad's and my first time to stay between us. It seemed Breccan didn't share the same opinion.

I rose from the couch I'd been relaxing on for the last couple of hours and stretched. The book I'd been trying to read lay discarded on the cushion. Knowing what we had planned for the day had made it hard to unwind. I kept imagining all the many ways things could go wrong. What if Lucy somehow got caught in the flames? What if Samuel failed to protect her? What if Petrik somehow woke during the day—an impossible feat, I know. But it didn't stop the fears from pestering me all night long. Lucy meant the world to me. I couldn't lose her. More than once, I'd had to stop myself from storming off to Vlad's office and insisting we put a stop to this plan.

Instead, I reminded myself of a few facts. One: Petrik would be dead to the world in his coffin. Two: Lucy wouldn't be alone. Three: She could accomplish anything she put her mind to.

In a few hours, I would go to sleep. And when I woke, it would be to a new world. One where Petrik was dead, I was free, and Lucy and I could return home.

Home.

Another thought that made me anxious. At this rate, I'd need to invent some sort of antacid for vampires. The idea of returning to Perish and seeing my family nearly gave me hives. The rest of Perish, I could handle. Hell, I'd just bite them if they pissed me off. But my family? That was a whole other hornet's nest.

I still hadn't spoken to my father, and my mother continued to refuse my calls. For all I knew, they straight up considered me dead. Maybe going home would help them see nothing had changed—other than my strictly liquid diet and new nighttime schedule. Or maybe my return would inspire a mob armed with pitchforks and fire.

The sound of Vlad's front door opening broke that train of thought.

"Please behave yourself," I heard Camilla whisper. "Vlad is stressed enough as it is without adding any of your werewolf antics into the mix."

Someone grunted a nonverbal response.

Could this be him? The infamous Samuel of the coffin-urination? I chuckled and strode toward them. But the second I turned the corner and spotted them, I froze.

"Holy shit," I murmured under my breath.

I wasn't sure what I'd expected.

Half man, half hairy beast? The way Vlad and Camilla had spoken about Samuel, I'd pictured some monstrous caricature of the Wolfman. Something more akin to the old movies. A beast lumbering around on awkwardly bent hindquarters with a face the shape of a wolf.

But this....

I whistled appreciatively.

Samuel was all man. And I mean *all* man. My gaze started at his feet and tracked up his six-foot five-ish height. The dude was massive, and his stacked muscles seemed to take up the entire entryway. He was like a giant lumberjack, especially considering he wore a plaid shirt—which, I shit you not, *strained* against his biceps—and dark, crisp jeans. When I finally made it to his face, I sucked in a sharp breath. The guy was beauty defined. And that was strange to think, considering he was male. But everything about him screamed *perfection*, right down to his piercing amber eyes.

If I wasn't taken, and happily so, I might have wondered if I could get a piece of that action.

"Who's this?" Samuel demanded, his voice deep like a wolf's growl.

"Anna," Camilla said. "Vlad's new paramour."

No one could blame me for being mildly gobsmacked. I hadn't seen a man this attractive since... well, ever. Don't get me wrong—I had zero interest in Wolf Boy here. And Vlad was downright luscious. But a girl could appreciate good art, right?

Samuel arched a dark eyebrow and raked me over with a scathing glare. "Really. Someone actually warmed up to Count Deadula?"

I tried not to laugh, but my lips twitched in response. Samuel's glare eased when he caught me stifling a chuckle, as though he realized I might not be the stuffed-up vamp he'd imagined.

"It's nice to meet you, Samuel." I offered my hand.

He slowly reached out, his giant, meaty hand engulfing mine entirely. "Sam."

"Sam."

I made sure to immediately release his hand. "Thank you for coming and for helping us with this."

His mouth cracked into a smile, and I damn near fainted. "Any time. Since you're a fanger, I assume you're not the one I'm escorting into the demon's den?"

"No. You'll be escorting Lucy. My best friend."

His head bobbed, and he took to studying his surroundings as though recommitting the place to memory. "Human?"

"Yup. And... uh..." I didn't know how to approach this. "She's..." I flicked Camilla a glance, then decided, *fuck it, just say it.* "Look, she's allergic to dogs. I don't mean any insult by this. I just want to make sure that you're not gonna set her off or something. We need this to all go down without a hitch."

Sam's brows shot up into his hairline. "Did you just call me a dog?"

"What? No!" I sputtered. Shit, this was awkward. "I just mean"—I cleared my throat—"ah, fuck. Look, Vlad mentioned that last time you were shedding all over the house, and Lucy is allergic to dogs. Well, fur. *Their* fur."

Camilla rubbed her brow and exhaled.

Sam crossed his arms over his chest. His massively manly chest. And holy crickets, I think those biceps were literally winking at me.

"The last time I was here, I was in wolf form," Sam commented. "I assure you, I don't shed while in human form."

"Right. Right. Sorry. I'll just...."

Footsteps approached. I glanced back and spotted Vlad approaching. He cocked his head and studied me, clearly confused by the sight of my flushed cheeks. I cleared my throat and stepped back. Thankfully, my fluster was from the things I'd said and not a reaction to his looks.

Vlad came to a stop next to me and eyed Sam. "Good to see you again."

Sam's mouth slipped to the side, but he didn't respond. Definitely no love lost between these two.

"Lucy's asleep," I informed the group, even though no one asked. Anything to cut through the awkward tension. "I could wake her if you want."

"Let her rest," Vlad said. "Camilla and I can go through the plan with Samuel. It won't take long."

No, it wouldn't. It was a rather simple plan when it came down to it. Break in, find Petrik's coffin, set him on fire, escape. All without dying or leaving any evidence behind that might harm Lucy in the future.

Cripes, I really did hate this. I hated that I had to rely on Lucy for this. She was just a human, for crying out loud. If the queen caught wind of this, she'd kill us *all*. Including Lucy. I needed to make sure that never happened. Lucy was the most important person to me.

My gaze shot to Vlad. Make that second most important. Tied for first? I couldn't decide. I just knew that if anyone ever tried to harm Vlad or Lucy, my face would be the last thing they saw—including the precious queen.

I turned back to Sam, my face wiped clean of all humor. "She set her alarm for eight a.m. She needs a good night's sleep before this, since she's been working on our schedule. Once she's awake, meet her in the kitchen, and I'll leave a note telling her where she can find you."

Sam nodded. He lifted his head and sniffed the air, his nostrils flaring. "I have her scent. I'll be able to find her wherever she is now."

Did that sound ominous to anyone else? And how the hell did he know which scent was hers? The house was full of stinky people. Believe me, I knew. "In the house, you mean?"

"Sure."

Before I could dig a little deeper, Vlad and Camilla led Sam into the office. Seconds later, the music cranked on, and I knew they'd entered secretive planning mode part *deux*. At least I didn't need to attend this one. Thanks to my extreme aversion to sunlight, I couldn't even be involved in the process. My idea, but I couldn't execute it, and I really hated that.

Sighing, I climbed the stairs to the second floor and started toward my bathroom. Maybe a warm shower would help soothe my nerves before settling in my coffin for the day.

After all this, Vlad and I really needed to investigate alternatives. I hated sleeping in the attic. Made me feel like some monster from a creature feature. Over the past two weeks, I'd researched UV Protection windows. So far, they claimed only to block ninety-nine percent. But maybe with the new interest in vampires, someone could look into inventing full protection windows. I hadn't had a chance to discuss it with Vlad, but that didn't keep it from percolating in the back of my mind.

"Anna."

I paused at the sound of my name and turned to find Eli in one of the guest rooms. He stood out on the room's balcony, a cigarette dangling from his lips. I'd never seen a vampire smoke before. Not that I'd met many yet.

I gave him a small nod, about to keep moving, when he waved me over. "I'd like to speak with you for a moment, if that's all right?"

I didn't hold back my sigh. Eli was exhausting at the best of times. I honestly had no idea what Vlad saw in him. The man constantly complained about his circumstances and made idle threats. Yet, he'd stuck around for the past two weeks to help protect me. The dude was a walking enigma.

"It won't take long. I just wanted to apologize."

Oh? Interesting.

I stepped into his room and spared a quick glance. His room was neater than mine, but then again, Lucy was bunking in mine. She'd done a lot of shopping over the past few weeks to supply us with everything we needed. Needless to say, my room was bursting at the seams with a new wardrobe for each of us.

Eli turned and gave me his back, leaning his elbows against the balcony railing. Mine didn't have a balcony. But it also didn't have this view. Vlad's land was spectacular. Even from here, I could see the surrounding swampland and wildlife. The world seemed so quiet right now, on the cusp of dawn, but that didn't stop me from taking it all in.

I came to a stop next to Eli and cocked my hip against the railing.

"Did Vlad ever tell you how we came to meet?"

"No."

Eli tapped his cigarette, knocking the ashes to the balcony floor. I couldn't imagine Vlad would like that, but I managed to keep my mouth shut for once.

"I fought for the Union Army, way back in the day. It seemed the thing to do back then." Eli shot me another glance as though to gauge my reaction.

I kept a blank face, even though inside, I grew excited. The one upside to being a vampire was having access to all these real-life historical figures.

"Unfortunately, I never saw the end of the war. At least, not as a human. I'll never forget that night. We thought the enemy was advancing, launching an attack on us. We heard the screams. But before we could retaliate, this *thing* swept in and massacred my unit." Eli dropped his cigarette butt to the ground and scuffed it out with his boot. "It wasn't until I lay bleeding to death that I realized it wasn't the Confederates, but a monster. Vampires back then took advantage of a good war to gorge themselves. The deaths were simply blamed on an enemy attack. I think he meant to leave us there, but just as he was leaving, I must have made a sound. He came back and stared down at me. I'll never forget the look in his eyes. At the time, I thought he was the devil coming to drag me to hell. He was leaning over me when another vampire appeared and, right before my eyes, tore off the first vampire's head. I doubt you've ever seen a decapitation, but it's messy. Quite a bit of his blood found its way into my mouth."

"And the other vampire was Vlad?" I asked, horrified.

"Good ole Drac. Never could resist a little decapitation. Nicest guy in the world, salt of the earth. But if you piss him off, he sheds that gentlemanly façade of his and unleashes the monster within. He's not Vlad Tepes, but our Vlad is hardly innocent. The longer you live as a vampire, the more you'll start to become one of us.

"Drac didn't realize what'd happened to me. He was simply disposing of a problem. The vampire who'd tried to kill me had been raiding up and down the front lines, massacring any human he could sink his teeth into. Vlad took him out and left."

A dark avenging angel.

"So, I became a vampire. Sired by a murderous monster. The first few months were the worst. I couldn't control myself. Without someone to teach me how to properly feed, I turned into the same monster as the one whose blood made me. I eventually gained control and learned how to hunt discreetly."

"I'm glad to hear it," I said.

"I ran into Vlad a few times over the next century or so. I eventually confessed to him how I knew him. Told him about that night. Vlad was horrified. It wasn't Vlad's blood that sired me, but his actions caused it. He told me all that he knew about my so-called sire, then invited me to live with him. I turned down his offer. I'd already learned how to be a vampire and had my own life. But from that moment on, we stayed in touch, coming to each other's aid whenever needed."

"Including now," I whispered.

Eli canted his head and stared at me in the darkness. "Vlad's never shown any romantic interest in anyone, vampire or human."

"Were you in love with him?" I asked, wondering if his dislike of me came from jealousy.

Eli chuckled. "Not even remotely. Our relationship is platonic. But I was curious about you when he came to ask me for help. Who was this woman who'd stolen Vlad's heart? And what do I find but an annoying newborn vampire hellbent on getting us all killed."

I sucked in a sharp breath. "What?"

"I've known Vlad longer than you ever will. I'm his friend and ally. Which means sometimes doing things your friend can't stomach. When it comes to you, he's like any other man in love. He's blind, made weak by you. He's made choices that could end his life. And I won't let that happen."

This was not the direction I expected this conversation to go. "I thought you wanted to apologize?"

"Oh, I do. But not for anything I've said."

"Then what the hell do you want to apologize for?"

Eli stepped back, kicked the extinguished cigarette butt off the balcony, then stared blankly at me. "This."

A loud thump resounded behind me. I whirled around and gasped at the sight of Petrik looming over me, his back blocking the moonlight behind him. I opened my mouth to scream, but Eli's arms came around me, his hand clapping over my mouth and smothering the sound.

Oh hell no!

This wasn't happening!

After all the training, all the preparing, I couldn't let *this* be how Petrik won.

I squirmed against Eli in a mad struggle to free myself, but the man's arms were like steel vices. I couldn't so much as budge. Camilla's training was proving useless! How could I defend myself if I couldn't even move? Eli was like some ridiculously strong boa constrictor, choking the damn life out of me.

"I will not let Vlad take the fall for your stupidity," Eli hissed in my ear. "Vlad never should have saved you that night. So, I'm going to fix this problem for him. Once Petrik's finished with you, you'll be nothing more than a stain on Vlad's memory."

My muffled scream barely carried across the balcony. I fought against Eli's hold, stomped his feet, kicked his shins, anything and everything I could think to break his hold. Nothing worked. Eli's cold grip held me hostage.

Petrik closed the distance between us, his icy gaze staring down at me. He lifted a hand and brought a lock of my hair to his nose. "I've been looking forward to this, little one."

Well, he could just keep waiting, because no way in hell would I let this happen.

I stilled my body, even held my breath. Eli probably didn't realize it, but his body instinctively responded by slightly relaxing.

It was now or never.

I wrenched my head to the side, freeing my mouth from Eli's palm. The second his fingers slid across my lips, I *bit*. My fangs tore into his fingers, and like a crazed dog, I shook my head, ripping through his flesh and muscle while his blood gushed into my mouth.

Eli sucked in a sharp breath, but not once did he cry out. Instead, he shoved me toward Petrik. I dug my heels into the balcony, then used what little momentum I'd gained to snap my head back. Pain bloomed across the back of my skull the instant I connected with Eli's chin, but it was enough to daze him.

With a sneer, I whirled around and implemented Camilla's first lesson of defense.

I grabbed Eli's face and shoved my thumbs into his eye sockets.

This time, he *screamed*. I grinned triumphantly. That scream was all I needed. Vlad would hear it and know something had gone terribly wrong. Unfortunately, I wasn't the only one who realized that.

The second Eli screamed, something hard smashed into the base of my skull, and I tumbled headlong into darkness.

23

Consciousness slammed into me with the force of a bus. My eyes snapped open, and I scrambled to my feet, absolutely terrified of what I might find. Last I remembered, Eli had betrayed me. Us. Everyone. And Petrik—oh, holy guacamole, Petrik.

Eli must have planned it all. He couldn't give Petrik permission to enter the house, so he'd stood on the balcony and waited for the perfect opportunity. Once he'd found me alone and lured me outside, kaboom, perfect opportunity.

For fuck's sake, I was going to kill him if Vlad hadn't already.

With a deep, unnecessary breath, I took in my surroundings.

Four concrete walls surrounded me, and two of those walls had windows. Windows that were starting to let in daylight.

"Oh, fuck," I whimpered and darted to the farthest corner, hiding in the weakening shadows.

I had no way of knowing how long I'd been unconscious, but considering I could see the darkness fading to the light, I could guess it'd been long enough.

Where the hell had Petrik taken me? What was this room? Where was Vlad and everyone else? Did Petrik kill them after knocking me out?

Panic spread through my limbs until they tingled.

"Okay, okay, calm down," I whispered to myself. Petrik wouldn't have been able to kill everyone in the house, right? Vlad and the others were younger, but surely four vampires could hold against one ancient one. I hoped. I *prayed*.

I couldn't lose Vlad, couldn't face an eternity of darkness without him.

No. I needed to focus on something else. Think rationally. Like how the hell I was going to get out of here before the sun turned me into fried vampire wings.

Petrik wanted me. Not Vlad. I had to believe

they were safe—it was the only thing that would keep me sane through this.

And even worse. I *had* to stay awake.

I wasn't even sure if that could be done. Vlad had once mentioned that vampires could remain awake when under duress, but could I do that? I was a month old, barely out of my training fangs. The only thing I knew was that once that sun rose, I was out like a light. If I allowed that to happen today, I'd never again wake up.

"Thought you might like it here."

My head snapped up with a gasp to find Petrik standing across the room, cloaked in shadows. Had he been there this whole time, watching me? My flesh pebbled into goose bumps. "What are you doing? Why am I here?"

"To enjoy one last sunrise," he said, pointing to the windows. "It'll be your last, of course, but I thought you might appreciate it."

"Why the hell would you think that?"

Petrik stepped out of the shadows with a nasty grin. "You were never meant to be one of us, Anna. Everyone knows that. It was sheer dumb luck that led Vlad to you."

"It was fate," I argued, shocked by my own words.

407

"Fate." Petrik tipped his head back and laughed. "Yes, I suppose the boy would believe that. He's always been a romantic, that one."

Vlad *did* have a romantic side to him, but right now, I needed his strength. I needed *him*.

"Did you kill him?" I demanded, forcing my voice out strong and steady.

"Does it matter? You won't be leaving this little place of mine. You'll remain here as a pile of ash for all eternity. I like it. The one who escaped my clutches, trapped with me forever."

Holy shit. He was downright insane.

"The queen has hair like yours, you know," Petrik mused as he stepped toward me. "Beautiful blonde hair. But her eyes are blue. Like ice. Like mine. Perhaps that's the reason I chose to take her as one of my children instead of ending her."

I shuddered and pressed my back against the wall.

The room brightened another degree. Dawn was approaching, and my eyes grew leaden with sleep. It was becoming difficult to keep them open. To stay focused. But I couldn't give in. If I slept, the sun's rays would sweep over me and reduce me to nothing.

"You, my little bird, are nothing like the queen, though. Where she is cordial and intelligent, you're brazen and ignorant. But you amuse me. Who would have thought you'd attract the attention of the famous Dracula?"

"If you're going to kill me, just do it," I snapped. "I'm tired of your voice."

"A shame," Petrik said, laughing. "For I dearly love the sound of it."

"Not surprising."

Petrik closed the distance between us in four strides. He grabbed my shoulders and slammed me up against the wall, rattling my brain. "Would you prefer to make this a little more exciting? I suppose I don't need you alive to watch you burn. Your corpse will do just fine."

I stared into his monstrous face and squared my jaw. The only thing that mattered was proving he *didn't* scare me. Not anymore. Funny how facing your worst fears helps purge you of them.

I lifted my chin and sneered. "Get *out* of my face."

Petrik's eyes widened a fraction, as though surprised by my confidence. Gone was the woman who'd cowered before him, who'd hidden behind Vlad rather than face him. I refused to give him the satisfaction.

As much as I wanted to lash out and strike him, I

didn't. I remembered John's warnings, that I was nothing more than a nuisance to one as powerful as Petrik. Striking him would accomplish nothing except getting my ass handed to me. Surely he'd soon leave, and then I'd find a way to escape. Even if it meant running out into the sun myself. I could smell trees in the near distance. Maybe they could provide cover before I burned away. Or maybe I could bury myself in the earth. So long as the sun didn't touch me, I'd be fine.

"This chamber of mine won't kill you," Petrik finally said. "There's space enough to move around and avoid the sun. Provided you can stay awake, of course."

So, he meant to torture me, then.

"Vampires *can* stay awake, you know," he continued. "I've never known a newborn capable of such a feat, but it can be done. We give ourselves to the darkness every morning. But that's because it's expected of us. I haven't been a slave to the sun for centuries now. As long as I keep out of direct sunlight, I can remain awake during the day."

"That's impossible," I whispered.

"Why? Because your precious Dracula told you so? He may be famous, but he doesn't know everything. With power comes great opportunity."

"And what about your queen?" I asked, grasping at straws. "What are you going to do when she decides your behavior has become a hindrance to her?"

"My sweet Genevieve would never harm me. She knows who I am better than anyone else. As long as she rules, I have my freedom." He released me and eased back into the shadows. "I think I'll stay. To see if you survive the sun."

It wasn't the worst thing he could do to me, so I took some relief in that. But the thought of being enclosed with him in this tight space for the next few hours didn't appeal to me. I couldn't think with him nearby. Couldn't plan an escape. Not that I even had a lick of an idea. The only way out was the door, and to reach the door, I had to get through Petrik.

"In case you haven't realized, no one will be coming for you," Petrik unceremoniously announced. "Your vampire friends are all crawling into bed right about now. Poor Vlad. I can only imagine how devastated he must be, staring at your empty coffin."

Relief washed through me. Vlad was alive, then. Knowing that bolstered my resilience.

My vision had grayed around the edges, but I had to keep fighting. This was the time of day when I tucked myself in and slept. If I succumbed to that need, I had a feeling Petrik would leave me exactly where I fell and let the sun take me.

I pressed my back against the wall and slid to the ground, tucking my knees into my chest. The first ray of sunlight eased into the room. I whimpered at the sight. Minute by minute, it crept across the floor, heading toward my feet. I had no way of knowing how long it would take to reach me. Not long enough, though.

What felt like an eternity later, my head started to droop.

No. Stay awake. Don't fall asleep. You'll die.

The sun touched the tip of my toes, and pain instantly shot through my body. My head snapped back up, and I screamed myself awake, tucking myself farther into the corner. Light bled through the entire cement room. Everywhere I looked, it spread. Petrik stood in the only remaining darkened corner.

What was his plan here? He couldn't leave the room and walk out into the light—it'd kill him. But there was nowhere in the room for him to hide. Did he intend to remain here all day, awake and watching?

Fire blazed across my feet, and I cried out in pain. The sunlight was like a cancerous cell, spreading, reaching. And it burned everywhere it touched. The scent of charred skin assaulted my nose, and I watched in horror as I started to burn. I couldn't move, though. Exhaustion had me trapped in the corner, pinned like a butterfly. I wanted to duck the sun's beams, run to the darkest corner of the room and sob, but I couldn't muster the strength.

"Ah," Petrik spoke. "Finally."

"Fuck you," I rasped, then screamed when the rays reached my ankles. It wouldn't be much longer now.

Petrik stepped out of the shadows and watched me with such intensity. It wasn't until that moment that I realized he was *enjoying* watching the sun torture me.

The sunbeam rose to my shins, and I moaned. The pain was damn near unbearable. I'd never felt anything like it. I had to move. *So move! Don't give in!* I turned and clawed at the wall, using it for leverage as I dragged my battered body across the floor. Every inch was pure agony, but I couldn't give up. Not yet.

I'd barely escaped the sun's rays when something massive slammed into the chamber door.

My head slowly rose, my energy depleted, but I managed to catch sight of the door bursting open, practically exploding at the seams. Fresh sunlight poured into the room, and I screamed when it washed over my hands.

Lucy and Samuel came barging into the room. Sam didn't even bat an eye before he lifted his arm and pointed something black and shiny at Petrik. I heard a soft puff of air and marveled at the sound of Petrik's immediate anguished scream.

He dropped to his knees, clutching at what looked like a massive chunk of wood protruding from his chest.

"What about stakes?" I heard my voice echo in my head, closely followed by Vlad's. *"Regretfully, quite effective at killing us."*

There was nothing regretful about this. I only hoped a single stake would be enough to take Petrik down. He was a thousand years old, after all.

Sam rushed forward, punched Petrik in the face, then slammed him to the ground and straddled his chest. Petrik barely twitched, his hands gripping the stake as though afraid to move it. Without hesitation, Sam unsheathed what looked like a machete from his side and pressed it against Petrik's throat.

"Wait!" I rasped.

Both Sam and Lucy both turned, and Lucy cried out the second she spotted me. She bolted to my side and ripped off her jacket before laying it across my back. It wouldn't guard against the sun, but I appreciated her efforts.

"Blood," I panted. "I need blood."

Sam shook his head. "Too risky."

My mouth felt drier than the Sahara Desert, and my throat had practically shriveled from thirst. I needed blood *now* if I was to survive this.

"Lucy," I moaned.

Her hands hovering above me as though afraid to touch me. I must have looked quite the sight.

"Ohmigod, ohmigod, Anna, what do I do? Take my blood!"

I shook my head, then gestured weakly to Petrik. I didn't trust myself to feed on her. Thirst blazed down my throat, and I knew I'd kill her if I so much as laid a fang on her.

"Okay, this might hurt. Just bear with me."

Her hands slipped under my arms, and she heaved my weight across the room. I bit down to keep from screaming. Once back in the shadows, my body relaxed, which brought about a new torment. My charred flesh didn't appreciate my slackening muscles. But I locked it all inside and kept quiet.

Lucy brought me to Petrik and eased me down on my back next to him. I could barely move, but I caught sight of his pale face. His eyes were closed, his mouth slack. By all appearances, he looked as dead as any other dead man. All from a stake?

I coughed, blowing up a puff of dust from the floor. "Is he gone?"

"Almost." Sam gripped the stake tighter. "The stake is made of hawthorn and was treated in holy water and monksblood—werewolf secret, so don't tell anyone. It will keep him restrained until I take his head. Just as a precaution."

I didn't nod for fear of my brain imploding. "Blood."

"Anna, he's ancient," Lucy warned me.

Right now, I didn't care. Someone needed to open a vein for me. Human, werewolf, or vampire, take a pick. I had no way of knowing what werewolf blood would do to me, and I couldn't risk draining Lucy. I didn't want to be gentle right now. I couldn't submit her to that.

So, with claw-shaped fingers, I grabbed Petrik's wrist and brought it to my mouth. I chomped into him with absolutely no manners, my teeth ripping through flesh and sinew. His blood poured into my mouth, and it took every last drop of strength remaining to swallow. I could hear the excess spilling out of my mouth and splashing on the floor, but it didn't matter.

Cool relief spread through my body, and my skin began knitting itself back together. Of all the blood in the room, Petrik's by far was the most powerful, and it healed me with every gulp.

But what else would it do to me?

Vlad had mentioned the repercussions of drinking ancient blood. The madness, the exponential power growth. Right now, I couldn't stop to consider the ramifications. I just knew I needed blood to heal.

"Enough," Sam barked.

I didn't let go.

"Anna," Lucy whispered. "Stop. You need to stop!"

Her panicked voice seemed to wake something in me, and I managed to release Petrik's mangled wrist.

Though still utterly exhausted, I managed to glance down at my legs to find my skin flush and pink. No injuries remained. Hallelujah. Now if we could get me somewhere safe, I could sleep.

"Look away," Sam ordered.

At first, I thought he meant me, then I realized he was speaking to Lucy. My head lolled against the cement floor, and I watched as Sam beheaded the bastard who'd tried to kill me. His head detached from his body with ease, *thwomp, thwomp, thwomping* as it rolled across the floor.

"Good riddance," I mumbled, barely able to get my lips to work.

"Anna, are you okay?" Lucy asked, leaning over me.

I stared up into her face but couldn't answer. Instead, I closed my eyes and let the darkness take me.

By SOME MIRACLE, I woke.

Darkness surrounded me, so I gave a relieved sigh and took inventory of my body. For someone who had been left out in the sun, I felt... well, good. Better than good. Hell, I felt amazing. Powerful. I probably shouldn't have munched on Petrik, but in all fairness, the asshat deserved it. I knew the Bible was all *forgive and forget*, but that would never happen.

I knew from the comfort beneath me that I was in my coffin. Lucy and Sam must have somehow managed to bring me home. I'd need to ask about that, considering the whole sun dilemma. Either way, though, I was home and alive. Ish.

KINSLEY ADAMS

Placing my palms against my coffin lid, I pushed it back, then climbed out. No lingering pain, no weakness, no debilitation whatsoever. Huh. Maybe I needed to drink more ancient blood. It certainly seemed to do the trick. Like a spinach smoothie—chock full of all those nutrients and vitamins a growing vampire needed.

I stretched out my neck and shoulders, then headed for the attic door. Had I been looking, I might have noticed some oddities. Oddity number one: the attic's ambience was far brighter than normal. Oddity number two: Vlad's coffin was still sealed. But I didn't notice either of these things until I climbed down from the attic and landed soundlessly on the floor.

Sunlight streamed in from *everywhere*.

I cried out and clutched at the attic ladder, about to dart back upstairs, when I noticed oddity number three: I wasn't screaming in pain.

A shuddering breath slipped past my lips, and I lifted my hand, studying it. Every window in the house was open, allowing fresh air to breathe through the house. Sunbeams scattered across the floor, creeping in from the windows themselves, though none had touched me yet.

422

What had Petrik said? That he hadn't needed to sleep during the day in centuries?

Was this because of his blood?

I crept forward, then dipped a trembling hand toward a pure sunbeam resting on the floor. The instant my digits dipped into the warmth, my flesh sizzled. I gasped and wrenched my hand back. Okay, so direct sunlight was still a no. But I was *awake*, in the middle of the day.

I brought my injured hand to my mouth and touched my lips.

Holy guacamole.

"Anna?"

I turned at the sound of Lucy's voice. Tears immediately welled in my eyes, and I rushed toward her, scooping her into a tight hug.

"Oof, woman. You're... really... strong," she wheezed.

"Sorry, sorry." I loosened my grip and rested my head on her shoulder. "Thank you so much for saving me. I don't know what I would have done without you."

It wasn't until I felt her body trembling that I realized she was crying. I pulled back and wiped her tears, then gave her a steady nod. "We're both okay and alive."

"Ish," she mumbled, uttering my favorite joke. "How are you awake?"

"Petrik's blood, I think. Vlad's told me multiple times that drinking ancient blood can bolster a newborn's power."

"He also said those vampires went insane, Anna!"

I cocked my head and pursed my lips. "I don't feel insane."

"That's what they all say. Betcha Petrik didn't think he was insane either."

We shared an awkward chuckle.

"Come on. Let's get you some blood," Lucy said.

I looped my arm through hers and followed her down the hallway, careful to avoid all direct sunlight.

"I'll see if we can get someone to close the windows."

"No, leave them open. Please."

She shot me a concerned look but eventually nodded.

The smell of the fresh air, heated by the sun, was a beautiful thing. I wanted to enjoy it for as long as possible.

Lucy sighed. "Vlad isn't going to like this."

"Yeah, but there isn't much I can do about it."

"How about you just stop drinking ancient blood for a while, 'kay?"

"So long as they stop trying to kill me, we're good."

Lucy chuckled.

"Care to fill me in on what happened after you and Sam saved me?"

She expelled a heavy breath, one that smelled of toothpaste. She must have just woken from a nap herself. Probably in preparation of spending the night awake with me. With my newfound resistance to the sun, maybe our schedule could return to normal. I might not be able to go outside, but at least I wouldn't be confined to my coffin all day now. And maybe sleep in a bed! So long as we blocked out all the rays.

"Once you passed out, Sam and I sat in that stupid crypt until nightfall. We couldn't risk moving you. I was worried that even the smallest amount of sunlight would set you on fire."

"You sat there all day?"

She raked her teeth over her bottom lip and nodded. "Then when the sun set and you didn't wake, Vlad immediately came to get you."

"Wait, I didn't wake up? How long have I been asleep?"

"A few days," she admitted. "It's been stressful on all of us. Especially Vlad. He hasn't moved from your side, waiting for you to wake up. He never admitted it, but I could see he was terrified. He mentioned once that you were taking too long to wake."

Holy shit. "I had no idea."

"Of course you didn't."

"Eli!" I suddenly shouted.

Lucy jumped at the sound of my voice and clutched a hand over her chest. "Shit, Anna. Scared the hell out of me."

"He betrayed us. He lured me out onto the balcony so Petrik could abduct me."

"Yeah, Vlad figured that out pretty damn fast. Eli tried claiming his injuries were from Petrik, but Vlad and I had been watching your training closely. Camilla taught you that... that disgusting attack in the beginning. Did you have to shove your thumbs in his eyes?"

"It worked, didn't it?"

"Only too well. Vlad said his eyes would heal—had Vlad let him live, that is."

"Eli's dead?"

"Ohhh yeah," Lucy muttered. "Vlad's... terrifying."

I frowned so hard my head started aching. "What do you mean?"

"Well, he may not be Vlad Tepes, but he took a page out of Tepes's book."

Oh, that didn't sound good at all. "What did he do?"

Lucy cupped her face and rubbed her temple. "He staked and decapitated the traitorous bastard, then stuck Eli's head on a pike out front for everyone to see what happens to those who betray him."

I whistled under my breath. Maybe a tad excessive, but considering Eli betrayed me, I really couldn't find it in me to care about his demise. I just hoped I didn't stumble across the head.

"He's been scary, Anna. Like, vampire scary. Angry. Violent. Losing you almost broke him, I think. He absolutely lost it at the crypt once we told him what happened. Utterly destroyed the entire thing. He demolished the building with his bare hands."

I sucked in a sharp breath. That building had been made of cement.

"Are you sure he's the right guy for you?" Lucy asked. "He's dangerous, Anna."

"No more than any other guy. And yes, I know without a doubt that he's mine."

427

Her lips pressed into a grim slash, and she eyed me. I sensed a question hovering on the tip of her tongue.

"Spit it out."

"How do you know he's yours?" Her words rushed together. "How do you know you're meant to be together?"

I pondered her question as we strode into the kitchen. One of the harem members stood next to the fridge, a popsicle hanging between her lips. Her eyes widened the instant she spotted me. She blinked her surprise away, then darted over to me with her arm extended.

"Thirsty?"

"Thank you... Malinda, is it?"

"Yes, Countess."

"Oh, please don't call me that."

She squished her lips together and lifted her arm higher. I cradled her wrist gently, then slowly eased my fangs into her skin. Warm blood filled my mouth, but that was all it was. Warm fluids. Frowning, I extracted my teeth and stared at the two tiny puncture marks. Her blood was fine, but it just wasn't hitting the spot for me.

"What's wrong?" Lucy asked.

I shook my head, then returned to my meal. Her

blood would suffice. Maybe it was because I'd just fed off Petrik. Perhaps I wasn't quite as thirsty as I'd thought.

After I'd had my fill, I drew back from Malinda and thanked her. She scurried away with a polite nod, the popsicle still dangling in her mouth.

"I know it deep down," I told Lucy, returning to her previous question about me and Vlad. "When I'm near him, I feel this connection. It's so strong."

"Could the connection exist because he's your sire?"

"No, it's far more intimate than that. I honestly can't explain it. It's just this knowledge I have. He's the *one* for me."

Lucy grimaced, then turned away.

"What's wrong? Do you not like him?"

"No, it's nothing like that." She waved a dismissive hand. "I was just hoping for a more useful answer."

"Useful? What do you mean?"

Lucy dug into the drawers and pulled out a bag of Cheetos. Then she hopped up onto the counter and ripped it open. The smell of plastic and cheese invaded my nose, and I grimaced. Even the blood in my belly soured. For a moment, I thought I might throw up, but the nausea quickly passed.

"So, obviously I met that Sam guy."

Seeing as how they murdered Petrik together, yes, I think I'd figured that out already. I frowned, wondering if she was trying to change the conversation. But from the reddening of her cheeks, it seemed safe to assume that this was all related.

And then it clicked.

"You like him?" I asked with a teasing grin.

She sighed and dropped the bag of Cheetos, then cupped her face. "He says I'm his mate!"

I blinked, convinced I'd misheard her. "I'm sorry. He said *what*?"

"That I'm his mate! He says he knew it the second he stepped in the house and caught my scent."

After a few seconds, I burst out laughing. "So, *that* was what he meant!"

"What who meant?" Lucy demanded, lifting her head to give me the stink eye.

"Sam!" I snickered into my hand. "He told me in a very deep and manly voice that he had your scent and could now find you anywhere."

"He said the same thing to me! Ugh. I'm really starting to dislike this whole paranormal nonsense."

I snorted. "Okay. Because what woman *wouldn't* want the Lumberjack Wolfman as her mate? And does mate mean the same thing to werewolves as it does vampires?"

"I think so," Lucy admitted. "I didn't ask him to elaborate. But I definitely got that feeling. Together... forever."

"Ohhh. Damn, girl!"

"He's just so... so... big!" Her cheeks flamed when she caught sight of my smirk. "That's not what I meant, and you know it!"

"I can think of a few more adjectives too. Sexy. Gruff. Manly. Stacked. Take your pick."

"Careful. Don't let Vlad hear you say things like that."

This time, I waved a hand. "He's snoozing away in his coffin. Besides, I can look. Especially because the only one I'm interested in has fangs."

"Oh, Samuel has fangs all right."

"Really," I hedged. "Do tell."

"Gah. You're such a lech!"

"In the flesh, baby girl. But let me guess—you plan on rejecting that manly hunk of muscle?"

"Reject him? Right now, I'm just trying to keep my damn hands off him!"

I burst out laughing. Now this was the type of gossip I was here for. Lucy never let her emotions get away from her before. I found it immensely enjoyable to see her step outside her comfort zone for once. And Sam seemed like the right guy for the job.

"Is he here right now?" I gasped, then gave Lucy a salacious wink. "Is he in your bed—*our* bed— upstairs right this second?"

"Cripes, Anna! You make it sound so bad."

I snickered. "That's my job."

"No, he isn't here right now. He doesn't particularly like Vlad. And with the mood Vlad's been in, Sam thought some distance would be best."

Insightful.

I glanced at the microwave clock and noted the time. Four-thirty in the afternoon. Another hour or so and Vlad would wake. Excitement zinged through my body. I couldn't wait to see him, especially after everything Lucy had told me. I just wanted to hold him, show him that I was perfectly fine, then maybe jump his bones.

"Where's everyone else?" I finally asked, shelving the wolfman conversation.

"Camilla, Rebecca, and Breccan left last night. They also felt it best to give Vlad some space. They were concerned with his mental health, but he refused their help. The only thing he wanted to do was sit and watch you sleep. They told me to call them when you woke up."

"Let's wait until tomorrow to make that call," I said. "It couldn't hurt to give the three of us one night of peace, right?"

Lucy nodded. "That sounds good to me. I really wasn't looking forward to another night of creepy vampires all standing motionlessly around the house, waiting for you to so much as twitch a finger."

Yeah, that didn't sound like fun to me either.

"Do you want to go see Sam?" I asked.

Lucy shot me a sharp glance, as though she understood exactly what I was doing. "You just want me out of the house."

"Maybe. But don't feel you have to. If you'd rather avoid him for a bit, that's fine too. But I definitely want to spend some time alone with Vlad tonight. I just don't want you to feel like I'm abandoning you."

"Oh, please. Go do what you need to do. I'm just glad you're okay and back with us again. These last few days weren't exactly my favorite."

I wrapped Lucy in a hug and breathed in her scent. "Yeah, same."

"I can't imagine what you went through in there...."

"Then don't." My voice came out harsher than intended. "It's best *not* to imagine it." Unfortunately for me, I knew the nightmares would hound me for the rest of my life. "We all just need to move forward and leave the past where it belongs."

Lucy nodded.

I released her from the hug and stepped back. "I'm going to go shower. I need to get all the grime from that disgusting place off me."

"And any residual Petrik stank."

"That too."

Lucy grabbed my hands, then with a naughty wink said, "Get some, girl."

I left the kitchen laughing, all the while wondering if she intended to do the same.

25

I'd BARELY finished towel-drying my hair when my bathroom door burst open. Vlad hovered in the doorway, wearing a cautiously optimistic expression. I drank in the sight of him, my heart practically bursting at the seams.

Neither of us said a word.

Instead, I dashed across the bathroom floor and threw myself into his arms. Vlad caught me, his hands bracing my ass as he stormed into the bathroom and slammed the door shut behind him. I angled my head and slanted my mouth over his, eagerly plunging my tongue into his mouth. My hands were everywhere, in his hair, cupping his neck, his face. I couldn't keep them still. I wanted to touch every inch of him—wanted *him* to touch every inch of me.

No more excuses. No more waiting.

If Petrik had won, we never would have had the chance to explore this passion for each other. And I refused to let that happen again. Time to seize this vampire by the fangs and impale myself on him. *Get it? Impale myself? Cuz he's Vlad?* I giggled against his mouth.

"Is this a joke you should be sharing?" Vlad murmured, his lips straying across mine.

"Later," I breathed.

Vlad didn't argue. Clearly, this wasn't the time to talk—and I couldn't have agreed more. His tongue had a far more important task to accomplish. And it was doing quite the thorough job at the moment. I loved the way he kissed. Desperate, with a sense of urgency that I found incredibly hot. Like he couldn't wait another second to take me.

He pressed my back against the wall, then tore his mouth from mine and moved to my throat. I sucked in a sharp breath when his teeth scored my flesh. He still needed to feed—I could *feel* the hunger within him. And I was more than happy to provide that for him, to once again experience his fangs buried in my neck. God, I wanted him to bite me.

But not quite yet. Anticipation would only make it that much better. The teasing thought of his fangs *and* dick buried in me at the same time made me shiver. Oh yes, please. A girl's got needs, and right now, that one was foremost on my mind.

As much as I loved the feel of him between my thighs, I couldn't strip in this position. And I needed to be naked, to feel his skin against mine. I squirmed down his torso until my feet were flat on the ground, then grabbed the edges of my towel and threw it off. Vlad sucked in a breath when he caught his first sight of me, but I didn't wait to let him look his fill. There'd be time for that later. Right now, I needed a good dicking. I needed to feel close to him, to feel him under me.

I grabbed his shirt and ripped it open, distantly aware of the scattering buttons. Whatever. He had people to clean that up afterward. The belt was next, then went his pants and everything else, until he stood stark naked before me.

My fingers instantly found their mark, encircling his hardened length. The feel of him pulsing in my hand seemed to soothe my inner horndog just a smidgen. Enough that I could tip my head back and meet his gaze while slowly stroking him.

"Anna," he groaned, leaning his forehead against mine.

I had the sense neither one of us wanted to take our time. A couple's first time together was usually slow and explorative with the intent of learning each other's body. But after everything Vlad and I had been through, time seemed like the enemy.

"I need—"

"I know what you need," he grunted.

He gripped my thighs and shot me back up into the air, balancing my legs on his shoulders. Before I could so much as move, he buried his face between my thighs. I cried out, my back arching away from the wall. Only his steel grip kept me upright, while his tongue unleashed the naughtiest and most pleasurable sensations within me. It was like he could read my body, knew how to lick and suck just the right way to send me into a euphoric tailspin. I shuddered against the wall and tightened my thighs around Vlad's head, not that he cared. The instant I orgasmed, he bit, sinking his fangs deep into my inner thigh. I almost screamed with pleasure, only managing at the last second to choke it back. The house was devoid of other vampires, but I didn't need to let every human know what we were up to in here.

Piece by piece, the world slowly returned to normal. But before I could catch my breath, Vlad unwound my thighs from his head and sat me on the counter, legs spread. He met my gaze, holding it for what felt like eternity, then drove his cock into me.

I cried out and let my head fall back, resting it against the mirror. Utter bliss. I couldn't believe we'd waited this long. We'd been insane to torture ourselves like this. Hopefully, we'd never need to go without each other again, because now that I'd felt him inside me, I never wanted to let go.

It was like my whole world made sense again. Like he was that last missing puzzle piece that I hadn't *known* was missing until the puzzle all came together. That elusive center piece. Now, my puzzle was complete. Time to frame it for all time.

Vlad gripped my hips and pulled me closer, softly grunting in time to his thrusts. I locked my ankles around his backside and matched his movements, riding him just the right way to spark that warmth within me once more. One orgasm certainly wasn't enough. And I was glad to see that Vlad seemed just as eager to push me over the edge again.

His hand came between us, and his thumb found that perfect spot. Every stroke brought me that much closer, until finally, colors exploded behind my eyes. I'd never had a multicolored orgasm before. It was like little fairy lights twinkling in the sky, stealing my vision.

I clamped around him, milking him for every inch he could give. His breath wavered for a beat before he shuddered and lost himself to his own release. His movements slowed, and his touch grew gentle, but he didn't pull out of me. Instead, he rested his forehead against mine and sighed contentedly. I joined him, my eyes slipping shut as I breathed in this moment.

Whatever I'd felt for him before this had just grown exponentially. Our connection was strengthened by this physical bond. And I loved it.

"I thought I lost you," Vlad said, breaking the silence after our mind-blowing sex. "I can't fathom living in a world without you. Don't scare me like that again."

I hummed and cupped his face. When he opened his eyes and met my gaze, I kissed him, allowing my lips to linger a second longer. "I found my way back to you. I'm not going anywhere."

Darkness shuttered across his face. "Do you want to talk about it?"

Did I? Hell no. But I could tell *he* needed to.

"There's not much to say. Eli betrayed us. Lured me out onto the balcony. Let Petrik take me."

I felt Vlad shudder. "And he paid for his crimes."

"So I heard."

"Samuel told me what happened in the crypt. The sunlight, your burns, drinking Petrik's blood."

I shivered—and not from pleasure. I never wanted to hear that name again, especially when there were far more pleasurable things we could be doing right now.

"How do you feel?" he asked, brushing my damp hair back from my face.

I took a moment to consider his question. Petrik's blood was potent and aged to perfection, but I understood Vlad's concerns. Since becoming a vampire, I'd had a myriad of ancient blood. Vlad's, Camilla's, and Petrik's.

"I feel fine," I told him. "Honestly. No madness or homicidal urges. Just the small surprise of waking earlier than you."

"Good." Vlad rested his forehead against mine and released a small breath. I felt the tension melt away from his shoulders and hated that I'd worried him.

Hoping to reassure him that all was well, I kissed him and reveled in his tongue's slow and seductive dance against mine. When he pulled back, I gave a small, displeased whimper.

"We'll need to discuss all this in further detail and decide how to proceed. The queen will eventually find out—"

I chased after that mouth of his and silenced him with yet another hungry kiss, one that made his dick twitch with eagerness. Only when we'd had our fill of each other did I pull back and smile at him. "Those are tomorrow's problems. Tonight, let's focus on each other. No thinking about the queen or any other vampire. Just you and me."

"If only it were that simple."

"We can make it that simple," I said. "We deserve this. We've waited so long for this moment. I don't want to spoil it with evil schemes."

"I thought we were the good guys?" he teased.

"Good is boring," I joked. "Now, what can I do to distract you from all this?"

With a salacious wink, I separated us, then slipped off the counter and strode to the shower in all my naked glory, swishing my hips just a little extra. From the sound of his chuckle, he'd noticed.

The shower would distract him from further questions—especially if I was in it and all lathered up. Once I had the temperature set to my liking, I extended a hand toward him and waited for him to take it. Then I pulled him into the shower and closed the curtain, sealing us away from the rest of the world.

Here, we could enjoy the heat and each other's body without any worries about what might await us out there.

And that was exactly what we did.

Tomorrow, everything would change. The queen would learn of Petrik's death and call for our beheadings. I mean, she was Marie Antoinette after all. I would be very disappointed if she didn't once try to sentence us to the guillotine.

But until then, I planned to spend every moment in Vlad's arms, because that was my happy place. And I deserved happiness.

EPILOGUE

Well, the shit definitely hit the fan this past month.

I met a serial killer, became a vampire, fell in love with Dracula—shh, don't tell him that. I haven't admitted it out loud yet—killed said serial killer, although that was more Sam and less me, and likely pissed off a queen. Not too bad. All in a day's work, right?

People continue to stalk me and Vlad. It's hilarious. They snap pictures of us when we're out and about. Pictures that literally only show our clothing. And the headlines are ridiculous. *The Count and Countess Out for a Midnight Stroll. The Count and Countess Looking for a Midnight Snack.* Just last week, someone did an entire article on a bathing suit I wore to the beach. Next thing I knew, the entire town sold out.

I asked Vlad how vampires had managed not to expose themselves prior to all this if we vanish in photos. He'd given me a long-winded explanation about how it was the vampire's duty to keep the secret, even if it meant silencing a photographer. That answer hit uncomfortably close to home, so I stopped digging. Thank goodness such extreme measures aren't needed anymore.

The Vampire Lounge has become the newest hot spot for all vampires, especially ones hoping to glimpse what they've dubbed "The Royal Couple." We aren't part of the monarchy, but that hasn't stopped anyone from calling us that. Bet Queen Genevieve is super pleased about that one.

And speaking of the queen... she's extended an invitation to us. I burned it, but unfortunately another arrived, and Vlad spotted it before I could destroy the evidence. Meeting the queen is literally the last thing on my to-do list, behind getting staked and resurrecting Petrik. Like, I would fight a zombie apocalypse before meeting her.

She chose her precious sire over me, so for all I care, she can rot in hell.

What about Lucy? Well, she's avoiding her

wolfman for now. She's a little overwhelmed and terrified by the concept of being someone's forever mate. Eh. I rather like it. But every time I bring it up, she plugs her ears and starts singing "The Itsy-Bitsy Spider." I love the girl, but I'm starting to wonder about her mental state.

Vlad spends most of his nights making me scream his name, all while monitoring me for any negative effects from Petrik's blood. He finds it quite amusing. It's all right. I got him back. A few times. *Wink.*

Camilla returned a few nights after I woke. She doesn't trust us to survive without her protection. Since she's a kick-ass fighter, I don't mind. She's continuing to train me, convinced I'm going to need it. She could be right—only time will tell.

Breccan left for home a few nights ago. Told us to call him if ever we needed help again. I like him, so I hope we do see him again in the future.

Rebecca never resurfaced after I woke. Whether or not she was part of Eli's dastardly plan, we aren't sure. Maybe Vlad's dismemberment scared her off. Hell, I refused to step foot out of his house until he took down that terrifying pike and burned Eli's head. *Shudder.*

Then there's my family. My mother finally

reached out again and begged to see me. I told her I'd think about it. Perish isn't my home anymore. New Orleans is. And Lucy, while avoiding her Lumberjack Wolfman, has no desire to leave either. If I do return home, it won't be without Vlad. He's a part of my life, and I wouldn't have it any other way. Rumor has it my brother finally told my dad. But I haven't heard a peep from him. Lucky me.

For a story with such a grim beginning, I must say it turned out rather well.

Of course, that could change. The queen still wants to meet us, after all. If I have any say in this, the answer is hell no, because meeting the queen will be the shittiest shit-show ever. But we all know how it goes when a monarch demands your presence. You aren't given a choice. So, I guess we'll see you then.

Hopefully.

LOVING DRACULA SNEAK PEEK

"Shh!" I giggled and clapped a hand over my best friend's mouth. "He'll hear you!"

Lucy—the aforementioned bestie—sniggered against my palm. An evil glint formed in her eyes two seconds before she slopped her tongue across my hand like a frigging dog.

"Ew!" I snorted a laugh, then smeared my palm —and her drool—across her face.

Seriously disgusting! Everyone knew the human mouth was a dirty, nasty place. Okay, yes, I was a vampire, and therefore impervious to all diseases, viruses, and bacteria, but that didn't mean I appreciated being bathed in her gross cooties. And yes, I understood the irony, considering I rather enjoyed playing tonsil hockey with my vampire boyfriend, Dracula, though he preferred to be called Vlad.

"I swear, you're as bad as Sam," I grumbled.

Sam was our local Wolfman—aka werewolf—*and* Lucy's mate. We couldn't forget that little bit, even though she desperately wanted to do so. My dear, sweet Lucy was trapped in the denial phase of their relationship. It'd only been three months since vampires had come out to the public. I think learning werewolves *also* existed had been the overwhelming icing on the mind-boggling cake for her.

Lucy wasn't the sort who rolled with the punches. That was my role in our relationship. I was the go-with-the-flow sort who made impulsive decisions which generally *always* landed me in trouble. Hence, why I was now a creature of the night. Since high school, Lucy had been my steadfast, austere counterpart. Always there to remind me to smarten up. Not that I ever took the advice.

I suspected this all had become a little too much for her. The same day she'd learned werewolves existed, she'd also learned she was mated to one. The wonderful Samuel Lowell had cemented our friendship by decapitating an evil vampire hellbent on murdering me, thereby saving my life. I owed him *all* the cookies—and no, I didn't mean dog treats.

From what little I'd managed to drag out of Lucy, she'd spoken to Sam a few times, but hadn't promised anything more than that. Though, she had admitted she was hot for his bod. I couldn't blame her. Much like Vlad, Sam ranked a solid twelve out of ten. Two very different men, but both absolutely mouth-watering. Lucky us!

Lucy swatted at my arm, then pointed at the television and howled with laughter. "I love this part. Anna, watch!"

I wiped my hand down my pants, then turned just in time to watch as the fictional Dracula leaned over a woman—also named Lucy—and bit her. When he started to drink her blood, it sounded like he was slurping it through a straw. I had to admit, there was a definite comedic value to that. One *my* Lucy found downright hilarious. The way she clutched at her sides and rolled across the bed had me snickering alongside her.

Since becoming a vampire, Lucy and I had made it our mission to watch every vampire movie out there. We wanted to compare fact from fiction with the goal of using the movies as research and references for a vlog post I was putting together. It'd taken me weeks to finally feel secure online again after the shenanigans that went down after I'd been turned, but I was ready to get back out there.

After my vampiric debut, the internet had gone *wild*. Reporters and gossip columnists had followed me and Vlad everywhere. They'd obsessively snapped our photos—which was hilarious, considering the only thing that showed in pictures were our clothes. I didn't quite understand why, but vampires cast no reflection. Our clothing wasn't magical though, so the photos of us were reminiscent of the invisible man and woman. All this had led Lucy to suggesting I continue my vlog—now that I was famous.

Becoming famous had always been a lifelong dream of mine. But that was the funny thing about dreams vs. reality. When you're finally handed the *one thing* you want more than anything, you suddenly realize it's nowhere near as great as you'd imagined. Fame was like that. I'd always thought it would be so cool to have people stalking me, begging for my photograph, longing to meet me. Yeah, it's not cool. Not at all. More than once, Vlad had to put on his scary vampire face to make people back off.

The movies were Lucy's and my way of relaxing —it let us laugh at my predicament and blow off a bit of steam. Pretty soon, we'd be going live with my first vlog post as a vampire. Fact vs. Fiction. Part of me was terrified. Would this only exacerbate the whole paparazzi issue? Or would it appease them if I made myself more available online? I was hoping for door number two.

When vampires first came out, the queen had issued a hush order to keep any eager vamps out there silent. But she'd lifted the order a few days ago. No one had come out in the open yet. Maybe they were too terrified of the public's response. Or maybe they were like my beloved and had absolutely no idea how to navigate the interwebs. I wanted to be the first. Which meant we needed to get on this, asap.

I hadn't told Vlad about it yet. And I wasn't sure why. Fear, I think. What if I failed? What if this all blew up in my face? I didn't want him to see that. I wanted him to keep adoring me. Either way, Lucy and I agreed not to show him until it was live. Best to ask forgiveness instead of permission and all that rubbish.

I focused on the movie. When we reached the scene where Van Helsing and company stuffed Lucy's room full of garlic in an attempt to repel the villainous Dracula, my Lucy was laughing so hard, tears spilled from her eyes.

Even my stomach was cramping from the hilarity. I choked on a stuttered breath, then dashed my own blood tears from my eyes before they fell. "Ohmigod, Lucy. Vlad's gonna hear you."

"So?" Lucy guffawed at the screen. "If ole Battikins pisses me off, I'm just gonna chuck some garlic at him."

I burst out laughing at the image, then clapped a hand over my own mouth to muffle the sound. Lucy *loved* the new nickname she'd come up with for him. It'd quickly become her favorite after she'd somehow managed to sneak up on Vlad—a feat I still had no idea *how* she'd accomplished—and startled him so badly, he'd spontaneously shifted into bat form. She'd just about laughed herself into an early grave that night.

Vlad didn't approve of our movie selection. Considering he was *the* Dracula, these movies possessed a completely different tone for him. I respected that. I'd gotten a taste of it myself, once I'd stumbled onto a public website that contained nothing but fanfiction written about me. Thousands of stories written by thousands of people. I'd tried reading a few but had stopped once I'd stumbled across the Anna x Lucy ones. I loved Lucy, of course, but not that way. And it weirded me out to read love stories about us. I had to imagine that was how Vlad felt about the movies based on him, especially considering his human wife's name had actually been Mina. Bet that felt like a donkey kick to the nuts.

Halfway through this ridiculous movie, I noticed Lucy's phone lighting up across the room. From the faint flicker in her eyes, she'd noticed it as well, but refused to acknowledge it. Which could only mean one thing.

"Sam?" I asked.

Her jaw tightened but she didn't answer. Like I said, denial, denial, denial.

ACKNOWLEDGMENTS

Thank you so much to everyone who helped make Dating Dracula what it is. Everyone who cheered me on when it felt like I was banging my head against a wall.

I'm not even sure where to begin. Dating Dracula took so long for me to finally get out of my head onto paper. And every time I thought I could *finally* work on it, another project arose that needed to be tackled first. But then camE the time when I could finally dedicate myself to it! It began as an urban fantasy concept, where Anna and Dracula were a married couple on the outs, due to Dracula's bloodthirsty ways. But that particular story never clicked with me. Then someone introduced me to the paranormal chick lit genre, and *boom*, everything clicked into place. The year of struggle made it worth it in the end. I truly hope you adore this couple as much as I do.

So without further ado, I need to thank a bunch of people!

Kayla Robichaux, my wonderful editor who just adores everything New Orleans; Molly Burton, my incredibly talented cover designer; C.E. Black and Debbie Herbert, because you two are my go-to when I'm stuck, and you're always so willing to help; my critique group, for helping me whip this book into shape; my soon-to-be sister-in-law (pfft, girl, you're already my sister) for encouraging and rallying me even on the days when I was too tired to write; and my husband, because, *always* and *forever*.

ABOUT THE AUTHOR

Kinsley Adams is a thirty-something-year-old author who stopped counting when she turned twenty-five. When she isn't writing uproariously hilarious romantic comedies, she's raising her womb-gremlin with the hopes that he might one day become the world's first Supreme Leader. You can find her online at kinsleyadams.com

If you enjoyed this book, please leave a review! Your support and feedback are greatly appreciated. And be sure to sign up for Kinsley's newsletter at kinsleyadams.com/newsletter for updates on new releases, sales, and more!

ALSO BY KINSLEY ADAMS

Made in the USA
Las Vegas, NV
11 March 2024

87056514R00277